# Heat IT UP

## OFF THE ICE - BOOK ONE

# STINA LINDENBLATT

**DIVERSIONBOOKS**

Diversion Books
A Division of Diversion Publishing Corp.
443 Park Avenue South, Suite 1008
New York, New York 10016
www.DiversionBooks.com

Copyright © 2016 by Stina Lindenblatt
All rights reserved, including the right to reproduce this book or portions thereof
in any form whatsoever.

This is a work of fiction. Names, characters, places and incidents either are the
product of the author's imagination or are used fictitiously. Any resemblance to
actual persons, living or dead, events or locales is entirely coincidental.

For more information, email info@diversionbooks.com

First Diversion Books edition June 2016.
Print ISBN: 978-1-62681-874-3
eBook ISBN: 978-1-62681-873-6

To Muumu and Vaari.

Even though you're in Heaven now,
you're always in my heart…

# Chapter One

## Sofia

Forgiveness. It doesn't matter how many times you say it, or if you say it five times fast, or even if you sing it in the shower to the beat of your favorite pop song. The meaning never changes. It's that word most of us don't even think about as we go through our day-to-day life. If someone bumps into us, we don't have to yell "I forgive you" as the person hurries off.

No, saying the word is easy, but meaning it…now that can be tough. Sometimes it's easier pretending. Pretending nothing is wrong and that you're moving on with your life.

Pretending. That's a much more interesting word.

I stare at the urinal, willing it to spontaneously clean itself. When it doesn't (stupid urinal), I pull on the rubber gloves and let out a long breath. With the industrial strength cleaner, which reeks of pine and disinfectant, I scrub the urinals, thankful no one back home can see me. And for the first time since I arrived in Helsinki, doubt slips in. What was I thinking?

I was thinking it would be great to get away from the memories haunting me every day. Sure, I could have stayed in Minneapolis for the summer and hung out with my friends, maybe even landed an athletic-therapy internship. But when I saw the ad in Student Services for the overseas work-swap program, and saw Finland listed, there was no way I could *not* do it. It was like destiny.

Only I hadn't imagined destiny would equal quality time with my new porcelain friends.

I finish the urinals, which are now clean enough to…I won't say eat off, because I don't think they'll ever be that clean. But they're shiny enough for Mr. Clean to give them his bald-headed stamp of approval.

Two guys walk into the bathroom. Awesome. I must've forgotten to put up the sign warning people that the bathroom's closed. Their gazes sweep over my body, hidden beneath this hideous brown uniform. From the expressions on their faces, they have quite the imagination. I wouldn't be surprised if my C-cup bra has magically transformed into a DD. My face grows hot under their scrutiny. They smirk at me and say something in Finnish, none of which I understand. Judging from their tone, they're not commending me on a great job. Too bad. A little recognition would've been nice.

Note to self: guys are jerks no matter what country they live in. It must have to do with the Y chromosome, where the douchebag gene is located.

As I contemplate waving the disgusting mop in their faces to chase them out of here, a girl my age, wearing the same hideous uniform as me, strides into the bathroom. She glares at the guys and lets loose a rapid stream of Finnish that leaves them chuckling. But more importantly, they back away, wave, and exit the room. Maybe she's my guardian angel.

Funny, I always imagined my guardian angel to be male. With hot abs.

"Hi," she says. "Fanni told me you'd be in here and we should have lunch together. I'm Maija." Relief washes through me at her ability to speak English, which sounds exotic buried in a Finnish accent.

I nod, having lost all ability to speak after not saying much in any language for the past week—with the exception of emails to Claire and my mom. *Earth to tongue. This is Houston. Will we have communication anytime soon?*

"Sorry about those idiots," Maija says.

"That's fine. Believe me, guys aren't any different where I'm from."

6

She makes a face. "I'm sorry to hear that. I thought it was only Finnish men who are idiots."

I laugh. "No, I think it's pretty much universal."

"Will you be finished in half an hour?" she asks as I give her the standard once over. She's about my height and slim, with dark blond hair pulled back in a short ponytail. Like me, she has a little makeup on, but nothing that will make us look glamorous—as if that would even be possible with the uniforms and sneakers. At my nod, she says, "I'll meet you in the staff locker room at eleven. Okay?"

"Sounds good."

With the new incentive ahead of me, beyond escaping this room as soon as possible, I move quickly to finish up and meet Maija as planned. After we scrub our arms and hands with more soap than I normally use in a week, she takes me to the staff lunchroom.

The windowless room only has enough space for two long tables, so we're forced to sit with four women who looked to be in their fifties. Maija introduces me and they smile. Or at least they smile until one speaks to me and Maija has to explain that I'm from California and I don't speak Finnish. That wipes away their smiles. It's not where I'm from that's the problem. It's that I don't speak their language. I can't contribute to the discussion, and Maija will have to translate. I don't even bother to correct her and tell her I'm from Minnesota. There's no point.

The women go back to their discussion. I take a bite of my open-faced cheese sandwich.

"I've always wanted to be a character actor at Disneyland. But not a Disney Princess," Maija says. "Have you worked there?"

I shake my head. "I'm from Minnesota, not California. But I know what you mean. I wanted to be one when I was eight after we went there one summer." The rest of the lunch break is spent with Maija asking me a gazillion questions about Minnesota.

"Why did you want to come to Finland to clean toilets?" she eventually asks.

Good question. "My mom's from Finland but I haven't been here in years. I thought it would be a great chance to spend time with my grandmother and get to know her better. Cleaning toilets was the added bonus." I laugh at her shocked expression about the toilets. "I'm kidding. When I signed up for the work-exchange program, I thought I'd get to do something related to what I'm studying at college." Especially when I found out I'd be working in a sports center. Silly me.

"What are you studying?"

"Athletic training." At her confused expression, I clarify, "I want to work with athletes who've been injured so they can play again. I'd love to work with a sports team one day." But it's a tough field to get into.

"What about you?" I ask Maija.

"I'm studying economics."

After lunch, and in preparation for Operation Scrub the Sauna, I pull on the oversized rubber boots in the women's staff locker room. Normally, I'm fairly graceful. Normally, I'm not wearing boots made for a six-foot-tall man.

With a resigned sigh, I stumble down the hall to the saunas. The boots make an awkward thunk, thunk, thunk on the tile floor as I do my best not to trip and land on my face.

The facility is open until ten at night, but management doesn't want to hire late-night cleaning staff, so instead the saunas are each closed for thirty minutes so we, or I, can clean and hose them down.

I spend the first half hour in the women's sauna, sweating like I'm running a marathon. A drop of sweat trickles down my back and I don't complain when the spray of water bounces off the top bench. It soaks through my uniform and bra. I'm tempted to turn the hose on myself and drench my entire body.

But that would be a little hard to explain should I bump into anyone on my way back to the staff room, especially my supervisor.

I finish the room and head for the men's sauna, my damp skin cooling off in the short distance. I knock on the pine-wood door, wait for a three-count, then crack it open. A blast of stifling heat hits me, along with the heady pine scent, which smells a million times better than the fake stuff found in disinfectants. "Hi, is anyone in here?"

When there's no reply, I inch the door open and peer inside just in case someone didn't hear me.

Once I've made sure no one's here, I push the door open and drag the hose in. A strand of hair falls from my ponytail and plasters itself against my face. I ignore it and get to work, placing the bucket with soapy water on the floor. It sloshes over the side and lands on my booted foot.

I spray the wooden benches, then grab the bucket and climb onto the first row. With a large brush, I scrub the upper bench. Even though it's hot, I manage to sing a new song that's been playing in my head over the past few days. It's the closest thing I have to music, and as exciting as this job is (ha!), it's better than nothing.

As I sing and scrub, I move my hips to the music in my head. I spray the bench, rinsing the soapy water. And like last time, the cold water splashes off the wood and hits my uniform. At the sound of laughter, I whip around in time to see two guys step into the sauna. Both are tall and covered in muscles, except the blond guy is much bulkier than his friend.

Both are naked.

Yikes! Without realizing what I'm doing, I shoot a blast of water at the dark-haired guy's leg, barely missing his man parts.

"Fuck," he says, echoing my sentiments, and jumps back. His friend bursts out laughing.

Fortunately, wooden railings separate me from the blond guy, and a two-by-four cuts across where *his* man parts are located. *Thank you, pine-tree gods, for your much-appreciated sacrifice! I owe you one.*

With mortification laughing at me in the corner, I jerk the hose in that direction and fumble to turn off the water. My face heats up more, which is hard to believe given where I'm standing. The blond continues laughing and I keep my gaze locked on the nozzle. It's not like I haven't seen a naked guy before. I have. My ex-boyfriend. And…well, that's it.

I finally manage to twist the traitor of a nozzle. If it had been on my side, it would've already cooperated and let me bail a minute ago. The water transforms from a blast to a spray. My breath comes out hard, almost a grunt.

The blond guy says something in Finnish.

"Sauna is closed," I say in their language. Or at least that's what I'm aiming for. God, what's wrong with this stupid thing?

The dark-haired guy takes the nozzle out of my hand, unconcerned by his nakedness—not that I'm looking. "Newton's third law of physics states that an object in motion will stay in motion if nothing acts against it."

I startle at his American accent, but don't wait to hear what else Newton has to say.

I bolt.

"Wait," the dark-haired guy calls out.

The only other thing I hear as I escape through the door is the blond guy. "Dude, I told you women don't like physics. It's boring."

# Chapter Two

## Kyle

Nik recounts what one boy said during training camp today. I laugh despite the growing ache in my leg. Nik's too busy telling me what happened, he hasn't noticed my slight limp. That, or he decided not to comment. As long as he doesn't mention it to his uncle, things will be okay. I don't want to risk my job. I live for coaching those boys and being on the ice again.

Even if it means my leg aches by the end of the day.

Nik pulls the sauna door open and heat instantly blasts us. I almost sigh in relief. Shortly after arriving in Finland for the summer, I discovered sauna heat helps with the pain in my leg after a day of coaching. Nik's apartment building has two saunas in it, but you can only use them once a week, on your assigned days.

We step into the sauna, Nik still laughing. A blond in a brown uniform turns around, her eyes wide. Before I can say anything, she blasts water at my good leg, almost hitting my package.

"Fuck." I jump back as Nik bursts out laughing. Ass.

The girl shifts the nozzle so it blasts water into the corner, and frantically tries turning the water off. Not once does her gaze shift in our direction. I repeat Newton's laws of motion in my head to distract where my thoughts are headed. The last thing she needs to see once she does look in our direction is me getting a hard-on. Unfortunately, I have no control over what goes on with Nik. Nor do I have any interest in checking.

She adjusts the nozzle, switching the water pressure from a

blast to a spray. Nik says something in Finnish. She replies, but even I can tell Finnish isn't her native language. I have no idea what she said, but the accent is all wrong for her to be a Finn.

I take the nozzle from her. "Newton's third law of motion states that an object in motion will stay in motion if nothing acts against it."

Shit. What the hell did I say that for? Apparently "Here, let me help" wasn't good enough.

I don't have a chance to say anything else. She runs.

"Wait," I call out and make a move to go after her, but my leg says to hell with that. And what am I planning to do? Chase her down the hallway, naked? Like that won't get me arrested.

"Dude, I told you women don't like physics," Nik says. "It's boring."

I turn off the water. "Physics isn't boring. It's the difference between you getting a goal or the opposition stealing the puck from you. Maybe if you appreciated it more, your scoring average would be higher."

"Hey, there was nothing wrong with my average last season."

I choose to ignore that and glance around. The benches are wet and the girl left a bucket of soapy water on the floor, along with a scrub brush. "What did she say to us?"

"Something about the sauna being closed. Who knows."

I groan. Not what I wanted to hear.

Nik shrugs. "I guess it was closed while she was cleaning, but now that she's gone, we might as well stay. The heat is still on." He climbs onto the top bench.

• • •

I wander along the sidewalk toward my apartment, my leg no longer aching. The warm, late afternoon sun is still high in the sky. Cars drive past on the busy road, along with the occasional cyclist. Everyone is in a rush to get home.

Everyone but me.

Ahead of me is the small park I've hung out in a couple of times since arriving in Helsinki two weeks ago. It's quiet here and a great place to work on my lesson plans for the next day. To think about each boy's strengths and weaknesses, and to figure out how I can help them become better players. That's why their parents spent money for the summer training camp for elite players.

I walk down the path to the pond and that's when I see her. At least I think she's the same girl from the sauna. Instead of the brown uniform, she's wearing denim shorts and a simple white tank top. Her endless legs are toned, and her long hair is still in the messy ponytail.

She watches a swan on the pond then crouches and lifts her camera, aiming it at the bird.

I'm about to walk over and apologize for what happened in the sauna when her phone rings. She answers it and sits on the neatly manicured, grassy bank. I sit a few yards away, waiting for her to finish her call. She doesn't seem to notice me.

I remove my notepad and pen from my backpack. I jot a few things down and study my coaching notes. I hadn't originally planned to become a coach. My goal had strictly been to play in the NHL. But once my little brother was old enough to strap on skates, I'd taken up the role of coach for his hockey teams. In the end, that had worked in my favor.

I glance at the girl again. She ends her call and returns the phone to her backpack.

Sensing she's about to leave, I push myself up to stand. My leg stiffened in the short time I was sitting, and when she looks toward me the limp is back. Recognition hits and she blushes.

"Hi, is it okay if I sit?" I gesture to the patch of grass next to her.

She nods and goes back to watching the swan.

"I'm sorry about what happened in the sauna. We didn't realize it was closed."

She smiles, a light blush hitting her cheeks. It's not a big smile, but it's better than nothing. "That's okay. I'm sorry I hurt you. You startled me…and…and I thought you were someone else."

"You didn't hurt me."

She frowns. "But you were just limping."

"It's nothing. My leg sometimes stiffens. Old childhood injury," I add, hoping she gets the hint I don't want to discuss it. I never do. "Who did you think we were when you blasted me with the water?"

"Just some jerks who harassed me this morning while I was cleaning the men's bathroom." She scrunches her nose in a way that makes her looks adorable. "Today was my first day, and they thought it was entertaining that I don't speak much Finnish. I guess I was a little tense when you and your friend came in."

"So how 'bout we start over. Hi, I'm Kyle."

"Sofia." She glances at her phone and scrambles up. "I have to catch my bus."

For a second, I think she's going to suggest we should get together sometime, maybe go for a coffee. But she doesn't. She rushes off. No hesitation or deliberation.

Like she never even considered it.

# Chapter Three

## Kyle

We're often faced with moments in our lives that we regret. It could be something as simple as buying the wrong toothpaste and hating the taste of it. It could be something bigger that changes our lives, sometimes for the better, mostly for the worst.

Or sometimes it's just waking up and realizing our mistakes from last night will haunt us for the rest of the day. I open my eyes and instantly recognize this is going to be one of those days. The bright light streaming into my room aggravates the pounding in my head. Shit.

My stomach churns, reminding me that it's dealing with the aftermath of last night, too. For now it feels somewhat stable, as long as I don't move. I snap my eyes shut and try to will myself back to sleep. That way when I wake up again, my hangover will be gone. I don't remember last night, and I'd rather not remember the after effects while I'm at it.

Cool fingers trace along my back and slip under the sheet wrapped around my waist. Despite the pounding in my head, I vaguely remember the previous evening. I went out with Nik, my former NHL teammate. We drank. I tried to forget the past year. I tried to pretend the ache in my leg hadn't worsened from an intensive day on the ice. And I tried to do what I promised my family I would do once I arrived in Finland: move on with my life.

The hand moves over my hip. I turn so I can see the girl who I'd hoped would make that all possible, even for a few hours. The blurred vision, with chin-length black hair, leans over me. I twist back around, reach for my glasses on the bedside table, and put them on. Last night, the girl looked like a hot version of Snow White. The morning after version looks like she ate the poisoned apple. Her face is pale and makeup is smeared under her eyes—not in a good way.

The good news, if you can call it that, is that we aren't in my room. Not unless a tornado hit mine and deposited a mountain of fashion magazines and women's clothing across the floor and furniture.

"Hi," Snow White purrs with a thick Finnish accent, and for a moment I'm tempted to close my eyes and see if she vanishes when I open them again. To see if I vanish to a new location, preferably my apartment. But something tells me that won't work, no matter how much I wish for it.

I stare at the ceiling, compounding my headache further as I struggle to remember what happened last night. I remember drinking. I remember playing pool and winning. I remember talking to my brother on my cell phone…

"Fuck," I mutter.

Snow White scoots over and whispers in my ear, "Yes, please." Her voice is the low murmur of seduction.

"The energy of light per unit of time determines its intensity. And right now, the light shining through your blinds is carrying too much energy."

She blinks, having no idea what I said.

"The light is bright and it's fucking with my hangover."

Her confused expression slips away, to be replaced by the familiar 'God, you're weird.'

"How did we get here?" I ask.

"You don't remember? I guess I shouldn't be surprised. You were kind of drunk." *No shit.* "Don't worry. I drove."

"My car?"

"No, my car. Yours is still at the nightclub. I can drive you back to get it if you want."

I push myself up to sit. My head argues that decision. It takes everything I have not to collapse back onto the bed. I check her alarm clock and groan. It's already 11:24 a.m.

"I need to go." I scoot off the bed.

She scrambles after me and grabs my arm. "Now? Can't we have a shower first?" Though from the way she says it, it's clear she's hoping for more than just getting clean. If it weren't for the hangover, and if I didn't have to talk to Cody, I'd be all over the shower idea.

"I have to be somewhere." I snatch my underwear from the floor. "I can get a cab."

"No, I'll drive you. Give me a second to get ready." She returns dressed in jeans and a tank top, her face washed and with the same amount of makeup as before.

She drives me back to the side street, lined with low-rise apartment buildings, where I left my rental car last night.

"Did my friend drive home last night?" If I was drunk, Nik would have been, too. Whenever we drink together, we pretty much drink the same amount as each other, although his tolerance is slightly greater than mine, given that he's about thirty pounds heavier.

"No, my friend drove him and his car back to her place. Your friend wasn't in any condition to drive. He wasn't too happy about that, though. Kept claiming he was sober enough."

That doesn't surprise me. It's only when a drunk driver hits your vehicle, kills your wife, and fucks up your future does it alter your perception of things, and you're less likely to lie to yourself about your state of inebriation. Nik wasn't even the one who stood by my side while I recovered from the accident. And Nik wasn't the one who encouraged me though every setback. That was entirely my family.

But Nik's the one who is there when I need to forget. He's the one I can turn to when I need to escape from it all. Hell, he's the one who gave me this opportunity in Finland to pull my life together.

"Tell her thanks for not letting him be an ass and drive," I say. "And thanks for not letting me drive and…and for last night."

"You're welcome." She hands me a pink scrap of paper with her name and phone number scrawled on it. "Call me." She then leans over and kisses me on the cheek.

"Okay," I say, even though I have no intention of doing that. She's nice and all, but I'm not interested in things going beyond a one-night stand.

I climb out of her car and squeeze into mine, which wasn't designed with my tall body in mind. None of the Finnish cars are—a fact my legs have grumbled about numerous times.

I turn the engine as my cell phone rings. Cody. I cringe and answer it. "Hey, dude." I attempt to mask the rough night that lingers in my voice—and fail.

"What's up?" my sixteen-year-old brother asks as I decrease the volume on the car stereo. I can barely hear the steady beat of the bass, for which my head is eternally grateful.

"Not much." *I'm just heading home to sleep off this hangover.* "What's going on with you? You ready for hockey camp next week?"

"Where were you last night?" His voice is rough, but not for the same reason as mine. He's pissed. Beyond pissed.

"I was out with friends," I say casually, the opposite of how I feel.

"You promised me. You said things would be different in Finland. But it's still the same shit. Nothing's changed." Mom must not be home. Cody wouldn't dare cuss in front of her.

I drop my head back against the headrest and close my eyes. He's right. That's what I thought would happen when I got here. Nik had planned to come to Finland for the summer, to help with his uncle's elite ice hockey training camp for boys. One of the coaches had backed out for personal issues and Nik convinced me to join him. His uncle was delighted to have another NHL player coach the teens, even if I was no longer able to play with the league because of my fucked-up leg. It was an offer I couldn't say no to, even if my family had reservations about it. It's great experience for my resume, something I need more of if I want to pursue a coaching career. It's a break from the painful memories. It's a timeout from my family's ever-watchful eye.

Who wouldn't have jumped at the position?

"It's not as bad as it sounds," I explain. "You just called me at a bad time last night."

"You went home with her, didn't you?"

"Who?" I say even though I have a good idea who he's referring to.

"The girl who answered your phone."

I'm not sure how to answer. Cody's sixteen. He's not an idiot. But I'm hardly going to admit I had sex with her.

"I thought you loved Gabby," he powers on.

I squeeze my eyes shut against the pain that has nothing to do with the hangover. "I did love her. But she's dead, Cody. Me not sleeping around won't change that. She's not coming back."

It's not like I'm even fucking all those girls to dull the pain of losing my wife. Gabby and I got married when we were only twenty. An idiot move, really. I didn't realize it at the time. I loved her, but I'm finally getting to do what I missed out on by settling down so young. And to hell if Cody thinks he can guilt me into becoming a saint or some born-again virgin.

A raindrop splatters against the windshield. A sullen cloud I hadn't noticed before darkens the sky.

"I know it won't bring her back," Cody grumbles. The same hurt and distrust I've heard in his voice so many times, since my accidental overdose, darkens his tone.

"Look, bro, I know I fucked up last year. But I promise it won't happen again. I'm not on those drugs anymore." I'm not on any drugs, other than the liquid kind. And even that I save for when I'm not coaching the next day. I'd rather put up with the pain than risk another accidental overdose, than risk being addicted to the drug, than risk showing up at work with an epic hangover. An asshole move like that could screw up my future career.

"But you're still hanging out with Nik," Cody says.

I glance down at my favorite t-shirt. The t-shirt that says: May the $\sum F = ma$ be with you. The t-shirt that Nik complained last night looked like I was entering a math contest instead of hitting the clubs. "There's nothing wrong with Nik."

"Dad says he's a hotheaded ass who's eager to milk the benefits of his fame."

Yeah, I do remember that conversation with Dad. I just didn't realize Cody had overheard it. I cringe at what else he probably also overheard when Dad forgot I'm twenty-four and not ten years old, and tried to ground me so I didn't come to Finland.

"I just don't want anything bad to happen to you, Kyle." Cody's voice cracks on the last part.

I might not feel guilty about the women I'm screwing, but I do feel like shit after he says that. "I promise you nothing bad is going to happen to me while I'm here. And I promise I'll be back home at the end of August. I wouldn't miss watching you play for anything." Even if it will tear me up inside knowing he's the one who has a shot at making his NHL dreams come true, while I only get to watch from the sidelines. I'll never again get to experience the euphoria of playing in the Stanley Cup playoffs. The dream of every hockey player.

The answering silence is louder than the rain hammering the metal roof.

He doesn't believe me.

I'm about to say something else, when I hear our father's voice on Cody's end. I can't make out what he said, but I pray to a God I don't believe in that Cody never mentioned anything to my father about what I was doing last night. I don't need any more lectures. I need some coffee and a shower. In that order.

"I have to go." Cody ends the call without giving me a chance to say goodbye, and without giving me a chance to repeat my promise. A promise that now feels oddly empty.

His disappointment at what I've become clings to me, but I'm too tired to think about it. I turn up the volume on the radio and pull away from my parking spot.

# Chapter Four

## Sofia

I pack my wallet, laptop, and camera in my backpack, and head for the apartment door. "I'm going to The Coffee Bar," I call out to the empty apartment. My grandmother has failed to join the twenty-first century. She doesn't have a computer, let alone Internet. I swear, we must be the only apartment in the building without it.

A loud knock on the door startles me. I open it and gape at the man in front of me—the man who looks like an actor from the soap *The Endless Circle*. The show is bigger in Finland than it is in the States, but Muumu and I bonded over it during my first day here. We both agree that the actor is hot.

The guy's short, spiky brown hair complements his warm brown eyes, and he has scruff along his jaw and upper lip. In a way, he's similar to the guy from the sauna last week, except Kyle's hair has waves and his eyes are light blue. This guy isn't as tall or built like Kyle either, though he still looks in good shape. Nor does he wear glasses, unlike Kyle.

And he's standing in front of me with a bouquet of white, pink, and purple flowers.

I scan the bright, airy hallway, searching for the TV crew. It's a joke. It has to be. Like in those shows where the unsuspecting victim doesn't realize she's being pranked until it's too late. Which means if it's true, I won't see the camera. I won't know I'm being pranked until it's over.

The guy doesn't say anything at first. He blinks like he can't

21

believe I'm standing here, like he was expecting someone else. "Hi, Sofia? I'm your date," actor dude says with a strong Finnish accent. Wow, he's good. "My name's Joni." He shifts on his feet and for a second looks unsure of himself, unlike the guy he plays on *The Endless Circle*.

"Sorry, I've got plans," I say as sweetly as possible. If this goes on air, I don't want to come off as a bitch. My friends back home might see it. "You're gonna have to prank someone else."

"Prank?" The way he says the word, it's like he's tasting it for the first time and he's not sure what to expect.

"Yes, prank. You know, joke?" I wave my hand in the air, gesturing at the hidden cameras. "You're the actor from *The Endless Circle*, and you're here to prank me."

"*The Endless Circle?*" If I thought he looked confused before, that's nothing compared to now. Not to mention he's looking at me, deciding if I'm crazy or not. And right now it's not looking too hot in the non-crazy department.

He holds out the flowers. "I'm not an actor. I work in advertising. And I create comics." The last part seems more of an afterthought and a light blush hits his cheeks. "Our grandmothers arranged for us to go out for lunch. Together."

"Seriously?"

He nods and a memory pops into my head of Muumuu and I watching the soap together for the first time and her mentioning Joni's name. At the time I thought she was talking about the actor. She meant this guy.

"Well, I'm un-arranging the date." I give him a quick smile. "Sorry, but thanks for the thought. It's nothing personal. I'm just not interested in dating while I'm here. I guess my grandmother didn't realize that."

"I understand." He turns and walks off.

I shut the door and lean back against it. Crap. The last thing I need is for Muumu to become involved in my pathetic love life, especially when I can't explain to her why it's so pathetic. That goes well beyond my Finnish skills.

Heck, it goes beyond my English skills, too.

I wait five minutes, my back against the door, before peeling myself away from it. Once I'm positive no one is out there, I open the door and peer over the metal railing to check the ground floor. The coast is clear.

At the cafe, I order a Diet Coke, sit in the far corner, and turn on my laptop. Claire responded to my email from yesterday, bemoaning, once again, that she has to wait forever to talk to me due to my WiFi situation. She has a million questions about Kyle.

I tell her what I can, which is nothing, and switch topics.

*You know the soap The Endless Circle? I swear there's a guy here who looks like one of the actors. He plays Eric Kincaid. He's hot.*

*And my grandmother is trying to set me up with him,* I type. I imagine Claire laughing at that. And then after she's finished laughing, she'll decide it's a great idea if it means I'll experience a steamy romance while I'm here. Anything to help me get over Ian and his death.

Correction. Anything to help me get past what he did to me. I'm long over what we had together, which wasn't what I thought it was. Not like back in high school when we were dating and he meant everything to me, and I thought I meant everything to him. We had even discussed our futures, which included both of us in each other's. Silly me.

Once I've finished my email to her, I surf the Internet, update my social media sites…and look up the cast of *The Endless Circle.*

According to one website, the actor who plays Eric is Brad McKinney. Not even close to a Finnish name, so there goes the theory about them being twins. Unless they were separated at birth.

After I finish, I wander around the neighborhood, the late afternoon sun warm against my bare arms and legs. I approach a wall covered with graffiti. Some words are in English, words you don't want young kids to read. Others are in Finnish or another language I can't read. Some designs are clumsy, while others are artwork in themselves.

I remove my lens cap from my DSLR camera and shoot photo after photo. I take a few pictures far enough away to capture most of the graffiti in the frame, including the surrounding concrete wall. Others are shot from a closer angle, so the design isn't recognizable. All you see are abstract colors and patterns. I get lost in those patterns, the contrast of curves and harsh edges.

I spend hours shooting close-up photos. The more bizarre and unrecognizable the picture the better. It's about the minute detail, that singular element so full of meaning, but which is lost in the big picture. It's the big picture everyone else sees because they're afraid to look closer, afraid to see the truth. Like how being far from home is messing with my head so I confused Joni for an actor.

The sun's still shining when I head back to the apartment. That's the best part about the location of Vantaa latitude-wise. It means more hours of daylight during the summer, so it's easy to lose track of time.

It's already after 6:33 p.m. Usually Muumu and I eat around five-thirty, so I know I'll be in trouble, especially if she knows that I'm not with Joni after all. But really, how much trouble can I be in if I can't understand her? All I have to do is look sorry and say *"anteeksi"* a few dozen times.

I reach out for the apartment door at the same moment it swings open. I'm not sure who is more shocked—me or Joni. He calls out something over his shoulder that includes my name. As I step inside the apartment, Muumu hustles into the hallway and flings herself at me.

Still hugging me, she speaks in rapid Finnish. I'm not sure who she's talking to, so I keep quiet.

After the hug fest is over, she turns to Joni, and I notice we're not alone in the hallway. A woman Muumu's age, with short white hair and a few extra cookies under her belt like Muumu, takes in the action. When she spots me watching her, she smiles and nods at Joni. I'm not sure how to translate that. It's either, "Hi. I'm Joni's grandmother," or "That's my grandson and I hope you'll fall madly in love with him and make me a great-grandmother anytime now."

I vote for the first option.

"Your grandmother was worried something bad had happened to you," Joni explains.

Perfect, a translator. No charades for this discussion required. "I'm sorry," I say to her in Finnish then switch over to English. "I was shooting photos and lost track of time." I glance at Joni, hoping he gets the hint what I need him to do.

Joni tells her what I said. Or at least I assume he does. For all I know, he just told her I was shooting penguins.

More rapid Finnish from Muumu.

"She was worried you got lost," he explains.

Muumu gestures at the kitchen and fires off more Finnish, except this time I recognize "*syödä*." Eat.

And inwardly I groan. Now I get why Joni and his grandmother are here. I shot him down for lunch; now they're making sure I can't shoot him down for dinner, too. Double groan.

Since I don't have many other choices, I sit at my usual spot at the small table, crammed into the equally small kitchen. Mina, the canary, chirps and Muumu coos back at the bird, then she and Joni's grandmother sit opposite to me, forcing him to sit next to me.

A long, red candle burns in the center of the table. Since when do Muumu and I eat dinner by candlelight? The groan from earlier is back, echoing off my ribs like wind trapped in a tunnel. Why does she have to be so freaking obvious?

While I'm one hundred percent against this plan, I can't deny that dinner smells amazing. Muumu made fish soup with chunks of salmon and vegetables in a milk broth. The dinner tastes great, and the company isn't bad either. I mean, other than when the meddling grandmothers keep asking Joni and me questions. Joni is forced to translate, and it's clear their questions are nothing more than a weak attempt to push us together through conversation. The kind of conversation you have during a first date.

"If you were a frog, what kind would you be?" Joni translates for his grandmother.

My mouth flops open for a second so I look like a frog, which wasn't the look I was aiming for. Our grandmothers watch my

25

reaction with great interest, leaning forward, eyebrows raised, and I get the feeling they weren't the ones who asked me the frog question. If it weren't for the mischief in Joni's eyes, I never would've guessed the truth: he did it on purpose.

"An extremely bouncy kind," I say, struggling to keep a straight face.

I wish I could understand what he said, because whatever it was appeases the two women. They grin and nod at each other. If I wasn't in front of them, I expect they would be rubbing their hands in glee at their attempts at match making.

"What did you say to them?" I ask.

"That you want to have fifty kids," he says with the same mischievous glint as before.

"Really?"

"Well, more like five."

I'm not sure what I want to do more—laugh or glare at him. Laughter wins, mostly because of his expression.

"You think I'm funny," he says. "Does that mean you will now go out with me?"

The laughter in me dies and I shake my head. "I don't date. Been there. Done that. No thanks."

Muumu speaks then gestures at him to translate what she said.

"Your grandmother believes that love makes us strong."

Focusing on my soup, I shake my head again. "No, it doesn't. Love makes us weak. And it makes us blind to what others see." During the last few months of my relationship with Ian, I knew he was cheating on me. He was on the football team and I suspected he was fooling around during their away games. I had brushed it off because I'd convinced myself that he still loved me. It was only recently that I realized I'd been too scared to let him go because it meant I'd be alone. And being with him was better than being alone.

Inwardly I snort at how stupid I was for thinking that. Being alone is better than risking your heart.

Joni chuckles. "You might have a point. But I don't think our grandmothers agree with us."

Both our grandmothers are beaming. I get the feeling neither plan to give up on this scheme to get me together with Joni.

Ha! I've got news for them—it's so not going to happen. I just have to figure a way to prove to them that my heart isn't open for business.

# Chapter Five

## Kyle

I enter the sports center, my duffel strap slung over a shoulder. The pretty blond receptionist, who's flirted with me several times, smiles at me. I nod and hand her the membership card. She waves it under the laser beam, confirming I am indeed a member. As if she didn't know.

After I finish working out, I head for the showers. If Sofia keeps to the same schedule as Friday, I still have a little time. I came here yesterday, hoping to see her again. I even asked someone working in the fitness center if he had seen her, but he didn't know who I was talking about. From what I could tell, the cleaning staff doesn't socialize with the fitness staff.

As I approach the sauna, showered and fully clothed, I see the sign Nik and I missed. A sign that I'm guessing says 'Sauna Closed for Cleaning.' But unlike last time, it guards the door, which has been left open a crack.

"I hear American girls love sex. Lots of sex," a male voice says. Laughter from more than one guy sets me on edge.

I reach for the door as a familiar female voice says, "Come near me and I'll spray you in the balls."

I open the door wider.

Three guys are standing in front of her, caging her in. They're large and look like they're friendly with weights—large but not as bulked up as Nik. And they're all dressed in jeans and t-shirts, despite the intense heat of the room, which means they didn't enter the sauna thinking it was open to the public.

"I'd listen to her if I were you," I warn.

The guys whip around at my voice, their surprise at seeing me evident on their faces. It vanishes when they realize they outnumber me.

"This has nothing to do with you," the guy in the center, who looks to be their ringleader, says. He's shorter than his goons by a few inches, but he's also the most muscular.

I clench my hands, muscles on high alert. I'd rather not fight these losers, but if it comes down to it, I will.

"Are you okay?" I ask Sofia.

She nods and a stray piece of hair flops from her ponytail. I push away the sudden need to tuck it behind her ear.

"I'm fine."

She shifts the hose away from the ringleader, so it faces the corner, then turns the water on. It bursts out the nozzle in a high-pressure stream, much like when she accidentally hit me the other day.

The guys wisely back away. The ringleader glares at me before the three of them leave. As soon as their backs are turned, Sofia slouches and the hand holding the hose starts shaking, the adrenalin aftershock kicking in.

"Thank you," she whispers. "Those are the jerks I was telling you about."

I place my hand on her upper arm, needing to do whatever I can to make her feel grounded, make her feel safe. "Are you almost finished for the day?" I want to talk to her but not here. Not when the sauna is so goddamn hot. Sweat trickles down my back and I've only been in here a few minutes.

"I just have to finish up in here then hit the shower," she says.

"Do you want to go get a coffee after you're done?"

She doesn't answer right away, and I'm beginning to think she's going to say no. "Okay. I should be ready in about twenty-five minutes. Is that all right?"

• • •

I wait for Sofia outside the main entrance. The door opens for the hundredth time and the blond receptionist steps out. She spots me waiting on the bottom step and her face lights up.

"Hi," she says. "I did not realize you were waiting for me. I would have been quicker if I had known."

My lips twitch into an apologetic smile. "I'm sorry. I'm waiting for someone else."

The main door opens and Sofia exits wearing a yellow sundress. I turn back to the other girl, but she's already gone.

"Sorry to keep you waiting," Sofia says once she reaches the second to last step. "There's a coffee shop around the corner that's pretty good."

"So, how come you're in Finland?" I ask as we stroll along the sidewalk. People bustle past us, rushing to catch their bus home or rushing to the train station. My leg stiffens, a combination of pushing myself hard at the gym and trying to keep up with the boys while skating. None of them know about my injury, and I want to keep it that way. It will only make me look weak in their eyes.

"My university offers an overseas work-exchange program," she explains. "So I signed up for it."

"But why Finland?"

"My mother's from here. So I'm staying with my grandmother in Vantaa, which is a town outside of Helsinki. What about you?"

"The uncle of one of my friends has a summer camp here for boys. Nik, the blond guy with me the other day, asked if I could help out after one of the coaches had to drop out."

"What kind of camp?"

"Hockey." I watch for recognition on her face that she knows who I am. I'm hoping she doesn't. I'm hoping that she's not another puck bunny who's only interested in me because I played in the NHL.

A light blush hits her cheeks. "Sorry, I don't really watch hockey. It's kind of sad, really. I'm an athletic training major but I don't watch much sports, except for maybe when the Olympics are on. Do you play or just coach?"

"I used to play. I don't anymore." I try to ignore the pain wrapping around my heart at the words and at how much I miss playing, but it's as strong as the pain in my leg.

"Because of what happened to your leg?"

So she does know about the accident. Which means she also knows who I am, or at least who I was. It shouldn't bother me but it does. As strange as it sounds, I wanted her to be oblivious to my past.

I nod.

"How old were you when you injured it?"

For a moment I have no idea what she's talking about. And then I remember. I told her my leg has a tendency to stiffen because of a childhood accident.

It wasn't a complete lie. When I was ten, I fell out of a tree and broke my leg. But it didn't end my hockey career.

"Ten," I say, "but it's something I don't like discussing."

She smiles and I become mesmerized by the way her pink-glossed lips curve up. "Okay. We'll talk about something else. Where are you from?" She gestures at the coffee shop at the corner.

"Minneapolis."

"Really? Me too."

I pull open the door to let her in and we're instantly greeted by the strong smell of coffee. If there's one thing I've learned since moving here, Finns live for their coffee and they live for it strong.

We order our drinks and find a quiet spot to sit next to the window. No one pays attention to us, unlike back home. It used to be hard going anywhere without being mobbed after I signed with the Bears. People would recognize me and want my autograph or a photo with me or they had tons of questions about the team. As flattering as the attention was, I don't miss it.

"What were you doing in Minneapolis before you came here?" she asks.

"I was working in the marketing department for the Minnesota

Bears. It was only an internship at the time, but they offered me a full-time position."

"And they let you take the summer off to come here? Wow, they must be a great organization to let you do that."

I take a sip of my coffee, stalling. Why should it matter what Sofia thinks about the truth? She's not my parents.

"I turned the position down. As much as I love hockey, I didn't love working in marketing. Unfortunately, I didn't realize this *before* I majored in it in college."

She visibly cringes. "What made you decide to study marketing?"

"My father felt I would have more career opportunities if I studied law, accounting, or marketing." He thought it would be a good idea in case my NHL career didn't work out. How right he was on that.

She tilts her head to the side. She's flirting but I don't think she realizes it, which makes her nothing like the girls I'm used to. "What did you want to study?"

"I love physics. I was the president of my physics club in high school." I chuckle. "I was a bit of a geek." Which made things challenging at first. The jocks didn't know what to make of me, and neither did the science geeks.

"How come you didn't study physics? Or biomechanics? I took a biomechanics course in college last semester. You would've liked it. You could've combined your love of physics with your love of hockey."

I sip my coffee. "I thought about it, but I would've needed to go on to grad school if I wanted to end up in something related to either of those. But if I had known that working in marketing would bore me, I'd have majored in something else." I wasn't against the idea of going to grad school, and I would have if hockey hadn't been my life. I would have majored in physics, despite what my father had said, but the course load would've been too much since I was also playing on the collegiate team. And I needed to play on the team if I had wanted to be drafted by a NHL team.

"So what do you want to do with your life?"

"I'm not sure yet. Maybe coach." Unfortunately, it's not the most stable position, especially at the high levels where I'd prefer to work. If your team doesn't do well, the head coach is often the first to go.

Sofia studies her mug, deep in thought.

"Once you're an athletic trainer, is there a particular sport you want to work with?" I ask.

She pulls her gaze from her mug, blinks the thought away. And damn if I don't want to get into her head and discover what she was thinking.

"Once you're a trainer, is there a particular sport you want to work with?" I repeat.

"I'm not sure yet. I have a clinical practicum this fall with a high school, and I'll be working with their different athletic teams. Maybe I'll know after that." She worries her lip again. "Can I ask you something? Well, it's more like I need help with something."

"Help with what?"

Her teeth go back to chewing on her lower lip. Lucky teeth. More than anything, I want to suck that lip in my mouth and taste her. But something tells me that's not part of what she's going to ask me.

"Well, you see." The words stumble from her mouth. "My grandmother's trying to set me up with her friend's grandson. I'm not interested. I mean, he seems like a nice guy, but I don't need the complication of a relationship."

I know what she means, but it doesn't stop me from asking the next question. "Is there something wrong with being in a relationship? Does it even have to be one? Why don't you just date him and have fun?"

"Because then I might develop feelings for him."

"And that's a bad thing?"

Her gaze returns to her mug. "The worst."

"How so?"

"It doesn't matter. Let's just leave it at I've done the boyfriend thing. It didn't work out well, and I'm not interested in going through that again."

"So you want me to fake being your boyfriend, so she'll quit trying to set you up with this guy?" This could be interesting.

She vehemently shakes her head. "No. No, nothing like that. I just need you to kiss me once. For my grandmother's benefit. After that, I can pretend I'm talking to you on the phone. She won't know the difference."

"Why don't you just tell her you're not interested in this dude?"

"She doesn't understand English, and my Finnish sucks, which makes it hard to tell her anything."

"Then how's she gonna know you're talking to me? Well, fake talking to me."

Sofia removes her phone from her backpack and holds it to her ear. "Hi Kyle." Her tone is all breathy and sweet. My junk tightens at the thought of her talking like that to me on the phone. She sounds like a girl talking to her boyfriend. "Can you believe that the Easter Bunny is Santa dressed in a disguise?"

I laugh, and the coffee goes the wrong way. I start coughing. "Do you always fake things this well?"

A blush sweeps across her cheeks and damn does she look hot. But it doesn't stop me from laughing again.

# Chapter Six

## Kyle

My grandfather used to tell me things happen for a reason. We might not always agree with them. We might fight them every step of the way. But in the end, it is what it is and a wise man will embrace them, learn from them, maybe even get knocked on the head by them.

Somehow, I don't think what Sofia is asking me to do is what my grandfather had in mind.

"Will you do it?" Sofia asks, once I stop laughing at the way she blushed at my comment. "Will you kiss me in front of my grandmother so she thinks you're my boyfriend?"

"If you do something for me."

"What's that?"

"I've been in the city for two weeks now and haven't seen much of it. I'll kiss you, but you have to explore Helsinki with me. Show me your favorite places." And keep me too busy to hang out with Nik. My father's right. When I'm with Nik, I do tend to get drunk. Sofia's the perfect excuse I need to keep me out of trouble.

She looks clearly dubious of my intentions.

I can't tell if that means sex with me is a no go, or a possibility if I play my cards right. "Just as friends. Promise."

It takes a few seconds but she nods. "Okay, but can we do this now before my grandmother gets any more crazy ideas?"

Sofia and I finish our coffee, then I drive her back to Vantaa.

"We don't have much time once we enter the apartment before my grandmother pokes her head from the kitchen," Sofia explains as we travel down a main street. Apartment buildings and pine trees border both sides of the road. "I want her to catch us in the act."

"So what you're saying is don't waste time with niceties once we're inside?"

"That pretty much sums it up. Yep." She points at a building. "Over there."

We drive past a hut on the sidewalk. Small metallic windmills spin in the breeze from a bucket next to the open window. On the other side is a display of magazines.

I point to it. "What's that?"

"It's a kiosk. You can buy all kinds of things from them, like stamps, bus passes, drinks, and ice cream. I used to love going to it as a kid, whenever my family visited my grandparents."

I turn into the parking lot. "I take it you used to come to Finland often?"

"Every year until I was fifteen. This is my first time back since then."

"Why did you guys stop coming?"

"There's a spot." She points at it. I wait for her to answer my question. When she doesn't after a few seconds, I drop it—her message clear.

We climb out of the cramped rental car, and she leads me to the far side of the building, to the entrance with an "A" printed on the square light above the door.

"I wouldn't be surprised if my grandmother's watching us."

I thread my fingers with Sofia's. Despite the warm ambient temperature, her hand is cold. "Are you nervous?"

Her eyes snap to mine. "Why would you say that?" Her shaky voice is a giveaway to what I suspect she's about to deny.

"You just seem nervous." One side of my mouth slides up. "Have you never kissed a guy before?"

"Sure I have. Remember? I used to have a boyfriend." She looks away.

I want to push the topic but this isn't the best time for that. Not if we're about to put on a performance worthy of a standing ovation.

Sofia doesn't remove her hand from mine, at least not until we're at the main entrance and she has to unlock the door.

We walk up the stairs to the first level. Unlike the apartment buildings I'm used to back home, this one is open in design. The stairs aren't hidden in a dark stairwell. Windows run from the floor to the ceiling, and I mean the ceiling of the building, not just the floor above us. Even the smell is different. It's a mix of pine, burning wood, and some sort of cleaner. It actually smells good.

Sofia leads me the short distance to the first apartment, which is around the corner. I look over the white railing to the ground floor.

"You ready?" she asks, her voice barely louder than a whisper. "Once we're in, we can start kissing." She gulps in a long breath and lets it out slowly. This is a first. No one has been scared to kiss me before. I'm not sure what to make of her reaction. Should I be officially scared, too?

Before she can change her mind—or I can change mine—she opens the door and pulls me in. I don't even have time to register the hallway before her mouth is on mine. Since we haven't established any ground rules for the kiss, I had no idea what to expect, and I hadn't thought to ask. So I'm almost surprised when she parts her lips and lets me in.

Damn if her soft lips, and the way her tongue plays with mine, doesn't send me over the edge. I thread my fingers through her silky hair, preventing her from escaping. My other hand makes itself at home on her hip. I'm drowning in the kiss. Drowning and wanting so much more. Drowning and never wanting it to end.

And for the first time I notice her scent, the sweet smell of apples that wraps around me. It's not overwhelming and I allow myself to drown some more.

My hand on her hip slides to her lower back. I press her toward me so that we're touching from head to toe. She moans against my mouth, sending electrifying vibrations through me. I don't remember the last time since Gabby's death that it felt this way when I kissed someone.

A polite cough intrudes on the moment and I silently curse

Sofia's grandmother. I pull away from Sofia, instantly missing her closeness, her touch.

Except it's not the person I was expecting who interrupted us. It's a guy who scowls at me like there's nothing he wants more than to kick my ass. Next to him is a woman who I guess is Sofia's grandmother. She's not eyeing me in the same way the guy is, but it's clear from the way the corners of her lips curve down that she's not happy with what she just witnessed.

"*Hei*," Sofia says. "Kyle, this is my grandmother…and Joni." She wraps her arm around my waist and snuggles close, her head on my shoulder. My arms automatically envelop her.

"*Tämä on minun poikaystäväni*," she says and I have no clue what it means. It goes well beyond my basic Finnish skills. All I know is that she didn't ask for a beer.

The old woman speaks and the guy replies, both in Finnish. Whatever they're saying is lost on me, but Sofia stiffens in my arm. Neither of them is happy to see me, that's for sure.

"What are they saying?" I ask her as Joni continues talking to the woman.

"I have no idea. Like I said, my Finnish sucks. It's a miracle I could tell them you're my boyfriend. Or I might have told them you're a zombie. I'm not sure."

Joni looks at us. "How come you never mentioned him before?" he asks.

She didn't think this one through, and neither did I.

Sofia doesn't respond so I jump in. "We broke up before we came here because…because of a misunderstanding. I'm coaching hockey in Helsinki this summer, and we bumped into each other in town."

Joni narrows his eyes. Whatever I said was the wrong thing to say.

"So this is the reason you don't believe in love?" he asks her.

Sofia tenses. Not enough to be noticed by anyone else, but enough for me to feel it with her body tucked against mine. "Um… no. That was due to my previous boyfriend. Kyle and I aren't in love," she rushes to add, squirming against me. Lying is something that clearly doesn't come naturally to her.

She turns to me. "Thanks...thanks for driving me home."

Joni's eyebrow goes up and I inwardly cringe at her mistake. If I was her boyfriend, she wouldn't be thanking me as if I were a colleague who had given her a ride home.

I pull her closer and do my best not to smirk at him. "I missed you." I kiss her cheek and breathe in her apple scent. "I didn't want to be apart from you longer than necessary. And if I could steal you away, I'd take you back to my apartment and make love to you all night." I make sure I say it loud enough for Joni to hear.

Sofia's face reddens and I grin. I'm not sure what's more fun: teasing her or tormenting him.

I kiss her gently on the lips and linger there for a long heartbeat before pulling away. Her eyes are still shut and I can tell I'm affecting her like she's affecting me. I'm not sure if that's a good thing or not, but for now I don't care.

She reopens her eyes as her grandmother speaks. Joni replies in Finnish. I have a feeling he's not translating what I told Sofia.

"I'll see you tomorrow." I lean in so only she can hear the next part. "I'll meet you at the same spot and at the same time as today."

All she can do is nod. I'm definitely getting to her.

Before she can change her mind about hanging out with me, I say goodbye and leave.

Usually after I kiss a girl, I don't dwell on it. I've kissed so many girls in the past year, they've all blended into one. But on the drive back to Helsinki, all I can think about is the kiss I shared with Sofia—and how I want to kiss her again.

# Chapter Seven

## Kyle

Nik isn't at the rink when I arrive the following morning. He left a note in our kitchen, explaining that he would be late today. That's okay. The summer camp isn't just about helping the kids with their hockey skills. Conditioning is a huge part of it, too.

"Okay, guys," I say to the group of fifteen-year-olds in the locker room. "Coach Tikkanen is going to be late. So you're stuck with me for this morning's drills. Grab your sneakers and join me on the soccer field."

The boys scramble to their lockers to retrieve their shoes and head outside.

"What is it like playing in the NHL?" Kai, one of the group's more talented players, asks as we walk. From what I've seen of him so far, he has a great chance of making it to the NHL if he keeps up the hard work.

"Tough and a lot of work," I say. "But it's worth the sacrifices to get there—if you're smart about it and dedicated."

"What about the girls?" Mikko asks, his English a little slower than Kai's.

"You mean the female hockey players?" Or the puck bunnies?

"The girls who want to be with hockey players." His eyebrows do a comical dance to get his point across.

"They're there too. But you guys are too young to worry about them."

From the way Mikko is grinning, it's obvious the last thing he's worried about is the puck bunnies. He's looking forward to them.

As I contemplate what my position entails when it comes to sex-ed and warning the boys about the dangers of puck bunnies, I push the arena door open and let the guys out. If they were seventeen years old, I'd discuss the pros and cons of "relationships" with these types of hockey fans. But as is, I don't need parents with pitchforks coming after me for stepping over any boundaries.

The temperature is crisp outside. Perfect for what we're about to do. I indicate to the boys carrying the equipment to put the tote boxes on the sidelines. No one else is on the field yet.

"Warm up first," I say. "Two laps around the field."

For a minute, I watch them run. My entire body twitches for me to join them. I want to so badly, but I have plans this afternoon that don't involve the sauna. Plans that don't involve my fucked-up leg causing me problems.

*Just one lap*, a voice in the back of my head demands. But what's the point of running only one lap if the boys have to do two? It makes me appear out of shape, which I'm not. Even before the physician gave me the okay after the accident to start physical therapy, I'd pushed myself hard. Anything to get me back on the ice again as quickly as possible. But it hadn't been enough for me to return to the Bears or to any other NHL team. No one wants a player with a bummed leg.

To distract myself from the need to run with the boys, I lay out the equipment for the first drill. I can always hit the gym after my afternoon with Sofia and use the stationary bike. My leg can handle it better than running anyway.

The first boys to finish the laps stop in front of the equipment. Once everyone is here, I give them a few minutes to get stretched out.

"We've been working on balance for the past few days, and now you're ready for something more advanced." I place my left foot on my right calf, and bounce the ping-bong ball on the paddle, keeping the bounces small and controlled. I continue until I've bounced the ball twenty times. Not once do I drop it.

I lower my foot. "I want you to start with ten bounces. You can work up to more as you get better at it. Then switch legs." Fortunately, no one asks me to demonstrate the skill with my left leg. I'm nowhere near as impressive with that leg. Nothing like I used to be before the accident.

I walk around the group as they attempt the exercise. Mikko sends the ball up high, but his paddle tilts slightly and the flight path of his ball is altered. He can't reach it in enough time, and it falls to the grass. "Keep the bounces small," I remind them. "You aren't trying to knock the moon out of the sky."

Several boys snicker and lose control of their balls. A few curses are muttered in Finnish. I recognize them from when Nik first played with the Bears. Now he swears in English like the rest of us.

Once they've finished the drill, I teach them two others. "Whenever you have a spare moment," I tell them, "you should practice the drills. Alone they won't improve your skills, but balance, agility, coordination, reaction time, and speed are all important to your overall performance."

Nik still isn't here, so I have the boys move onto the agility part of our dryland training. "Do you guys know what the crab walk is?"

They exchange looks. I'm sure they know what it is. They just aren't familiar with the English word for it. I demonstrate what I want them to do. While they crab walk to the pylons, I let my thoughts drift to Sofia and the kiss. It's not the first time I've thought about it. It was all I could think about last night.

The question is will I get to kiss her again? She made it clear yesterday that she doesn't want a boyfriend and she doesn't believe in love. She also made it clear that she isn't interested in dating casually. Which means she doesn't view our time together as anything other than hanging out as friends. Now I have to convince her that kissing me again is a good idea, even if we are just friends.

The boys return to the start line, performing the crab walk backwards. By the time Nik shows up, the boys have done leapfrog, the wheelbarrow, and several other drills to work on their agility.

"Miss me?" Even though he sounds amused, he looks tired. All those puck bunnies he's been hooking up with are wearing him out.

Smirking, I slap him on the back. "Absolutely. I don't know how I survived without you."

The boys return to the sideline as they complete the final drill. Nik and I have them each grab two yo-yos from the tote. Last week, the boys worked on their coordination by using two yo-yos simultaneously, one in each hand. They start first with that drill.

"I won't be going to the gym with you after work," I tell Nik, keeping things vague. The last thing I want to mention is Sofia. Yesterday morning, he pointed out that he wanted to tap her. Not that he's seen her since the sauna incidence.

He simply nods, his attention focused on the boys.

I'm impressed at how far they've come since last week. They've obviously been practicing in their free time.

Nik and I demonstrate the next drill. We both take a yo-yo and I grab a tennis ball. We get the yo-yos going and toss the ball between us. We're not trying to screw each other up. It also means I need to focus on the ball and not on yesterday's kiss.

But tell that to my brain.

I've practiced this skill numerous times with Cody since the accident, helping him improve his coordination. And several of those times I'd fucked girls just before meeting up with him. But this is the first time I've had a pair of luscious lips on the brain while doing the drill. Reciting Newton's laws of motion won't help me now.

I'm not the only one who's distracted. Nik doesn't seem to be anymore mentally here than I am. He tosses the ball to me but it misses his intended target by a couple of feet and I dive to grab it.

Call it testosterone and competitive stupidity.

My bad leg impacts with the hard ground and a grunt jerks from my throat. Pain shoots up my leg and I groan. I lie still for several seconds, the pain temporarily paralyzing me.

Nik crouches beside me. "You okay?"

Nodding, I push myself up. While Nik gets the boys moving on the drill, I excuse myself and limp to the locker room to grab some over-the-counter pain meds. The entire way, I curse my leg and the drunk asshole for screwing things up for me.

Now I have to hope his stupidity doesn't mess up my plans this afternoon with Sofia.

# Chapter Eight

## Sofia

Yesterday's kiss has turned me into a mess. The entire time I was working, I couldn't focus on what I was doing. And yesterday, when Joni coughed and interrupted Kyle's kiss, I wanted to stomp on Joni's foot for his crappy timing.

But last night, while the memory of the kiss mocked me, I reminded myself that only *I* felt that way about it.

*Even Samantha's kisses were hotter than yours. I couldn't help myself.*

Luckily, Kyle and I won't have to kiss, again. The last thing I need is to embarrass myself again with another one. And the last thing I need is to become a basket case for the rest of the summer because of a single kiss. On the bright side, whenever I need to act sappy on the phone while I fake talk to him, I just have to think about the kiss.

"Sofia?"

I blink and return to the real world. Kyle's in front of me, but unlike yesterday, he isn't carrying a duffle and his hair isn't damp. He's wearing jeans and a plain blue t-shirt that gently hugs his muscles, and enhances the blue in his eyes behind his sexy glasses. The overall effect is enough to knock the air from my lungs.

I smile at him, hoping he hasn't noticed me checking him out. Not that it should make a difference. He's doing the same. His gaze takes in my denim shorts and shell-pink tank top.

"Have you been to the marketplace on the pier yet?" I ask.

He shakes his head.

"You'll love it." I always have, ever since I was a kid.

I lead him along the busy sidewalk, weaving around people hurrying in the opposite direction to where we're headed. "Thanks for helping me out yesterday."

He places his hand on my lower back. My skin tingles at his warm touch. "Did we convince your grandmother?"

"I'm not sure. I guess I'll find out soon enough."

"Do you think we convinced the grandson?"

"I don't think it matters if we convinced him," I say. "It's his and my grandmothers who need to be convinced. I doubt he's even interested."

"Oh, I can guarantee he's interested." Kyle pauses and lightly grabs my arm, stopping me. "I'm interested in getting to know you better, so why wouldn't he be interested too?"

I roll my eyes and start walking. Kyle easily catches up with me in a few strides.

"Doesn't matter," I say. "It's not going to happen. With either of you."

"I don't get it. You've got two guys interested in you, and you're not interested in either of us?"

"Should I be?"

"Why wouldn't you be? We're not bad looking."

I snort. "Shallow much?"

"I was just getting started on our virtues," Kyle says, grinning in a way that should be illegal. It's breath-stealing-adorable and he's not playing fair. "Or at least my virtues. I can't vouch for the rest of his."

I laugh. I can't help it. "Okay, what are your virtues?" Not that it changes anything.

"Well, obviously I'm funny."

I laugh again.

"See? I make 'em laugh every time."

"That doesn't count."

"Why not?"

"It just doesn't. Next." I move around a woman pushing a stroller as we continue along the sidewalk. Quaint low-rise buildings made of brick, with stores on the lower level, line both sides of the busy city street. A tram rambles past.

"I'm great at chasing assholes away while you're cleaning the sauna," he points out. "Doesn't that make me the protector of your virtue?"

I bite my lip to keep from laughing. It doesn't work.

"Told you I'm funny."

I shove him on the arm. "Keep going."

"I'm a great kisser, right?"

"And immodest too." I point left at the intersecting street, desperate to change the topic, hoping he hasn't noticed my now flushed face. I don't need to start thinking about how great his kisses are. I'm trying to forget them, not relive them. "This way."

We turn down the street as Kyle says, "And let's not forget that I know all kinds of useful facts about physics."

"So you're gonna get me all hot and bothered with your sexy physics talk?" My hands fly to my face. *Oh God! I can't believe I said that.*

He gently removes my hands from my face. The grin on his face is the sun shining on a cold winter day. "Right now, there's nothing I want more than to kiss you after that comment." He leans down, his lips inches from mine. I can't move. I can't speak. I can't even think. All I can do is stand still as his breath caresses my face.

But just as I think he's going to kiss me—and I'm not sure if I should let him or not—someone bumps into my side and sends me flying. Before I have to make an emergency crash landing on the sidewalk, and suffer from a serious case of road rash, I catch my footing and straighten at the same moment Kyle reaches out to grab my arm.

A homeless guy, who smells of alcohol and puke, sways on his feet and yells in Finnish at me. Kyle's face darkens as he glares at the guy.

I snatch hold of Kyle's hand and pull him away. "It's not worth getting into a fight over. He's so drunk, he doesn't know what he's doing."

Kyle threads his hand with mine, preventing us from being

separated again. Ian didn't hold my hand very often, so this feels odd yet nice.

"We're almost there." I continue walking.

We cross the street and I inhale the briny smell of the Baltic Sea ahead of us. "There." I point at the crowded pier where well over fifty booths are set up. Canopies of various colors keep the rain and sun off the merchandise. In the distance, a tall, majestic church stands proud, its green steeples reaching to the sky. Seagulls shriek overhead, looking for discarded food. "That's the famous marketplace."

A long historic building made of yellow and red bricks, and with tall white wooden doors, sits near the open market. I lead Kyle there first. Inside, the air is filled with an assortment of aromas, most notably the pungent smell of fresh fish. We wander down the aisle. On either side, booths beckon us, each one specializing in a different food item. Meats. Cheeses. Fish. Baked goods. Open-faced sandwiches. Desserts.

Kyle buys bread, Edam cheese, and thinly-sliced, processed reindeer meat, which I convinced him to try. We then walk outside and check out the other booths, which sell mainly fresh fruits, mushrooms, and vegetables. I buy peas, still in their pods, and tomatoes for Muumu. Kyle buys strawberries.

After we pick up sodas from one booth, we head to Esplanade Park, not far from the marketplace and sandwiched between two main roads. Historic buildings, several stories tall, line the street opposite the waterfront. A variety of specialty stores are located on the first floor of each building, with apartments and offices above them.

The giant greenish statue of Johan Ludwig Runeberg, a Finnish poet who is long since dead, stands proud in the park, on a stone pillar surrounded by flowers. We walk past, to the grassy space where kids are playing soccer, and find a quiet spot to sit. Kyle opens the container of strawberries. I bite into one and moan at the sweet taste. I eat another one and juice trickles down my chin. I moan again. God, these are good.

Kyle watches me, an odd expression on his face. He leans over and presses his lips where the juice dripped. I freeze, unsure what to do, but then he moves his mouth to mine and my brain screams at me to not let the kiss go further than this. I'll regret it if I do.

My body is less willing to comply.

Kyle's tongue traces along my lower lip.

*"Sorry, babe, but sex with you was…boring."*

I pull away and duck my head, pretending to be fascinated with a blade of grass. I can feel Kyle's gaze on me as he tries to puzzle me out.

"Do you have a boyfriend back home?" he asks.

I shake my head while examining another blade of grass. Anything to avoid looking at him.

"I had a boyfriend. He used to play collegiate football. I guess I'd suspected for a while that he was cheating on me whenever his team was away, but I was stupid and looked the other way, positive that since no one had mentioned it to me, I was just being paranoid." I shrugged. "I know lame, huh? But I was in love with him and love makes you naïve." Or maybe it just made *me* naïve.

"One day my best friend wanted to go to a party because there was a guy she was interested in," I continue. "I showed up at the party to find my boyfriend and a girl getting hot and heavy on the couch. I swore off boyfriends after that." I wrap my arms around my bent knees, pulling them to my chest, guarding my heart. "As the therapist of my best friend's mother would no doubt say, I have trust issues."

"Not all guys cheat on their girlfriends."

I give him a sad smile. "That's right. Some wait till they're married before they cheat. Just ask my mom." A seagull lands on the grass and pecks at a piece of forgotten garbage. "My father cheated on her with a student in his class. His college-aged student who was obsessed with him." Think *Fatal Attraction*, minus the boiling bunny. "I found out about it when I showed up for classes one day during my sophomore year of high school, and a classmate took great delight in sharing the details with me and everyone else at school.

I spent two months dealing with the aftermath." The taunts worm their way back in, and I close my eyes, keeping him from seeing the pain. The pain that intensified when Ian cheated on me.

In my dad's defense, he did try to end it with her after his better judgment finally kicked in. She wasn't too impressed, having some wild delusion that he would leave his family for her. On the bright side, she didn't try to kill my mom in the bathtub or blow us up or anything like that. But she did tell the faculty of International Law and Policy about his indiscretions. Dear old Dad lost his position and Mom dumped him.

So, yes, I have trust issues. Who wouldn't after that? How can I trust the next guy isn't going to demonstrate the same lack of better judgment that escaped both my father and Ian?

I open my eyes but I still can't look at Kyle. "I've long since decided I'm cursed. But try telling that to my grandmother." I finally look at him. "Do you think Joni would translate for me?"

He doesn't say anything, but I can see the pity in his eyes.

"So you've written off guys completely?"

A small boy blocks the soccer ball and dribbles it to the other end, darting between the opposition. The other boys struggle to steal the ball from him. They don't succeed.

"Have you ever been in love?" I reply.

His attention focused on the boy, Kyle's expression changes, a cloud drifting over the sun. "I was in love once."

Before I have a chance to ask him my next question, he stands and offers me his hand. "C'mon, let's go."

"Where're we going?"

"Remember our deal? Let's explore."

Works for me. Anything to move away from this conversation. I remove my camera from my backpack.

"You're a photographer?"

"Not professionally." I focus on the small boy and press the shutter release button as he kicks the ball toward the goal. "I love exploring the world through the lens. Searching for the story no one else sees 'cause they're too busy looking at the wrong things."

I show Kyle the picture in the viewfinder.

"Wow, that's really good."

"Thanks."

We wander around the pier. I take random shots of whatever grabs my attention. A mother carrying her baby in her arms. A discarded candy wrapper. A weathered old woman working alongside an equally weathered old man in a booth selling fish. After each shot, I tell a story about it. Some are kind of sappy (like with the elderly couple). Others leave Kyle laughing.

"You have quite the imagination," he says, chuckling after my rather twisted version of *The Little Mermaid*. He grabs my hand and pulls me to him. His warm breath brushes against my ear and sets off a round small fireworks in my lower belly. "And you're very talented."

Just when I think he's going to kiss me again, he pulls away. Leaving me both thankful he didn't kiss me and disappointed.

# Chapter Nine

## Kyle

Like yesterday, I wait for Sofia outside the sports center. Despite the clouds, the breeze is warm. Perfect for what I have planned.

I didn't have any accidents today while coaching. No dramatic saves that resulted in me hurting my leg like yesterday. Fortunately, by the time I met up with Sofia, the pain had dulled enough for me to walk around without limping.

I don't have to wait long before she steps from the building, wearing shorts, sneakers, and a fitted white t-shirt, and bounces down the steps. Something inside me shifts. Just a small shift. Nothing that would register on the Richter scale.

"Hey," she says, smiling. "Where do you want to go?"

"Linnanmäki Amusement Park."

Her smile fades. "Are you sure? I mean your…"

"My leg will be fine. We can take a bus there. It'll be fun." I raised my eyebrow. "Where's your sense of adventure?" Based on what we've both been through, fun is exactly what we need. A fresh start, even if it's for only a short time.

She laughs, and the sound reminds me of aurora borealis. Rich, full of wonder and mystery, and so damn beautiful. "Is that a challenge?"

I wink at her. "It is. And maybe it's just the start of my diabolical plans to see how far your sense of adventure goes."

"Okay, you're on. Challenge accepted."

We catch the bus to Linnanmäki, then wait in line to buy tickets for the park.

"Just so we've got it straight, this isn't a date," Sofia says, putting her wallet back into her backpack after I refused to accept her money for the ticket.

I smirk. "Is that your way of getting out of kissing me?"

"No. Yes. I mean there won't be any more kisses."

"Not even if I decide it's part of the challenge?"

She rolls her eyes. "How can us kissing be part of the challenge?" Her gaze drops to my lips. "We've already kissed."

A slow smile grows on my face at the memory of the kiss and the way she had moaned against my mouth. "But that doesn't count," I say.

"Why not?"

"Because we did it for the wrong reasons." Before she has a chance to argue, I ask, "What do you want to ride on first?"

"Your challenge. Your choice."

I scan the area, checking the choices. "How are you with heights?"

She bites her lip for a second and that's the only answer I need. I slip her hand into mine and squeeze it. "You'll be fine. I'll be with you the entire time. And these rides were designed to work with physics, not against it. Nothing bad will happen."

"Unless I lose my lunch."

"And if you do, it's not the end of the world, right?"

She looks at me like I'm nuts but eventually nods. "Okay, let's do it."

We walk to the tower ride and join the long line. "You said you took biomechanics last year. Did you enjoy it?" I ask.

The smile from earlier slips back on her face. "I did. I wasn't sure I would. Math and I aren't actually besties, so I avoided physics in high school. But I managed to pull off a B in biomechanics." The smile brightens. "I wouldn't mind learning more physics. From you."

"Like what?"

She thinks for a second, her focus on the ride in front of us. The people in the seats around the base suddenly shoot up, screaming, to the top of the tower. They stop, free fall, then bounce up again.

She tears her attention away from the ride, her face paler. "How do Santa's reindeer fly?" she asks, her face without a hint of humor.

With an equally straight face, I reply, "While the rides here have to abide by the laws of physics as we know them, Santa's reindeer are able to ignore those laws since they are…they are magical."

"I knew it!" She laughs. "Okay, tell me something that has to do with physics and hockey."

A light in my chest flickers on. A light that had burned out after the accident. She remembers what I told her the other day. Which makes her nothing like the puck bunnies who are only interested in fucking me so they can tell their friends that they screwed a NHL hockey player. They never ask anything about me and I never volunteer anything, either. Sofia's different. She's interested in the real me and nothing less.

"What do you know about impulse?" I ask.

She bits her lip, again, as she thinks. "Not much. It has to do with momentum."

"That's right. It's based on Newton's second law of motion. It's the force applied for a given amount of time. The greater the force, the greater the impulse. If you have two hockey players charging down the ice toward their respective pucks during a drill, the one who hits the puck the hardest will send his puck traveling further, assuming the time of contact between the puck and the stick is the same between the two players."

"And if one player screws up on the follow through," she says, "the contact time is less, and the puck won't go as far even if the force was the same as with the other player?"

The warmth inside me spreads at how she's listening to what I'm saying. "Exactly. You got it."

She asks me a few more questions as we wait. We're almost near the front of the line when she sucks in a sharp breath. We're in the next group to go on the ride. The physics Q&A isn't enough to relax her.

"We don't have to do this if you don't want to," I tell her.

She watches as the people in the seats jerk upwards. The muscles in her shoulders visibly tighten. "No, I'm good."

"Let's play a game."

She pulls her attention from the ride. "What kind of game?"

"One person makes a statement about the other person, and if it's false, the other person has to tell the truth or do a dare." I used to play this game with Cody. I spent more time doing the dares than telling the truth.

Sofia peers at the ride again. "Okay, you ask first."

"All right. You ready?"

She takes a deep breath then nods. "Ready?"

"You once played spin the bottle and had to kiss the class geek."

She laughs and some of her tension drains away. "Is this your way of getting me to kiss you at the end of our non-date date?"

"Hey, just answer the question."

"False. The bottle landed on a girl. Who later came out of the closet in our senior year and everyone thought she was a lesbian because of my kiss."

The corner of my mouth slides up. "Can't say I'm surprised. You're an amazing kisser."

Sofia's face flushes but she doesn't have a chance to say anything because the line moves forward. We take our seats and I reach for her hand. She willingly accepts it. Within seconds, I swear there's no circulation left in the hand she's gripping.

The ride jerks up and my stomach stays behind on a slight time delay. She screams. Her hand releases mine and she grabs the safety harness pressing against her shoulders. She screams like everyone else as we rapidly ascend, then we drop, and for a moment my stomach feels like it was left behind, again.

After a few more rapid ascents and descents, the ride returns to the ground. Sofia's smiling, and I have a feeling it has nothing to do with the ride being over.

We climb down from the seats and she kisses my cheek. A quick kiss. One filled with gratitude, nothing more.

"Thanks," she says.

"For what?"

"For taking me on that ride. For challenging me to do something I didn't think I could do. For being there for me." She scans the nearby rides. "Okay, where to now?"

We walk around the park, riding whatever ride Sofia's comfortable with…which surprisingly includes the roller coaster. We also play arcade games while throwing out the occasional question in our True and False game. I fight to keep the limp from being noticeable as the ache in my leg builds. It's not bad yet, but since I didn't have a chance to sit in the sauna after work, it's worse than it might have otherwise been.

"You dated the high school mascot in your senior year." She sips her smoothie through her straw in a way that's incredibly hot. As in, I'm-getting-hard-against-my-jeans-zipper hot.

"True or false," she prompts.

"False. Our mascot was a bulldog. An actual bulldog. You *were* the high school mascot in your senior year."

"True. But it wasn't anything sexy. We were the woodchucks and no one else wanted to do it, mainly because the mascot had to do this stupid dance." She demonstrates, shaking her ass, which does nothing for my situation.

Rain splatters against my arms and my head. Scattered shrieks pierce the air as the rain picks up in intensity and people run for cover.

"We might as well catch our bus now," Sofia calls out. Her damp t-shirt clings to her body. The image in my mind of peeling off her clothes and finding the body I know is buried underneath also doesn't help my situation.

"Good idea."

We walk to the bus stop, the rain no longer bothering us. We're already wet. The entire time I wonder if I should risk kissing her again, but in the end it doesn't matter if I want to kiss her or if she wants me to kiss her, her bus is waiting at the stop.

"Thanks for the fun. See ya later," is all she has time to say.

And I'm left alone, watching her climb on the bus. It drives away as I wonder what the heck I'm going to do. Sofia is getting to me in a way no girl has in a while, and I'm not sure what I should do about it.

Or if I should do anything about it.

# Chapter Ten

## Sofia

The day I walked out of my pity party for one had been the first warm day of spring. Young green shoots were poking their way between the dead brown grass. The early buds were forming on the trees and bushes. Birds were chirping from the branches in my backyard. That was the day I decided to spend the summer in Finland and get a fresh start.

My plan might've been to have a fresh start, but so far it hasn't happened. The same tired Sofia stares back at me in the mirror. My long blond hair is pulled back in a ponytail. The same way it has been for the past year. I can't even remember the last time I had a haircut.

I take a deep breath and make a decision. Muumu is watching TV on the orange vinyl couch in my room (aka the living room). She nods at me as I enter and tells me I can change the channel if I want. I tell her I'm good, although I'm not sure if it has the same meaning in Finnish as it does in English.

Taking my phone with me, I step out onto the balcony. Laughter greets me from young kids running around the playground one level down. Tall apartment buildings and birch trees surround the area. Even years after I was last here, the area looks the same.

I Google hair salons in Vantaa and I call one to book an appointment for myself and for Muumu. Luckily, the girl who answers the phone speaks English.

"I have a cancellation for one o'clock this afternoon. I can fit you both in then. Is that okay?"

Not only can she fit us in for hair appointments, she can schedule us in for pedicures and manicures. Perfect. Let the girl-bonding session begin. My grandfather died a few years ago and Muumu has lived alone ever since. Who knows when she last did something nice for herself. In the short time I've been here, she's done all kinds of nice things for me.

I return to the living room and sit next to Muumu on the couch. With my smart phone, I Google translate the words I need to help me. I don't use my phone for translating too often because it's a major drain on my phone plan. Plus, I've learned the hard way that it's not always the most reliable method. The translations have been screwy more times than they've been correct.

Maybe sensing I want to say something, she looks expectantly at me. I say the Finnish word for haircut and I point to her then me. Her expression is blank at first, as she tries to figure out what I said, but after a few seconds she nods. I pretend to paint my fingernails and toenails. Again, I point to her then me.

She nods and I let out a relieved breath. That was easy enough. I tell her the appointments are today, as well as the where and the when. Her eyes light up at the news.

My phone pings. I check the text from Maija. I haven't heard from Kyle today, but Maija and I have plans for tonight. I respond to her text confirming we're still on. I've already told Muumu that I'm going dancing with a friend tonight. The first thing she asked was if it was Joni. I might have rolled my eyes.

Muumu's show finishes and a *Friends* episode comes on. I laugh at something Rachel tells Ross. Apparently, Rachel and Ross are just as funny with Finnish subtitles, because Muumu also laughs, albeit a second later because of the delay in translation. By the end of the show, we're both laughing hard.

Muumu drives us to the hair salon and day spa in time for our appointment. She's normally animated, but this Muumu is like a kid on candy. She's as excited about our girl-bonding session as I am, which makes me feel a million times better already.

We arrive five minutes early and are directed to the seats in the corner, where we sit and wait our turn. Muumu picks a tabloid from the coffee table. I select a hairstyling magazine and flip through it. I need a change, but nothing too drastic.

Something to represent the new me.

# Chapter Eleven

## Kyle

My phone rings as Nik and I walk along the sidewalk to the dance club. I check to see who it is—my brother, Cody—and accept the call. "Hey, what's up?"

"Nothing much. What are you up to?" His tone is in the gray zone between interrogation and casual. Which way it falls depends on how I answer.

And since lying to Cody is out, given the loud music spilling onto the streets… "Coaching the guys is going well, but they're nowhere near as talented as you." Who knows if he's buying my bullshit. They're all equally talented. "Nik and I are just checking out the local night scene."

My brother groans. He thinks I'm out to get wasted and laid. To forget about last year.

Except this time, he's wrong.

I'm here to forget the girl who's starting to get to me in the short time I've known her. She's not what I need. What I need is exactly what I've been doing since the accident—living the life I gave up to get married so young.

"I promise, I'm fine," I say. "I'll call you tomorrow. Promise." And this time I won't be hung over. Or at least I'll try not to be.

I promise Cody I'll be careful tonight and end the call.

The nightclub is similar to any other back home. But instead of the normal college crowd, here you've got your college-crowd smorgasbord from all over the world.

Nik's face lights up and he straight-lines for the bar while scanning the crowd. He's not just hunting for an easy lay for himself. He's searching for a girl with female friends so neither of us go home empty handed.

I leave him talking to a group of girls Sofia's age, and walk to the bar. Contrary to what Nik wanted, I haven't been back here since the night I went home with the girl who looked like a sexy version of Snow White. I order drinks for us and join him and his groupies. I listen to the introductions—and forget their names the instant I spot her on the dance floor. Her long brown hair swings against the olive brown of her shoulders. Her purple dress skims her curves. Gabby.

Except it isn't Gabby. But that doesn't matter. Just seeing her is a stabbing reminder of everything I've lost. I swallow back the pain and the memories of the last time I saw her, bleeding next to me in the car.

One of Nik's groupies says something to me. I block her out as I down my beer like it's a life preserver to keep me from drowning. Once the drink's finished, I return to the bar and order two more. I don't give a damn what I promised Cody or my parents. I need this. I'm not planning to get wasted. Just a little buzzed to get me through the evening.

I return to Nik and gulp back some beer. He glances at the two bottles in my hand but doesn't say anything. The girl who tried to talk to me earlier asks him a question. He nods and they head for the dance floor. Her friend asks me if I want to dance, but since the Gabby lookalike is there, I shake my head and go back to drinking. She quickly loses interest in me and chats with her friends. In Finnish.

As I contemplate the pros and cons of bailing on this fun-filled evening, my gaze catches a familiar blond. A familiar blond who looks...different. Her long blond hair now swings just above her shoulders. She looked pretty before, but now she's hot. I blink, positive it can't be Sofia. It must be another look alike. The universe hates me that much.

She's with a girl and a guy, and is laughing. My eyes scour the crowd near her. If Joni's here, I don't see him. I let out a slow breath and the tension that's been building trickles away like water from a faulty faucet.

I continue staring at Sofia until she must've sensed me watching her and looks over. She smiles and everything instantly feels better with the world. Without saying anything to the girls, I walk over to her, bumping into people as the alcohol kicks in. Shit. Not how I want Sofia to see me.

I stop in front of her. Her smile wavers and she glances at the dance floor, her mind spinning over something. She then grabs my hand. The warmth of it seeps into my skin and sobers me a little.

"Let's dance." She pulls me toward the crowded space.

We don't get that far. As if summoned by my thoughts of her earlier, Snow White steps in front of me and rests her hand on my chest. The seductive curl of her lips makes it clear she wants a repeat of the other night. "Hi, Kyle."

# Chapter Twelve

## Sofia

The woman steps closer to Kyle, her manicured hand still on his chest. Everything about her is the opposite of me—if you don't count my newly manicured fingers and toes.

She's about my age, but her chin-length black hair and slim fitting red dress scream sophistication. Her long legs appear never ending, especially with her stilettos and short dress. She's obviously not living out of a suitcase with only a limited supply of clothing.

I glance down at my short skirt and the white tank top that Kyle has seen me in before.

"I've missed you," she purrs and my stomach twists. "My bed's been lonely without you." Her hand moves south, stopping just above the waistband of his jeans. She either hasn't noticed me standing next to him or just doesn't care. Clearly I'm not much competition as far as she's concerned.

And she's right.

I step away and return to Maija and her boyfriend. Guys like Kyle aren't interested in girls like me, not when they can have women like the one now whispering in his ear about all the hot positions they can do tonight.

My stomach pinches at the thought. Silly stomach. But really, what did I expect? He knows I'm not interested in a boyfriend and that my last one cheated on me. Kyle's probably already guessed why Ian did that. It doesn't take a genius to figure out I wasn't all Ian had hoped for. This woman knows how to please a man; I'm a million miles from there.

"Hey," Kyle says, catching up to me. "I thought we were going to dance." His words hold a slight slur.

"You were busy." I cringe inwardly at how petty that sounded. Kyle doesn't seem to notice.

"Sorry about that. She surprised me by showing up like that."

"Who is she?" I glance around but can't see her anywhere.

Kyle doesn't say anything. He reaches for my hand and tries to pull me to the dance floor. I hold my ground.

"I'll still dance with you," I say, "But I just want to know who she is?" And if you've slept with her.

He releases my hand. His shoulders slouch forward, my words knocking the wind out of him. "She was a one-night stand. Nothing more than that. I haven't seen her since then. At least not until tonight."

"Okay." I smile, the movement small but genuine. "Thank you for being honest with me." I place my hand on his biceps, the muscle hard from hours in the gym. "And I believe you owe me a dance."

We manage to find a spot on the crowded dance floor, our bodies pressed together. I wrap my arms around his neck and move my body with his. It's been a while since I last went dancing. I've missed it. I just didn't realize how much until now.

I turn around, my back against his chest, my arms around his neck. My tank top raises, exposing my stomach. His fingers trace the skin above my waistband. Tiny shivers glance across my skin at his touch and I suck in a sharp breath.

I move my body to the beat, the song fast yet sensual. The limited space keeps me against Kyle, and he takes advantage of the situation. His slight state of drunkenness has to do with that, too. His lips press the skin on my shoulder. Then his tongue flicks lightly against it, turning my legs into molten lava. It's a good thing his arm is around my waist, keeping me upright; otherwise, I'd melt onto the sticky floor.

The feel of Kyle's lips on my skin triggers the memory of them on my mouth, all of them good, which is part of the problem. I haven't been able to stop thinking about him since the kiss. I haven't stopped craving him since the kiss. Even at Linnanmäki, when he challenged me to face my fear of heights, I wanted to kiss him, really kiss him. But I couldn't.

His lips continue their path, marking their way along my shoulder. He pushes my hair aside, and his mouth is back to teasing me. As if it has a will of its own, my head drops to his shoulder, encouraging him to keep going. My brain tells me to stop this from continuing further. My body says to hell with it. I deserve this just once.

The song slows, but we stay the same, moving in a way that makes me dizzy with want. His hands slide down my hips. I sway against him. His breath is raspy in my ear and he moans, the sound barely heard over the loud music.

I turn around to face him and rewrap my arms around his neck. My gaze falls on his mouth. I want to kiss him so badly. Maybe things will be different with Kyle. Maybe he can teach me to be a better lover. Maybe he can give me the confidence I'm missing, like he did at the amusement park when it came to my fear of heights.

I kiss him. Lightly. Hunger gleams in his eyes. Hunger and uncertainty. Before I can speak, his mouth is back on mine and I welcome him in.

His kiss is as amazing as I remember. Our tongues stroke, glide, feel in time to the music and the swaying of our bodies. Nothing else exists. Just us. And the kiss.

Kyle's hands drift from my hips to my lower back and pull me closer. Every cell in my body hums, until I'm positive the vibrations in the floor are caused by me and not the music. Our swaying stops. The kissing doesn't.

It's not until someone bumps against us that I realize the music is no longer slow. Kyle takes my hand and leads me off the dance floor, my breath still ragged. He pauses, looks at a group of girls and the guy from that day in the sauna, then heads toward Maija and her boyfriend.

His expression looks torn, but I can't tell what he's torn about. Is it because he's with me instead of those girls? If they gave him the chance, would he go home with one of them?

"Is something wrong?" His thumb slides along my lip and pulls it away from my teeth. Until then, I hadn't realized I was chewing it.

"No, I'm good." I glance over my shoulder at the girls again. I've never done a one-night stand before. I've only been with Ian. I flirt with guys all the time, but when it comes to taking things further, the art of seduction is lost on me.

I look back at Kyle. I guess there's a first for everything.

I introduce Maija and her boyfriend to Kyle. Kyle and Toivo hit it off immediately, and start talking hockey.

Kyle's friend joins us with his three-girl entourage.

Maija pulls me aside. "Watch out for the girl in the pink shorts. I heard her talking to her friend in the bathroom. She's very interested in Kyle, if you know what I mean." I know what she means. The girl isn't touching him, but she's close enough that if she shifts slightly, there'll be a lot of bodily contact.

"Thanks for the warning."

Maija wraps her arms about her boyfriend's waist. I do the same to Kyle, sliding between him and Pink Shorts. She gives me the death glare but moves back a step. Kyle gives me an amused grin. I almost reach up and kiss him, but decide it might be too much. He's not territory to be marked.

Kyle's not the only one looking amused at the situation. His friend, Nik, keeps eyeing both me and Pink Shorts, as if he expects us to Jell-O wrestle at any second.

I'm not sure if Pink Shorts thinks we're in some sort of contest, and Kyle is the prize, but she moves to his other side and rubs the front of her body against his hip. Maybe if I were another girl, I'd kiss him and tell her to back off. Instead, I move away, realizing my plan isn't working, and toy with the swan charm around my neck. I'm not her. I'm not trained in the art of seduction.

I don't get too far. Kyle tightens his hold on my waist. "Where do you think you're going?" He chuckles against my cheek.

I lean against him, victory coursing through me.

With a huff, Pink Shorts leaves to dance with her friends and some guys, and I'm left contemplating the next step in my plan.

And come up with a blank.

Not paying attention to Kyle and Toivo's current conversation, I covertly watch the girl with Nik. She's wrapped around him, her hand on his butt, her mouth on his neck. Half of his attention is directed at her, the other on the guys' conversation. He takes a break from listening to them to shove his tongue down her throat and grab her breast.

Ewww. *Lesson plan aborted.* I quickly return my attention to Kyle and Toivo.

Maija and her boyfriend soon say their goodbyes. I'm about to leave with them, so they can walk me to Muumu's car, when Kyle stops me.

"Do you have to leave? I thought maybe you could stay and protect me."

"Protect you from what?"

He nods toward Pink Shorts and her friends.

I start to laugh but it turns into a yawn. "I should go. I have to drive home."

"Then let's get out of here. I'll walk you to your car." He tells Nik he's done for the night, and his friend winks at me. Inwardly I groan. I might want to have sex with Kyle, but I don't want Nik to know about it. Then again, what difference does it make? If I have sex with Kyle, he won't want anything to do with me after that. Isn't that how it goes with one-night stands? He had sex with that woman from earlier and he wasn't interested in sleeping with her again. Was that because she wasn't so hot under the covers after all, or because he doesn't do repeat business?

A sad ache slams into me. Is that really what I want? Exploring Helsinki with Kyle has been more fun than I ever expected. Am I ready to risk it for sex-ed 101?

As I deliberate the pros and cons of my plan, we walk to where a man's stumbling to the driver side of the car. His girlfriend is sitting in the passenger seat. My entire body goes numb at the realization of what he's about to do.

"Hey buddy," Kyle says. "You aren't driving, are you?"

The man responds, but his words are slurred. I can't tell if he answers in English or Finnish. He turns and opens the door.

Before the man can climb in, Kyle grabs hold of his shoulder and whips him around. The man staggers but manages to steady himself with the car door. The girl in the car shrieks at us in Finnish.

"You're too fucking drunk to drive," Kyle yells in his face.

The man shoves Kyle away and slurs what I guess to be obscenities. Kyle's jaw tightens and he shoves him right back, pushing him against the car with a lot more force than is called for.

I don't know where the man gets his strength from—maybe from fear or from anger or from the alcohol—but he knocks Kyle's arms off him and swings at Kyle. Kyle's own anger isn't enough to dull the effects of the beer he drank. And he's not fast enough to block the blow. The man's fist slams into Kyle's jaw.

# Chapter Thirteen

## Sofia

There's a misguided belief that a woman needs a man to protect her. He's the hero of her story, the one who makes her feel loved and safe. To hell with that.

Sometimes men need saving, too.

I grab the jerk's arm and attempt to yank him from Kyle. None too thrilled at my attempts to intervene, the man lashes his hand out at me. His ring digs into the flesh below my right eye, and gouges the skin. Blood trickles down my cheek but there isn't time to worry about it. Kyle lies sprawled on the ground, stunned, his glasses on the asphalt near him. The man sneers at him and moves his leg back, ready to kick Kyle in the ribs.

"Kyle!" I scream out.

Kyle looks over at the man, and rolls out of the way. He staggers up but doesn't move fast enough. The booted foot hits him low in the ribs, below his arm, and Kyle collapses to his knees.

I throw myself at the man. It's a stupid move, but it's all I can come up with to buy Kyle time to get up.

The man's girlfriend goes back to shrieking and jumps into the brawl. She grabs hold of my hair and yanks my head back. I cry out in pain.

Just as I expect them to both turn on me and beat me to a pulp, someone yells in Finnish and the woman is lifted off me. Dazed from being hit in the face, it takes me a minute to realize two cops have stepped in. The man and the woman are talking to them in

Finnish. The man slurs while the woman's shrill voice digs into my brain. Kyle is still on the ground but is now sitting, his glasses back on his face.

"He was going to drive while drunk." I point at the man. "Kyle was stopping him before he got behind the wheel and killed someone. He assaulted Kyle and kicked him in the chest." I kneel next to Kyle and tenderly touch where the boot hit him. He flinches.

His gaze lands on where the ring dug into my cheek. I can't tell if the cut is still bleeding, but it stings like crazy. He cups my cheek in his hand and brushes his thumb below the cut. "Did he do that?"

I nod.

The cop crouches next to me. "The man assaulted you?" His voice is gentle yet firm. English comes easily to him.

"I was pulling him away from Kyle and he hit me."

"What about the woman? Did she do anything?"

"She was in the passenger seat and shrieking for most of it. When I tried to keep the man from kicking Kyle again, she grabbed my hair." My scalp still hurts from the vicious attack. I can't imagine it will be too thrilled next time I brush my hair.

Realizing that Kyle and I are the innocent ones in this whole mess, the cop asks us more questions and lets us go. Kyle and I walk back to my car. I had suggested that I could drive him to the hospital to have his ribs checked out. He waved it off, claiming he's not hurt.

"Why don't you come over to my apartment and I'll deal with your cut?" he says once we reach my car.

I hesitate for a moment. The one-night stand I was considering is now a distant thought. He won't be in any shape for it to happen. Knowing that is a huge weight temporarily knocked off my shoulders. "Okay."

I drive us to his apartment and we walk up the first flight of stairs. But as his breathing increases with the exertion, it becomes clear from the grimace on his face that his ribs bother him. How much, I can't tell.

"What floor are you on?" I ask.

"Sixth."

"We're taking the elevator." I don't give him a chance to argue. I walk to it and press the up button. The elevator opens soon after and we enter, both lost in thought. The doors reopen on his floor, and we walk down the short hallway to his apartment. He opens the door and lets me in.

The place is bigger than Muumu's apartment, but that's because it has two bedrooms instead of one. Kyle points to the door at the end of the hallway, where it turns into a T-junction, and tells me he'll meet me there in a minute.

I end up in the bathroom. Even though two guys live here, the place is clean. The navy towels are lined up neatly on the towel rack. The tub is clean, and so is the sink. Not at all what I was expecting.

I check the damage to my face in the mirror. The cut isn't deep, only half an inch. It might not leave a scar if I'm lucky, but there's no way I can hide it from Muumu. And how the hell will I explain what happened? She's going to freak. Or maybe I can pretend I accidentally walked into a branch. With me, that's highly believable.

Kyle returns with a first aid kit. "Okay, jump up." He pats the counter next to the sink. Once I'm up, he nudges my legs apart and steps between them. He examines the cut, his fingers tracing the skin below it.

And I examine his lips.

An electrifying buzz hums through my body, starting from where our bodies touch. I'm both vulnerable and on fire, and I don't want the feeling to end.

"True or false," I whisper. "You have a pet Chihuahua in Minneapolis."

His chuckle is a low, sexy rumble. "I prefer bigger dogs. My parents have a golden retriever."

"Those are my favorite breed."

His gaze drops to my lips for a heartbeat before tearing away. He removes gauze from the first aid kit, rips the package open, and leans around me to turn the tap on, placing his hand on my hip. His ocean scent eases its way around me, embraces me, fires me up. His chest glances mine, and the electric buzz intensifies to the point where I'm ready to forget the cut. I want him. All of him.

Water splashes in the sink behind me. It stops and Kyle moves slightly back. His eyes focus on my cheek and he dabs the cut. The cold, wet gauze soothes the stinging. Next, he opens the Steri-Strips and applies them to my cut, sealing the edges together. His gaze shifts from my wound to my eyes and he drinks me in for a long second.

My heart flutters against my ribs, like Mina in her birdcage when she gets excited. With Kyle as close as he is, I wouldn't be surprised if he can hear it. Heck, I wouldn't be surprised if his neighbors can hear it.

As if some magnetic force pulls us together, we drift toward each other, hesitate, then our mouths collide. Tasting. Wanting. Thriving. I moan as his tongue teases mine. Normally I wouldn't find his beer taste so erotic, but everything about this man gets me excited. Even when I know he shouldn't have this affect on me. Even when I know I should walk away and protect my heart.

But I can't, and it goes beyond wanting to have sex with Kyle and temporarily forgetting the past. There's something about him, his sense of humor, his tenderness, his thoughtfulness, that makes me want to learn everything there is to know about him. To know all his secrets and his dreams.

I tangle my fingers in his hair. The soft strands curl loosely around them. My legs wrap around his hips as if they have a mind of their own. My short skirt hikes up to the tops of my thighs. I'm exposed, vulnerable, but I don't care. I want to feel him next to me. Against me.

The thickening length in Kyle's jeans presses against my panties and the aching throb beneath. Kyle leans in, and I moan in his mouth at the sensation rocking my body. My fingers tighten their grip on his hair. But just as I think he's going to do me right here on the counter, he pulls away from my lips, breath ragged, and rests his forehead on mine.

"We need to stop," he whispers, though he sounds like stopping is the last thing he wants. My body silently groans in protest. *I* silently groan in protest. But then I remember why he'd want to stop, and it's not because he isn't interested in me.

I finger the hem of his t-shirt and inch it up until I've exposed the skin where the guy viciously booted him. Kyle reaches down and whips the fabric over his head, then tosses it onto the floor. I catch the tail end of the wince on his face from the movement, and my gaze skims over his hard chest, covered with a scattering of fading scars, to where he was hit on his side. A bruise the size of my fist is already forming. The bruise is faint, but by tomorrow it will be black.

I touch it, my finger tracing over his skin. "Does it hurt?"

"It's fine."

"And you're lying." I jump down from the counter. "Go lie on your bed. I'll be right there." I start to leave, but realize I have no idea where his room is. I don't exactly want to step into his roommate's by mistake. I turn back to Kyle. "Which one's your room?"

"The one across from the bathroom."

I locate the kitchen and rummage through the drawers until I find a small plastic bag. I open the freezer and remove the ice cube trays. After dumping ice into the bag and tying it up, I track down Kyle's room.

I find him lying on his bed, eyes closed, t-shirt still off. I kneel next to him. The bed dips under my weight but his eyes remain closed. "Are you sleeping?" I whisper.

"If I am, don't wake me up. I don't want this to end."

I frown. "You don't want the pain to end?"

He peers at me. "No. I don't want to wake up and find out I only dreamt you were in bed with me."

I wiggle a little closer to him and place the icepack on his ribs. "I got some ice to help with the bruising."

He closes his eyes again. "That wasn't quite what I imagined in my dream." His words fade with the final ones and his breathing eases.

I yawn, the events of the evening heavy on me like a blanket, pulling me into a state of sleepiness. I blink it away, and cover Kyle with the bedding.

"Please stay," he mumbles, but I can't be sure if he's awake or saying it in his sleep.

"Okay." I climb under the covers with him, remove his glasses from his face, and lean over him to place them on his nightstand. "I'll stay for a few minutes." To keep the ice against his bruise.

• • •

The room is dark when I wake up, other than a faint glow from the curtains next to the bed. There's something off about its location. I'm not at Muumu's.

Panic seeps in, like rainwater after a storm, giving life to my fears. It takes a few moments as my eyes adjust to the darkness for me to remember I'm with Kyle, in his bed. It takes even less time to figure out what woke me up as the panic fades away.

I twist around to find Kyle moving restlessly in his sleep. He mutters something but the words are too soft to hear. I can't understand what he's saying, although one thing is clear, he's having a nightmare.

"Kyle?" I say quietly so not to scare him. When that doesn't get a response, I place my hand on his arm, and say a little louder, "Kyle, it's okay. You're having a nightmare." But despite my words, he's still restless. He still looks vulnerable. Maybe even more so than I felt earlier when we were in the bathroom.

I click on the bedside light. A soft light fills the space around us, leaving the room in long shadows. The restlessness and murmurs stop, and Kyle slowly opens his eyes as I stroke his bare arm. His face twists in confusion.

He blinks, attempting to bring me into focus since he doesn't have his glasses on. The confused expression eases from his face. "You're here," he whispers.

"You were having a nightmare. You wanna talk about it?"

He shakes his head. "No." A sad smile ghosts his lips. "Can I hold you for a bit?"

I place the bag of ice water on the floor, and shift closer to him so our bodies touch. "Sure."

He drapes his arm over my waist, and his fingers stroke lazy circles on my lower back. His intense gaze locks on my eyes for a heartbeat, then drops to my lips.

In an easy move that lasts both a brief moment and a million years, he lowers his mouth to mine. Our bodies shift, so I'm lying on my back and he's on top of me. The weight of him sends a thrill through my body that matches the one the kiss ignited.

We deepen the kiss, the passion and lust growing stronger with each passing second. Needing more of him, I wrap my leg around his hip, then place my hands on his butt and encourage him to rock against me. He does and the throbbing between my legs builds, climbing toward the peak I sense coming, but have never reached before. I push away the thought that maybe that's why Ian had found sex with me boring, and a moan escapes my lips.

"Oh, God, please," I beg.

Kyle pauses, pulling back slightly, his eyes dark with want. But want isn't the only the emotion peering back at me. He's deliberating something.

Before I can ask what's wrong, his hand inches under my tank top, and with a skilled flick of his fingers, my bra comes undone. My body screams that it needs to feel Kyle, all of Kyle against me. I sit up and remove my tank top and bra, and toss them to the floor.

His fingers trace along my shoulder and glide between my breasts. His thumb teases a nipple and a soft gasp falls from my lips. "So beautiful," he murmurs, his mouth returning to mine.

We lay back down and kiss, pouring every emotion, every desire into it, before his lips move away. They travel along my neck and chest, leaving a trail of goose bumps. He swirls his tongue around a nipple then takes the hard bud into his mouth. Like he did with his thumb, he teases me with each flick of his tongue, and pushes me closer to the release waiting for me at the peak.

He switches breasts and teases the second one into submission like he did the first. He then plants tender kisses along my ribs to my belly button. He hits my ticklish zone and I giggle.

I open my mouth to ask him about his bruised ribs, but don't get far as his fingers skim along my inner thigh and trace the edge of my panties. I inhale sharply, the sound quiet yet rough. His fingers then shift and brush against the seam of my entrance. The throbbing between my legs grows stronger, more desperate. My body jerks in response and I moan softly.

I want to touch him, to feel him, but he's too far away to reach. All I can do is tangle my hands in his loose curls.

He hooks his fingers on my panties and slides them down my legs. Once they reach my ankles, he removes them and tosses them onto the floor to meet up with my bra and tank top. He pushes the hem of my skirt up and separates my legs.

Panic floods me, and I fight to keep afloat. It was never like this with Ian, and I'm not sure what I'm supposed to do. Part of me wants to run. To hide. To not feel as vulnerable as I do now. The other part, the much larger part, wants to take my lesson much further. That part wins and I relax, closing my eyes briefly.

"God, Sofia, I want to taste you so badly."

Before I realize what he means, his tongue strokes and swirls against the oversensitive nerves between my legs, stoking the fire there, pushing me further and further toward the crest. Promising to take me to the stars and beyond.

I've never had a guy go down on me before. Clearly I've been missing out.

Unable to help myself, I squirm against Kyle's tongue. He slips a finger inside me and then another. They press against the soft lining, and a small wave of pleasure fans out from the spot. A mind-numbing taste of things to come.

A moan trembles from my lips, pleading for him to continue. He slowly pumps them in and out while his tongue continues its magic. I expect him to stop at any second, so we can physically share this moment together, but he doesn't. And the next thing I know, the throbbing radiates out, exploding between my legs, sending an aftershock that shatters my body.

I scream Kyle's name along with "Oh, God."

He moves up my body and kisses me deeply before pulling

away. I reach for the zipper of his jeans, but he wraps his fingers around mine before I can do anything.

He moves off the bed, putting distance between us. At least with Ian, he'd flop next to me on the bed once he was done and hold me. Kyle can't get away from me fast enough. A sinking feeling sits heavy in my belly. I screwed up. Again. And I have no idea what I did wrong so I can do it right next time.

"I'll be right back." He leaves the room, shutting the door behind him.

I pull on my underwear to the sound of the shower raining against the tub. Struggling to push away the pain and disappointment at what just happened, I retrieve my tank top from the floor and spot a silver chain with dog tags on the nightstand. They aren't the cheap kind. They're the kind you give someone you care about. A hockey stick is engraved on one side. On the other side are the words 'Forever yours, Gabby.'

The apartment door clicks open. A man speaks in what is supposed to be a hushed voice, except he's too drunk to realize he's anything but quiet. A female giggles, followed by a thud.

I hastily reach behind me and drop the dog tags on the nightstand. Without giving them another glance, I yank the rest of my clothes on and walk into the hallway.

"*Hei.*" Nik stumbles as he tries to kick off his shoe.

Knowing he's too drunk to think before he speaks, I ask, "Who's Gabby?"

The female who was all over him at the nightclub giggles, again.

Nik looks confused for a second then his face lights up. "She's Kyle's wife."

A pain similar to what I felt when I found out Ian was cheating on me slashes through my chest, destroying what little faith had remained that not all guys are like Ian and my father.

I should have known better.

# Chapter Fourteen

## Kyle

I turn the freezing water off and stand in the bathtub, letting the goose bumps remind me that I'm an idiot.

When I woke up from the nightmare, the last person I had expected to see was the very person I'd been dreaming about—Sofia. I had been reliving the night of the accident, which was typical for my nightmares. What wasn't typical was that Sofia was dead in the passenger seat of my car, not Gabby.

I'd been so relieved that it had only been a dream, I let all logic slide. Yes, I want Sofia. No denying that. But she's been hurt before. The last thing she needs is someone like me messing around with her then walking away.

I hadn't meant for things to go that far, but once I started, I didn't want to stop. I didn't want to ramble off some random physics facts in my head to take away my need for her. Yes, I should have walked away, that would have been the smart thing to do. But instead, I let my desire to be with her, to taste her, overrule all logic. And in the process, I let down my wall just enough. That's the only explanation I have for the nightmare.

I bang my fist against the tile as the accident plays in an endless loop in my head. I squeeze my eyes against the pain of hearing Gabby scream seconds before the collision. Except now it's Sofia's face I see, like in the nightmare.

God, I'm so screwed up.

I yank on my boxers and jeans, and leave the bathroom. A

girl giggles from Nik's room. It's not Sofia. The muffled sound belongs to someone who's been drinking too much, and will giggle at anything he tells her.

I return to my room…and stop dead in my doorway. Sofia's not in here, and neither are the clothes I tossed on the floor when I removed them from her.

I bend over and pick up the dog tags Gabby gave me our last Christmas together. They're a reminder of how fucked up my life is, not that I need a reminder. I could've sworn the dog tags were on the nightstand the last I looked. But the last time I paid attention to them was several nights ago. Have they been on the floor all this time and I didn't see them until now?

I walk into the hallway and spot the cell phone next to Nik's oversized sneakers. I pick it up. It's not mine and it's not Nik's. It could belong to his latest conquest.

Nik's bedroom door opens and my roommate walks out in all his naked glory. It's an annoying habit of his that he does with great frequency when "entertaining."

"Dude, put on some clothes, would you?"

Nik shrugs and walks to the kitchen. I follow him, even though I'd rather be in my room than find out what he's getting for his sexual entertainment.

"Does this belong to your *friend?*" I show him the phone.

He opens the fridge. "Dunno. Maybe it belongs to that plaything you brought back with you." He straightens, a can of spray whipping cream in his hand. "And by the way, you're welcome."

I frown. "Welcome for what?"

"Making sure she doesn't think there's gonna be a third period."

I feel my frown deepen. "What do you mean?"

"She asked who Gabby was. I told her your wife." He grins stupidly and waits for me to high-five him.

The only thing I want to do is slam my fist in his face. Inwardly I cringe. I'm not normally violent, even on the ice. But in the span of a couple of hours, I've broken my record for physically lashing out at someone or contemplating doing so—if you ignore my constant craving to punch the lights out of the drunk who stole my career and Gabby's life. But since he's dead, I don't.

"Fuck," I mutter.

Nik's grin widens. "I bet you did. Nice piece of ass she had."

I fist my hands. Definitely going for a record. "Don't ever talk about her that way again." Not that there will be an "again" after the stunt he just pulled.

Nik's grin wavers at my harsh tone. I hand him the phone. "Can you ask the girl in your room if this is hers?"

He nods and leaves. He returns a minute later. Shaking his head, he gives me back the phone. "No, it's not hers. At least you won't have to go around Finland to see who the shoe fits." He chuckles at his stupid analogy. I glare at him.

But he is right about one thing. It's not hard to figure out who it belongs to. Now, the problem will be returning it to her. Correction, returning it and getting Sofia to talk to me again. Because if I've guessed things correctly, she's put two and two together and come up with me as the major asshole who's cheating on his wife while he's in Finland. Like her ex-boyfriend cheated on her and her father cheated on her mother.

And now I have to prove to her, somehow, that she's wrong.

# Chapter Fifteen

## Kyle

One of the advantages of not getting drunk is that hitting the gym the next morning isn't so painful. Nik is still asleep in his room when I leave to go to the sports center. Judging from how wasted he was last night when he came home, I don't expect to see him anytime soon.

The sports center isn't too busy when I arrive. It's still early, but not too early for the cleaning staff to be working. I approach a woman mopping the floor. "*Hei*. Is Sofia working today?"

It's Sunday, but since she never mentioned last night if she's working today, the odds of her being here are miniscule.

The woman gives me a blank look. "Sofia?"

I've learned some Finnish since coming to Helsinki, but this is beyond what I can say. "*On Sofia*"—I point to the mop—"*tänään?*"

The woman laughs, which isn't too surprising. Between my Finnish and pointing to the mop, I've asked her if Sofia is a mop today.

I'm about to give up and head to the weight room when Rafu, a therapist from the building's physical therapy clinic, approaches us. The woman is still laughing.

He nods at me. "Can I help you with something, Kyle?"

"Maybe. I'm looking for an American girl who's working here for the summer. Her name's Sofia. I was just wondering if she's here today."

"Where does she work?"

"She's studying to be an athletic trainer, but they've got her cleaning toilets."

Rafu talks to the woman. She responds in rapid Finnish. "She's not working today," he tells me. "Sorry."

"That's okay. I figured I'd ask since I'm here." It's probably just as well she isn't here. Now that Sofia thinks I'm a cheating asshole with a wife back home, talking to her in public might not be a bright idea. Who knows how she'll react.

I thank them and walk toward the weight room. Like the rest of the building, the area is quiet, with only a few diehard exercisers working out. Toivo and his girlfriend are by the bench press.

"*Hei*," I say to them. "Do you need a spotter?"

"That would be great," Toivo replies.

"I'll let you two work out and talk hockey," Maija says, "and I'll be on the rowing machine. Have fun!" She walks away.

The best part about Toivo is that he's serious when it comes to training. He's not at the gym to socialize. We push each other hard, focused on the workout and on nothing else. It's not until we're finished that I start wondering why I'm even worried about what Nik's dumbass comment could mean for me when it comes to Sofia.

*Because she's a friend*, I remind myself. Yes, I'd be more than happy to screw her if she gave me another chance. But I also don't want to fuck up what we have between us. She's not a puck bunny. Unlike them, she wants to be friends.

But thanks to Nik, I might've lost her as even that.

Toivo and I finish off our workout and join Maija. As far as I can tell, Sofia hasn't told her yet that I'm a cheating douchebag of a husband.

"Do you want to have coffee with us?" Toivo asks as we head for the locker room.

"Sure. But I need to use the sauna first." I explain how the heat helps my injury. Like with Sofia, I'm vague as to how I got it, but even though he hasn't said anything, I have a feeling he knows who I am. And I have a feeling he knows about the accident. I have no idea if Maija also knows, but if she does, it's only time before she inadvertently mentions it to Sofia.

Maija splits off to go to the ladies' locker room. The men's sauna is busier than I expected, and it keeps Toivo from asking questions once he notices the scars on my leg. But he also doesn't seem too surprise to see them, confirming he knows who I am and what happened to me last year.

"Can you do me a favor?" I ask. "Can you not tell Maija about them or about who I am?" At his puzzled frown, I explain what I mean.

"Maija knows you used to play hockey for the Minnesota Bears. I told her." He cringes. "I'm sorry. I had no idea it was supposed to be a secret. But why don't you want Sofia to know that you used to play in the NHL?"

"She's different than the girls usually interested in me. Different in a good way. I'd rather she just see me as a regular guy." And not a man to pity because he lost everything important to him, no thanks to the stupidity of someone else.

"I'll talk to Maija but I can't guarantee anything. She's not into gossiping, but if she thinks Sofia should know, she will tell her."

"Thanks." That's better than nothing, I guess.

Nik texted me while I was in the sauna and wants me to call him back ASAP. I tell Toivo I'll meet him and Maija at the coffee place he mentioned. By the time I arrive, he has already asked her not to say anything to Sofia about my previous career.

"So you want me to lie to her?" Maija says.

"Not really." I tell her the same thing I told Toivo. "I just don't think she needs to know. That was my past and I'm focusing on my future." I don't mention what that is. If Maija's like most other girls—excluding puck bunnies—she's thinking happily-ever-after thoughts about me and Sofia. She doesn't need to know the truth—that Sofia isn't part of my future.

Maija remains torn between what she wants to do and what I've asked of her. In the end she lets out a hard breath. "Okay. I won't tell her. But if it comes out, you can't tell her I knew. This is between you two."

"Thanks."

One problem down. Next up? Dealing with the lie Nik told Sofia.

# Chapter Sixteen

## Sofia

I tie up my sneakers. Muumu emerges from her bedroom, smiling. She's in her bathrobe and has curlers in her hair. She asks me if I'm going for a run, but other than that I don't understand what she's saying, even though she says it slowly. You'd think after being here for almost a month, I'd at least be a little bit more fluent in the language. But noooo. I still suck at it.

And maybe that's why I notice whenever she says Joni's name. It's pretty much the only thing I recognize in that long string of Finnish.

"*Hei, hei,*" I say and open the door...to discover why she's been smiling ever since she left her room. Joni is standing in the hallway in his running gear. "Hi?"

"I thought you might like a running partner." His gaze drifts over my tank top and running shorts.

"Have you been waiting all this time?" I never told him when I run, but I suspect someone has. I look at that someone. She nods her encouragement.

"Maybe a few minutes," he says. "I won't talk if that's what you prefer."

It is what I prefer. I can't daydream if I'm talking or listening to someone. I don't want to be rude, though, so I avoid answering the question. "Can we run by the lake?"

He tells Muumu something that causes her smile to widen.

"She's responsible for this, isn't she?" I say as we leave the apartment. I shut the door behind me.

"She worries about you."

That might be so, but I suspect it's more than that. She hasn't asked about my "boyfriend" since I kissed Kyle in front of her, but she's mentioned Joni's name a few times.

"Give me a second," I tell him. "I just remembered something I have to do." I return to my bedroom to grab my phone from my nightstand. It's not there. I don't have time to look for it, so I stand close enough to the doorway to be heard, but not far enough for them to see what I'm up to.

Unfortunately, Joni is here and understands what I'm saying, so I can't fake talk like I demonstrated to Kyle when I first asked him to help me out. But since I'm more concerned about Muumu than Joni, it doesn't matter if he understands me or not.

"Hey, are you busy?" I say to the phone. I laugh as if Kyle had just said something funny, but all I can think about is how the joke is on me. Kyle is married and he cheated on his wife by not only kissing me, he went down on me. The laugh sounds phony to my ears.

Pushing away the memory of what his roommate told me, I close my eyes and remember the feel of Kyle's tongue against mine. And then my thoughts turn south and I remember the feel of his tongue on my girlie parts. A small moan slips out. Awesome. Now it sounds like I'm having phone sex. "I'm just about to go for a run." The words come out all breathy. Oh well, whatever works.

Since Joni can understand me, I add, "Have fun coaching today, babe. I miss you." The ache between my legs echoes that sentiment. Clearly it's already forgotten that Kyle's married.

I fake end the call and return to the hallway where Joni and Muumu are still standing. "Sorry about that. You ready?"

Muumu tells me to have fun and goes into the kitchen. I can't tell if she fell for my act and finally realizes I'm not single.

Unless…unless she's spoken to my mom and Mom confirmed that I don't have a boyfriend. I've always been open with her about these things. She has no reason to believe I'm keeping a boyfriend from her. Oh crap. Maybe I need to tell my mom what I'm up to. If I'm lucky, she'll tell Muumu to back off.

Joni and I walk down the stairs and exit the building. The sun is shining and promises to be another warm day. Without saying anything to each other, we start with a light jog, heading along the sidewalk. A few cars drive past, but nothing like the weekday morning traffic.

Needing to burn off my frustration at what happened last night, I pick up my pace. Joni easily matches it. I get the sense he's holding back so he can run with me.

"You and that guy aren't really dating, are you?" he says.

I stumble on a raised crack in the sidewalk. That's what I get for not paying attention to where I'm running. "Why would you say that?"

"I can just tell."

And the award for worst actress goes to…

"I'm curious," he continues, "why are you pretending that you're dating him?"

"It's nothing personal. It's just I don't want to be involved with anyone. But you try explaining that to my grandmother. Even if she could understand what I tell her, she won't understand my reasons." I conveniently ignore the part about how I was involved with Kyle twelve hours ago. What happened with him only further cemented my resolve.

Joni laughs, the sound slightly distorted because we're running. "If you're going to break my heart, can you please explain why you don't want to be involved with anyone?"

I consider picking up the pace so neither of us is able to talk, but the least I can do is tell him the modified version of the truth. Besides, who else is going to translate for me when it comes to Muumu?

"I had a boyfriend last year who I loved. We'd been together for several years but he didn't love me like I thought he had." I keep my gaze glued ahead, not daring to turn to see Joni's reaction. "He was cheating on me." The word 'cheating' cuts through me and I can barely breathe.

How could I have been such an idiot last night? And what is it with me and males who are only capable of cheating? Which just proves, once again, that I'm cursed.

"I'm sorry to hear that," Joni says, "but not all guys cheat."

I give a spluttered laugh. "My track record proves otherwise." This time I do pick up the pace.

"What do you mean?"

"My father cheated on my mother. And it turns out Kyle has a wife back home."

"I don't think being your fake boyfriend counts as cheating on her."

I throw him a look, momentarily forgetting he doesn't know what happened between Kyle and me last night.

"Granted the kiss didn't look good," he quickly adds, "but it was all acting, right?"

"Yeah, it was acting," I mumble.

"Good. And you're not cursed. You just need to find the right guy."

"I guess you've never had your heart broken." If he had, he wouldn't be so quick to judge.

"That would be where you're wrong. I was in love with a girl. Like you and your ex-boyfriend, we dated for years. I was getting ready to propose to her, when she up and left me for the lead singer of a rock band. I won't say that it didn't hurt at first, but then I realized it was what it was, and I can't waste my life because one girl hurt me."

We run down the path that leads to the lake. A man jogs past us in the opposite direction, but other than that, we're alone.

"And you can't let your ex-boyfriend and father cause you to waste your life," Joni adds. "You need to take a chance. You might be surprised."

He's got that right. Except the surprises haven't been happy ones. I shove away the image of the dog tag with Kyle's wife's name on it, and race Joni to the fork in the path. With his long legs, it doesn't take much for him to overtake me.

He stops at the junction. "Which way?"

Fortunately, unlike with life, it doesn't matter which way we go, it ends up the same place. "This way." I pick the path on the right, and continue along the packed dirt. With just the two us running, it's like we've disappeared from civilization. All that's left is the untamed wilderness.

Running at a slower pace, and allowing my breath to catch up with me after sprinting to the fork in the path, I ask, "Do you run every day?"

"You can say that. I play football. And when I'm not playing it, I'm training for it. So, yes, I run every day."

"Football, huh? You don't look like a football player." And then I get it. "Oh, you mean football as in soccer. So how come not hockey?"

He chuckles. "I'm not much of a hockey fan. I prefer running over skating."

"My best friend would love you. She hates hockey. She plays with our university women's soccer team. She's brilliant at it." Too bad Claire isn't here. She and Joni would make a cute couple. A voice in the back of my head begins to point out that he and I would make one too. I flick it away before it can finish the thought.

We continue running. Joni does most of the talking, because as fit as I am, he has longer legs and doesn't have to run as hard to keep up with me.

"What are you studying at university?" he asks. I explain my degree. "Do you know how to...what's it called when you wrap tape around the ankles so you reduce the risk of hurting your ankle while playing football?"

"Taping."

"Can you do that?"

"Yes."

"The wife of one of my teammates does that for us, but she's pregnant and could use some help. Would you be interested? It's a volunteer position, so we couldn't pay you."

"No, that would be great. The more practice I get the better." Plus, it would look good on my resume.

"Good. I'll drop off the summer schedule later. We meet two evenings a week."

And since I'm no longer hanging out with Kyle, this will work for me.

We're silent for several minutes, focused on running as we finish the loop around the lake, before Joni says, "The day I showed up for our date wasn't the first I'd seen you."

I glance at him. "It wasn't?"

He shakes his head and returns his attention to the path. I do the same so I don't trip over a rut. "I saw you in The Coffee Bar a few days before that. But I'm not like those guys in the movies who see a beautiful girl and talk to her."

I snort. Right now beautiful isn't the adjective I would use to describe me. I'm sweaty, have zero makeup on, and my hair was shoved into a ponytail before I left. A few stray pieces have wiggled their way loose and are sticking to the side of my face.

Joni either doesn't hear the snort or chooses to ignore it. "I was worried I'd sound…I'd sound cheesy if I said anything. I didn't realize you were the same person my grandmother was trying to convince me to go out with."

I laugh. "Convince?"

"Let's just say you weren't the only one who was resistant to the idea of being set up. I figured if you were so great, why didn't you have a boyfriend?"

The same thought I'd had about him.

"I saw you a few other times at The Coffee Bar. You must like it there."

"Muumu lives in the stone age. It's the only nearby place that has free WiFi."

"You can come to my apartment anytime and use mine. I live near you, and I wouldn't mind practicing my English."

I almost trip at the comment. There's nothing wrong with his English. "Okay."

A smile brighter than the sun appears on his face. God, am I making a mistake going to his apartment? But then he already knows where I stand on dating, so maybe it means nothing beyond me getting to use his WiFi.

As we run back home, Joni points out his building. I arrange to meet him there in an hour and race home to shower. If I'm lucky, Claire will be on the Internet at the same time as me.

Muumu isn't home when I enter the apartment. She's probably upstairs, scheming with Joni's grandmother. I hurry to get ready, wanting to leave before she comes home and I have to tell her where I'm going.

I search through my purse for my phone, so I can call Joni and check that it's okay to go over early. The phone isn't there. I hunt around my bed. Nothing. I had it last night when I went out. I check the back pocket of my skirt. Still nothing. Crap. Where the hell did I put it?

I sink onto my bed, but in my dazed stupor, I misgauge the edge and fall to the floor. *Earth to Universe, can you cut me a break here?*

I had the phone at the nightclub, but that's the last I remember seeing it. Maybe it fell out of my pocket when Kyle got into the fight with that drunk loser and I tried to protect him. I didn't see it on the ground, but his injuries had distracted me. It could have fallen from my pocket without me noticing.

Or I could have lost it at the nightclub.

I can't do anything until the place opens, so I head to Joni's apartment, cursing myself the entire way for paying more attention to Kyle than I did to my phone. I can't even phone him to see if maybe I left it at his place. I have his number.

Programmed.

In.

The.

Freaking.

Phone.

And after what we did last night and after the revelation that he's no better than Ian and my Dad, I can't bear the thought of seeing him face-to-face again.

The corners of my mouth flick up at the thought of sending Muumu and Joni over to get it for me. I'm sure she would give Kyle an earful if she knew the truth. Sure, he wouldn't understand what she said, but her tone would say it all.

I chuckle as I imagine Kyle's expression if that happened. He's not one of those jerks who would tell her where to go. He would just listen to her, and every now and then mention an interesting physics fact.

My heart oddly aches at how much I already miss his physics explanations, his thrilled grin whenever I ask him questions about the topic, and our True and False game.

Joni's apartment is similar to my grandmother's, except the furniture spells bachelor pad. Framed superhero movie posters hang on the opposite wall to the large screen TV, and echo the theme of a number of books on the shelves next to it.

I set my laptop on the dinner table. While I wait for it to start, I pick up the open sketchpad. When Joni doesn't protest, I leaf through it. Each page either has a comic-style sketch on it or an actual comic strip. They aren't all the same. Some are of your typical male superheroes, along with their big-breasted heroines. Others are PG friendly, with adorable wide-eyed animals. The male lust-filled comics are written in Finnish, the animal ones in English.

I read a few of the animal ones and laugh. "These are really good."

Joni blushes. I've never seen him do that before and it's cute. "Thanks," he says.

"Do you do this professionally?"

"I would like to, but it's hard to break in to."

I flip another page. "So what's your daytime job?" Judging from the furniture, it's not cleaning toilets like me.

"I work in advertising, in the graphic department. I love it, but I love that more." He nods at the sketchbook in my hand. "I'm lucky my two loves are related." He is lucky. I love photography, but it's tough to make a living in it—just like it is with his comics.

I turn the page and my face heats at the image on the paper. "That's me?" I squeak. The low cut, black bodysuit that lookalike me is wearing reveals a cleavage and big breasts that I don't have in real life. My blond hair flows down my back, contrasting against the stark color of my outfit. Joni has drawn it so there's a slight breeze blowing through my hair, which is glowing in the light. I'm a combination of innocent and kickass, especially with the whip to match my ensemble.

Joni coughs and shifts on his feet, clearly unsure how I'll respond to this sexy version of me. "I drew it when I first saw you in The Coffee Bar. Sorry. I never expected you to see it."

I giggle, more from nervousness than amusement. I'm not sure what to make of this. "It's too bad I had to send my outfit to the dry cleaner, or else I could have worn it when we ran."

Joni pulls out the seat next to me and sits, his gaze fixed on the drawing. "I saw you that day and knew I had to draw you. The sun was shining through the window at just the right angle and I couldn't resist. I hope you don't think I'm creepy now."

"No, it's great. Do I have any special powers?" If comic me has breasts guys fantasize about, then I can at least have special powers, too. It's only fair.

His gaze moves from the picture and I have a feeling he's not seeing me in front of him, the girl in shorts and a tank top. He's seeing the fantasy version of me.

"What kind of powers would you like?" he asks softly, mesmerized by my mouth.

I run the tip of my tongue over my lower lip, relieving its sudden dryness. It's not until he leans toward me that I realize maybe, just maybe, that wasn't the smartest move on my part. Does he think I'm trying to seduce him?

I almost bust out laughing. A seductress, I'm not.

Joni keeps moving toward me. I should move or duck out of the way, but I'm frozen in place. Maybe that's Joni's special power.

His lips touch mine for the briefest of seconds. He pulls back and his gaze roams over my face.

"I want special powers that let me know when a guy is lying to me," I whisper. I don't have to elaborate. I can tell Joni knows what I'm talking about.

Sighing, he stands and nods at my laptop. "I'll let you get to work."

"Thanks." An odd sort of ache spreads through me as he walks away. Would it be so bad to give him a chance? What's the worst that can happen—other than he cheats on me and becomes another notch in my curse belt? Maybe something great could happen between us, and I'd never have to face Minneapolis and my painful memories again. That would be a definite perk.

Except, his kiss didn't incite the same reaction I got when I kissed Kyle. Joni's kiss was nice. Sweet. But shouldn't I at least feel something more?

But then, look where something more always gets me.

I email Claire and fill her in on everything, even though she's thousands of miles away. While it would be better to talk to her face-to-face, she's the only one I can really talk to. Well, almost talk to. I can't quite bring myself to tell her everything that happened last night. I'm not sure how she'll take the news if I tell her the full truth.

Instead, I tell her how Joni kissed me and how Kyle has a wife back home. I don't tell Claire that he cheated on his wife, but even on email Claire is brilliant at reading between the lines.

'Would it really be so bad to give Joni a chance?' she types. 'Just for fun. It's not like you're staying there permanently. You deserve to have fun.' *After what Ian put you through* is the part she doesn't type. She doesn't need to. The words hang there, a ghost from my romantic past. I can almost imagine her arms around me, hugging me, like she did all the time after I found out the truth about Ian. And that makes me miss her more than I thought would be possible.

Thirty minutes later, I'm finished with the Internet. Joni offers to walk with me back to Muumu's.

"It's okay. I need to check on my grandmother," he says after

I tell him it's not necessary. "I'm all she has, other than her friends who are the same age as her. My parents and sister live too far away. And my mother was an only child."

Since I don't mind him walking with me, even though an awkwardness now exists between us after the kiss, I tell him it's okay. I'd love to have the company.

We walk back to our grandmothers' building, chatting about Joni's comics and my frustration at not being able to speak the language yet.

"If you want," he says, "I can help you. You could come over in the evenings and I can teach you some Finnish."

"That would be great! Thanks."

As we approach our grandmothers' place, a familiar figure walks toward us. At first Kyle doesn't see us, but then he looks in our direction and the world goes still, everything suspended mid action.

# Chapter Seventeen

## Kyle

I push the buzzer for the building and wait. A crow in a nearby tree caws. If it's sharing its secrets for dealing with misunderstandings, I wish it would do so in English, because I need all the help I can get. Something tells me even the most eloquent physics fact won't help me here.

No one answers. I try again. Still nothing. There's always a chance Sofia looked out the window and is now avoiding me. If that's true, the only way to give her back the phone is to track her down at the sports center, but if I do, she might not give me a chance to talk to her.

I press the buzzer once more, then turn away from the building and walk toward my car. I could wait with my vehicle until she shows up, but who the hell knows when that will be. All I know is I can't walk away. Bit by bit, Sofia has slipped into my life and I don't want to let her go. She's the one ray of light in my otherwise pathetic life. She makes me want to do better, be better. Something I haven't felt in a while.

And not for the first time since last night, I realize that if Sofia hadn't shown up at the nightclub, I would have gone home wasted. My parents and Cody were right.

I am a mess.

I look up from the ground and as if my thoughts summoned her, Sofia walks toward me. With Joni. *Shit.*

Sofia seems as shocked to see me as I am to see her with Joni.

Joni is the only one who isn't surprised. His expression tells me he's swooped in to pick up the pieces. His expression also warns me he's not about to give her up if he can help it. I might only be thinking about friendship with her, but he's thinking about something more, and for some reason that's settling in my stomach like a huge pile of boulders.

Sofia's shocked expression transforms to pain. I put that pain on her face. While Nik might have been the asshole who told her I had a wife, I'm the one who held onto the fucking dog tag as a reminder. Not a reminder of what Gabby and I once had. It's a reminder of the asshole who destroyed everything because he figured it was okay to toss back a twelve pack and get behind the wheel of a deadly vehicle.

The image of Gabby dead in her seat flashes in my head. I clench my jaw together so hard, I'm surprised my teeth don't disintegrate.

"What are you doing here?" Sofia says, her voice cold.

The knot inside me tightens. Joni folds his arms across his chest, ever ready to be her protector.

"I found this." I hand her the phone I discovered in Nik's apartment.

Sofia turns it on, and some of the tension in her body eases, but there's still plenty to keep her heart frozen against me.

"Can we talk?" I glance briefly at Joni. "In private."

"I don't think that's a good idea." He steps closer to her and places his hand on her lower back. If I hadn't been paying close attention to Sofia, I might have missed her slight flinch at his action.

"I don't have anything to say to you." She attempts to step around me. I reach out to stop her and my fingers brush against the soft skin of her arm. An electrical undercurrent spreads up my hand and travels throughout my body. She gasps, and that plants a tiny seed of hope. Despite what she might believe, she can't deny she felt the same reaction I experienced. The same electrical undercurrent she didn't have when Joni touched her.

"What Nik told you...it was a lie."

"Why would he lie and say you're married?" Joni asks, frowning.

He's not frowning out of confusion. He's frowning because he doesn't believe me.

But I don't care what he thinks. I only care about Sofia. I narrow my eyes at him. "This is between me and Sofia." I turn to her. "Can we go somewhere and talk?"

Sofia looks between me and Joni, torn as to who to believe, who to trust. Taking comfort that she didn't instantly tell me to go to hell, I place my hand on her arm. Joni's frown deepens.

If it weren't for what's at stake here, I'd rejoice at his reaction.

She raises her chin. "Whatever you have to say you can say it in front of Joni."

Joni's frown smoothes out. He doesn't smile, but the corners of his mouth twitch in their own victory dance.

I let out a heavy breath. If this is the best I'm going to get, it will have to do. It's better than no chance to explain my dumbass roommate's lie.

I nod. "Okay...I was married. My wife's name was Gabby, but she died over a year ago."

Sofia's face softens. "I'm sorry."

I can tell she wants to ask how Gabby died, but she doesn't want to bring up that pain, and I don't want to talk about it. My entire body tenses, waiting for Joni to ask the inevitable question, but when he remains silent, the tension drips away.

"But why did your roommate lie to her?" Joni says, asking the other question I hoped wouldn't come up.

The returning tension slams into me full force.

Shit. How do I answer this without revealing what happened between me and Sofia last night? If she's mad at me now, that revelation will push her too far and she'll never forgive me.

I'm about to pretend I didn't hear him and change the subject when Sofia says, "I'd like to know why too." The way she says it, cautious and full of pain, I can tell she already knows the answer.

"Because...because he saw us kissing and was concerned Sofia would"—shit, I'm going to whip Nik's ass for this. I have no idea what to say to prevent further damage—"He was worried she would get the wrong idea—"

"And think there's more to your fake relationship than there really is," Joni finishes for me. I'm not sure if I should cringe at what he said or be relieved. He's saved me from explaining what happened last night between me and Sofia.

The 'what happened' that I can't stop thinking about.

"But he got it all wrong," I say to Sofia. "There is more to the relationship. Or at least I want there to be more." It's not until the words come out that I realize how true they are. I do want more than just a friendship with her. How much more I don't know though.

Joni stiffens. Sofia stares at me, several different emotions flickering on her face, uncertainty ranking on top. I hook my finger under her chin, then guide it up and kiss her. It's a tender kiss, nothing that would steam up a car window. Nothing like the fake kiss I gave her for her grandmother and Joni's benefit. But it's enough to show her and Joni that what I feel for her is more than I've felt in a while for any woman.

And yes, there's a bit of marking my territory going on here, because let's be honest, no way in hell am I letting her end up with Joni. "Nik's got a summer cottage. He's invited a few people to join him next weekend. I'd like it if you would come with me."

Joni huffs and I try not to grin, my focus still on Sofia.

"I'm not sure that would be a good idea," she says. Her words are cautious, but there's no mistaking her slight intrigue.

"It's a great idea," I say. "You can keep me out of trouble. And I bet there are tons of abstract photo opportunities waiting for you."

"What kind of trouble?" Joni's tone is as cold as Sofia's was when I first showed up. That doesn't surprise me. If our places were reversed, I would have zoomed in on that too.

"Dude, it's just an expression. She's safe with me. Promise."

"I'm in," Sofia says. "Joni, you'll need to explain to my grandmother so she doesn't worry about me. If I try, she'll never figure out what I'm telling her."

He blinks then his forehead scrunches. "I don't think this is a good idea, Sofia. You don't even know him very well. You can't go off for a weekend with him. It's too dangerous."

I barely manage to keep from rolling my eyes. "I'm not a serial killer."

"Maybe not. But you could be a rapist."

"And so could you," I fire back.

Sofia backs away from both of us, eyes searching us for signs of serial killer or rapist tendencies. Her hand tightens around her phone. I step closer to her and lean down so my mouth brushes against her ear. "I didn't hurt you last night and I would never hurt you." I press my lips against her cheek.

Then I walk back to my car.

# Chapter Eighteen

## Sofia

It's that moment I live for, if you subtract scrubbing the urinals from the equation. It's time for Operation Scrub the Sauna. Cue the fanfare.

As I thunk, thunk, thunk my way to the women's locker room in my not-so-stylish, oversized rubber boots, a man in his thirties wearing athletic pants and a plain t-shirt walks toward me. I've seen him around the physical therapy clinic in the sports center.

He stops in front of me. "Sofia Philips?" I nod. "I'm Rafu Jarvinen. Kyle Bennett mentioned you're studying athletic training back home."

"That's right."

"I work in the physical therapy clinic here and one of my part-time assistants is away next week. Would you be interested in covering for her then? I thought it might be good experience for you and I would certainly appreciate the help. I'm short staffed as it is at this time of the year."

I look down at my uniform to make sure I still have it on. Surely he realizes I already have a job here, unless he means the position is for the evenings and weekends. "What are the hours?"

"She works Mondays to Thursdays from three until eight in the evening."

"I'd love to do it, but I don't finish this job until four." There's also the matter of helping Joni out with his soccer team like I promised.

"I can talk to your boss and see what happens."

Luckily my boss is all for it, especially since it's only for the week. Rafu is the one who comes to tell me the news. "She feels bad that you're working here as a member of the cleaning staff when you could be doing something career related." Maija told her what I'm studying back home during my first week here. While I don't regret my decision to come to Finland for the summer, even if it is just to clean toilets, I'm ready to do handsprings down the hallway, in my uniform and rubber boots, at his news. The goal for the summer was to become the new me, the one who has thrown out her pity-party decorations and has a fresh start.

I'd say this is another step in the right direction.

After work, Maija and I walk to Stockmann, the huge department store where I love to shop. Somehow, I need to steal away and buy condoms. I've never had to buy them before now. Ian always took care of that, plus I was on the pill. I stopped using it after he died. Figured there was no point to it after that.

Since Maija needs to buy her mom a birthday present, we head to the kitchen department first.

"How about oven mitts?" I hold up a cute red pair with reindeer on them.

"I was thinking more like kitchen…" Maija scrunches her forehead in the way she always does when struggling for the English word she's searching for. "I can't remember the word for it."

It takes us a few attempts before I guess it: utensils. We search the shelves, my thoughts all over the place, other than on helping Maija.

She lays her hand on my arm. I startle. "Are you okay?" she asks.

"Huh? No, I'm fine."

Her head tilts to the side and she studies my face. "You seem distracted."

"I need to get, um, something after this."

She picks up a small knife. "What?"

*It's not a big deal.* I'm sure she and Toivu are sleeping together. *Just say it.* "I need to get some…some condoms. For this weekend."

She looks down, trying to hide the smile on her face, and switches the knife in her hand for another one. "And is there a certain person you need them for?"

She knows about Joni and what Muumu's been up to, but she has also seen me several times with Kyle and told me he obviously likes me. Last week, before we hit the nightclub, she declared that my life is way more exciting than *The Endless Circle*. I'm not so sure about that.

"I'm going away for the weekend with Kyle." At her grin, I add, "We're staying in a cottage with a bunch of other people. I want to be prepared just in case." Just in case we decide to go to home base—or whatever the hockey equivalent is.

"Good idea." The grin remains on her face and she inspects the knife in her hand. "I think I'll get this one."

We join the line to pay for it, then head to the clothing department. After searching through the clothing racks and the stacks of clothes on the tables, I find a few more tank tops and a pale pink skirt.

"Sofia," Maija says, next to a rack of swimsuits. "You should get this for your big weekend." She holds up a white string bikini that looks more like a piece of lace than a swimsuit. "It will be perfect."

"I have a swimsuit."

"A one piece or a bikini?"

"A one piece." A boring black swimsuit.

"I bet Kyle will prefer this one more."

"I don't know." It's a lot sexier than what I'm used to wearing. I take the bikini from her and try it on in the fitting room. The bikini is lined and does this cool trick where it looks like I have more cleavage than I do. Perfect.

A tiny voice in the back of my head asks me if I'm really ready for this. Confident me from the dance club has gone on vacation—to the moon. "*Sorry, baby, but sex with you was…boring.*" The voice is a perfect imitation of Ian's.

Chewing my lip, I step out of the cubical to model it for her. "What do you think?"

She nods. "You'll definitely need condoms this weekend."

• • •

Joni is waiting for me when I get off the bus near Muumu's building.

"Have you made a decision about this weekend?" he says before I have a chance to say hi.

"You mean, am I going away to the cottage with Kyle?" I nod. I haven't told Kyle yet. I was about to call him, once he got off work. "I am. I know you don't like him much, but he's a nice guy."

Joni snorts at the nice guy part.

"It wasn't his fault I was upset at what his roommate told me," I say. "If anything, you should dislike his roommate for lying to me."

"So, after what your old boyfriend did to you, you're ready to trust Kyle with your heart?"

I stop abruptly. "Who said anything about my heart? I'm just having fun with him, like I'm having fun with you."

"Except you've never kissed me like you kissed him," he mutters.

My face heats at the memory of what else I've done with Kyle that I haven't with Joni.

Tension brushes against us like the hot July breeze. This isn't how I wanted things to be between Joni and me. I wanted us to be friends. I thought we were friends. But I can't be friends with him if he's going to be jealous over something that might not amount to anything. It's not like Kyle is my boyfriend. I'm not really sure what he is.

And it's not like I'm looking for a boyfriend. Maybe summer fling is a better description—like Claire suggested. Once Kyle and I return home, we'll go back to our own lives, which won't include each other. He has his degree and there's no guarantee he'll stick around Minneapolis.

I straighten and start to cross the road. Joni follows. "I hope it's okay with you, but I won't be able to help out with your soccer team next week. The physical therapist where I work asked if I could cover for one of his staff members who will be away. It will be great experience." I'm practically bouncing up and down at the news, like a cheerleader buzzed up on caffeine.

"That's great. Are you still able to help out this week?"

"Absolutely. How's your grandmother?" If he's here, it must mean he was visiting her.

"I haven't seen her yet. I was visiting yours."

That can't be good. "Mine? How come?"

"I went to see if you were home yet, so we can begin your Finnish lesson."

I cringe. I never told Muumu where I was going after work. Usually I get home late from exploring Helsinki with Kyle. But he had something else he had to do today after work, and even though I'd told Muumu I was coming home early, I ended up shopping with Maija.

"Sorry, I went shopping with a friend from work," I say. "Let me drop my stuff off and we can get started." And hopefully he doesn't tell Muumu what I've been up to and she doesn't ask to see what I bought.

We go upstairs to the apartment, the tension between us a little lighter than before, but not by much. I can't tell if it's because I can't help out with his team next week or because I'm spending the weekend with Kyle. Or maybe both.

I open the front door and moments later Muumu pops out of the kitchen. She asks me a question and I look at Joni for the translation. He doesn't give me one. He replies to whatever she said. Her expression brightens and she looks at me expectantly. When I don't respond, because I have no idea what I'm responding to, she rushes out another sentence or two. She wants to see what I bought.

"Clothes. Nothing exciting," I explain.

He tells her some version of that and she replies. "She said even better," he says. "I don't think you're getting out of this. You might as well show her."

It could be worse. I could have raided Victoria's Secrets and really given Muumu something to freak over.

I unzip my backpack and remove the skirt and tank tops. Before I realize what's happening, the bikini gets caught on the skirt's zipper and tags along for its grand unveiling. It falls from the offending piece of metal and flops on the floor.

Muumu picks it up while I inwardly groan at her anticipated reaction.

She inspects it, turning the skimpy pieces of fabric in her hands. Laughing, she says something else to me and hands the swimsuit back.

Joni chuckles. "She says you will look much better in it than she would. And I have to agree with her. She also suggested that you wear it for our Finnish lesson." He laughs at what is no doubt a confused expression on my face. Why would I want to wear a bikini to learn Finnish? Unless this is an ancient Scandinavian trick I don't know about to appease the language gods so learning the language will be a breeze. And if that's true, I'd wear a thong if it will help me speak fluent Finnish.

If I had a thong.

"I'm taking you to the lake for our lesson," Joni explains. "And your grandmother made us a picnic to bring with us."

While I'm not sure the bikini part is a good idea, I'm all for studying by the lake. I put my stuff away, hiding the condoms in my suitcase so Muumu doesn't accidentally find them. Then grab my Finnish language books I bought back in Minnesota. If Joni is disappointed that I didn't change into the bikini, he doesn't show it.

My cell phone weighs down my pocket as we walk to the lake, impatiently waiting for me to call Kyle. But I can't do that in front of Joni. That's not fair to him. He wants to spend time with me. He doesn't want to spend time with me while I'm talking to Kyle on the phone—or texting him.

The beach, which is just a long, narrow stretch of sand that extends to the wooded area surrounding the lake, is busy when we arrive. We find a location not far from a group playing soccer, and spread out the blanket. Joni passes me a soda and we settle in for some serious studying.

"You need to roll your R's," he tells me after fifteen minutes of trying to teach me how to pronounce numerous words.

"I *was* rolling my R's."

He gives me a look asking me what planet I'm from. I respond with my own look: the planet that doesn't require me to roll my freakin' R's.

"Okay, let's try something else." He flips through my book and starts reading the sentences, without letting me see them. "*Mitä minä sanoin?*" he adds after a pause.

I let my brain absorb the words. "You said, 'What time is the movie?'"

"Very good. Do you know your numbers?"

I recite them from one to thirty. I can go higher but that took long enough.

"*Haluatsä nää elokuva mun kanssa?*"

Blink. I have no idea what he said.

"*Varo!*" a male voice yells and before we can see what he's talking about, something solid slams against my arm.

"Ouch!"

The soccer ball rolls a short distance before stopping at a pair of men's sneakers. The skin on my arm stings from the impact and I can tell it's going to bruise.

"*Anteeksi!*" the owner, a guy Joni's age, says. Scooping up the ball, he yammers away, the words lost on me.

"Sofia," Joni says, "this is Markus. He's on my football team." To Markus, he says, "Sofia's the first aider joining us. She'll be taping ankles."

Markus nods at me then winces. "Sorry about hitting you with the ball."

I flash him a brief smile. "That's okay. I'll survive."

"Do you guys want to join us?"

Joni and I exchange looks, then scramble up.

"What did you say before I was attacked by the ball?" I ask, taking my position on the sand.

"I wanted to know if you want to see a movie with me."

I don't have a chance to respond. Markus kicks the ball and the game is on.

# Chapter Nineteen

## Sofia

Muumu watches as I slide out the small baking sheet from the toaster oven, revealing the grilled, open-faced sandwiches. The melted cheese oozes over the tomato slices.

"*Hyvää.*" She grins at my culinary masterpiece.

I place two on each of our plates and set the plates on the table. I've already made the salad.

Muumu sits and bites into a sandwich. "Mmmm. *Herkullista ruokaa.*" This is followed by something I loosely translate as "Are you going to see Joni play soccer?" Or she could have asked if I'm making sandcastles with him. Tough call.

I tell her yes. I don't bother telling her that I'm checking my emails at the café first. That's beyond my level of Finnish. Instead, I ask her if she wants to see a movie tomorrow night. Yes, Joni's language lessons are paying off. And thankfully American movies aren't dubbed in Finnish. Hello, subtitles.

She pulls out today's newspaper and checks the listings for the local theater. She points to the romantic comedy that looks good and we make plans to see it.

Once I'm finished with dinner, I clean my dishes and head to the café. There, I order a Diet Coke and sit on an empty seat next to the window. Because I haven't checked my inbox since yesterday afternoon, there's a bunch for me to go through. Some are from Claire, who is eager to hear more about my non-existent love life.

*Spending the weekend with Kyle at a cottage by a lake*, I type. I never told her that Kyle's wife is dead. I referred to her as his ex-wife. She might not be as excited about me hanging out with him if she knows he's dealing with that level of loss. A dead ex-boyfriend is nothing like a dead wife.

She responds soon after, *I didn't realize things were getting serious between you two.*

She only knows that he's my fake boyfriend and we hang out whenever our schedules allow it. Which turns out is fairly often.

*I'm not spending the weekend alone with him*, I reply. *We're meeting up with a bunch of people he knows.* A romantic weekend for two, it's not.

Not that I want a romantic weekend for two. We're just friends. Friends who happen to kiss. That's all.

Mom has responded to my email asking if she can talk to Muumu about her scheme to hook me up with Joni. All I get is a message that she's going away for the weekend. She doesn't mention who it's with though. And since I don't want to bring up how I'm going away for the weekend with Kyle, I let her email slide.

And finally, I read the email I had missed when I first scanned my unopened messages. It's from my university regarding my fall clinical experience.

> *Dear Ms. Philips,*
>
> *We're sorry to inform you that Westbrook High School is no longer able to offer you the clinical placement for the fall due to funding cutbacks. We are doing our best to find you an alternative practicum.*

I stare at the screen, unable to believe it. This had been a great opportunity and now it's gone. And worst yet, all the best placements went early. Chances aren't good the university will be able to line me up with something similar.

I reread the email several more times. Nothing changes. It really is true. I'm currently short a clinical placement. A clinical placement that is not only necessary for experience, it's necessary for me to graduate next year. *Shit.*

I shutdown my laptop. As I pack up my stuff to leave for the soccer field, my phone pings.

*Kyle: You're currently fantasizing about me...True or false?*

The corner of my mouth twitches up. *Maybe,* I type back. I had thought about him several times today, even though I probably shouldn't have. Against all my plans, Kyle is getting under my skin. I haven't decided yet if that's a good thing or not.

*We're just friends,* I remind myself once again.

*Me: You're getting all hot and steamy over this text...True or false?*

I hit send before realizing how lame it sounds. Ugh.

Kyle responds as I walk out of the cafe. *Maybe. You?*

*Well, considering I'm walking to the soccer field to tape a bunch of players' ankles...*

Kyle knows what I'm referring to. I told him about it after we "made up."

He doesn't send me any more texts. A slight twinge of disappointment zaps me like static. I'm not sure why. It's not like I've ever had phone sex or sent sexts. I have no idea what to do.

And it's not like I would actually do that with Kyle. It's not like that between us.

*Right. Because he never went down on you.*

Inwardly, I roll my eyes at the voice. It was a one-time thing. From what I've seen of him, he's a player. I wouldn't be surprised if his text to me was just foreplay before he heads out for the bar with his roommate to pick up more one-night stands.

The new twinge of disappointment hits me harder than before. I do my best to ignore it and practically run to the field where I'm meeting Joni's team.

I arrive and Joni introduces me around. Dabria, the coach's pregnant wife, takes me to the sideline where she has the supplies set up. "I'm so glad you can help me. For practices, we're mostly here to provide first aid, but some of the men need their ankles taped. Joni said you know how to do that."

"That's right."

She and I don't have a chance to talk again until we've finished taping ankles. Then we sit back on the bench and watch her husband lead the practice. While they might not be professional players, they take the sport seriously. It's no wonder Joni's in good shape.

"Joni said you're staying with your grandmother," Dabria says.

"It's just for the summer, then I'm returning to the US to finish my athletic training degree." At least that was the plan until the dilemma with the canceled practicum. I do my best not to think about it, but it's like an annoying mosquito bite that won't stop itching.

"So nothing is going on between you and Joni?" she asks.

"He's a nice guy, but I'm not interested in him that way." And even if I were, I wouldn't want to risk falling for him. Not when my heart could end up being a casualty or I could have to deal with a long-distance relationship that fades over time. It isn't worth the effort.

Besides, it's not Joni who inconveniently fills my thoughts. It's the dark-haired guy with glasses and a love for hockey and physics who's the guilty one.

"Do you want to work with athletic teams once you're finished with your degree?" Dabria asks. "Or do you want to work in a clinic?"

I glance at the guys running around the field. "I've done both as part of my clinical training, but I like working with teams more." The idea of working with a team and getting to know the players appeals to me. I don't mean getting to know them on a personal level, but to know them enough to understand how best to work with them. To see the benefits of my job when the injured player can play again.

We watch the guys run through their drills. Markus, the guy from the beach last week, cuts one way but his knee has other plans and he goes down. I'm already on my feet, charging across the field before Dabria has a chance to stand up from the bench.

I dropped next to Markus who is writhing in pain. I check his knee, careful not to cause more damage, then ask Joni and another player to help him to the bench. Once they're there, I elevate his leg and apply an ice bag to the swelling joint. I don't even have to think what I'm doing. It's instinct.

The coach has Joni and the other player help Markus to his friend's car, and his friend drives him to the hospital so his knee can be checked out. The game resumes.

"You're sexy in action," Kyle says behind me. I startle at his voice. I had no idea he was here.

I turn to him. He's wearing jeans and a light gray t-shirt that skims his developed chest and abs. Lucky t-shirt. "Hey, what are you doing here?"

"I didn't have anything exciting to do, since the person I'm exploring Helsinki with now has a life beyond that." He glances at the field where the team is playing, then leans down and kisses my jaw. "And maybe I missed hanging out with you."

His lips linger against my skin and my entire body buzzes at his touch. My brain tells me to step away from him, but I can't for the life of me remember why. My body says to hell with that. I move my head so my lips can brush against his. But before I get that far, Kyle stumbles into me and lets out an exhaled grunt.

He turns toward the field. Joni jogs to where the ball rests on the grass a couple of yards from us. The rest of the team watches. And now I remember why my brain wanted me to step away from Kyle. Him kissing me while I'm volunteering as a first aider is hardly professional.

"Sorry," Joni says. "It wasn't meant to hit you."

Kyle mutters something under his breath that sounds close to "sure it wasn't."

Joni picks up the ball and tosses it into play.

"Are you okay?" I ask Kyle. "Where were you hit?"

"It's no big deal. I've had worse playing hockey."

"I guess that's true." Hockey isn't known for being a friendly sport, which might be why I've never been into it. Too much fighting. "If you want, I can take you for an ice cream to make you feel better." I press my lips together to keep from grinning. It doesn't work.

"You've got a deal. But in the meantime, I'll wait over there." He points to a group of birch trees a safe distance away.

"Are you sure? There's still another half an hour left."

"Did I mention you're sexy when you're working?" His gaze travels down my body.

I laugh and give him a small shove on the shoulder. "By the way. Thanks."

"For what?"

"For telling Rafu Jarvinen about me." At Kyle's confused expression, I explained, "He asked me if I'd be interested in covering for someone next week in the physical therapy clinic. So thanks for suggesting me."

"I didn't. I was looking for you yesterday at the sports center before I went to your grandmother's. I might have mentioned to him what you're studying." He shrugs.

"Thank you anyway." I give him a quick kiss on the cheek. "Okay, off you go. I'll see you soon."

He salutes me and walks away. He's limping, but not as bad as he has been. He has his good days and his bad. Right now seems to be a good day.

"Who's that?" Dabria asks, a knowing glint in her eyes.

"A friend." My face heats at the memory of what my "friend" did to me the other night.

Dabria laughs. "Your friend's hot."

I look back at Kyle. "You're right. He is." But he's a lot more than that, too.

I return my attention to the game. The remainder of it goes down injury free. During the final minutes, Dabria and I put away our supplies, and I thank her for letting me help out. We exchange numbers in case we need to get in touch with each other about the practices and games.

We're finishing up when Joni jogs over. "So what did you think?" he asks.

"You were great out there." I'm about to ask him why he kicked the soccer ball at Kyle, but I have no proof he intentionally did it. And why would he anyway?

The guys collect the equipment and carry it to the parking lot. I say bye to everyone and join Kyle.

"Are we still on for ice cream?" I ask him. Ever since I suggested it to him during the practice, it's all I can think about.

"Sounds good."

We walk to the café where I checked my email earlier. I order mango in a waffle cone. Kyle orders chocolate. I then lead him to the playground I used to go to as a kid. It's huge and made of wood instead of plastic. The benches are occupied, so we sit on the grassy knoll near some trees and watch the kids play.

"How's your ice cream?" he asks.

"Yummy. You wanna try some?" I hold out my cone for him to lick.

But instead of sampling the ice cream, his lips find mine and the tip of his tongue traces along the seam of my mouth. I automatically open up and let him in.

My tongue brushes against his and I savor the taste of chocolate. And it's good. Really good.

Our kisses become more heated, a taste of what's to come this weekend. I moan softly. Kyle pulls away. Screams of laugher float over to us, reminding me where we are. Kyle's kisses have that effect on me—the effect of making me oblivious to our surroundings.

"You're right," he says with a wiry smile. "Your ice cream is good."

I laugh. "So is yours."

We watch the kids run around, carefree. They don't have to worry about their careers, a topic which is foreign to them. They don't have to worry about how their practicum has been canceled.

I try pushing away all thoughts of what it means for my final year and for my future, but they refuse to budge. It doesn't help that I'm here and can't talk to my counselor in person.

Kyle strokes my lower back with his thumb. "Hey, where did you go?"

"I'm right here."

"Right. But I'm not buying it, Sof. What's going on?"

My eyes widen. In the short time we've been hanging out together, he already knows me that well. Which means he can probably tell when I lie. "I found out today my practicum for the fall has been canceled."

"Can you get another one?"

"Hopefully, especially since I need it to graduate. But it won't be the same. This one was with a high school, which meant I'd be working with sport teams. That's what I want to do once I graduate and get my credentials. The experience would've been perfect."

"I'm sorry," he says and I can tell he means it. But since he can't do anything about it, I change topics.

"What's your favorite part about coaching?" I ask.

He doesn't have to think about. "Working with the kids. What about yours with athletic training?"

"Knowing I make a difference. It's hard to explain."

He nods. "No, I get what you mean."

We finish our ice creams in a silence. With Kyle, I don't have to talk all the time to avoid the awkward dead air that leaves some people fidgety. It's nice. Comfortable.

I check the time on my phone. 8:40 p.m. I scramble up. "I should go. I need to study."

Kyle frowns. "Study? For what?"

"My certification exam. It's in March, but I'm getting a head start on it while I'm here." Since I don't have the same distractions as I do back home. Another perk of spending my summer in Finland.

Except now that I've got a lot going on, it's getting harder and harder to find time to study.

Kyle pushes himself up. "I can give you a ride home if you want."

"Thanks." I can easily walk home, but I'm not ready to say bye to him yet.

We return to his car and he drives me back to Muumu's apartment. I'm about to climb out when he grabs my arm and pulls me back to him so only a few inches separate us.

"Will I get to see you before Saturday?" His gaze drops to my lips.

"I'm not sure. I'm taking my grandmother to see a movie tomorrow." Kyle works late Wednesday and I'm volunteering on Thursday with Joni's team.

"Then this will have to do until then…" He kisses me long and hard, our tongues exploring, tasting, teasing. I'm breathless by the time we pull apart. Breathless and wishing tomorrow were Saturday.

# Chapter Twenty

## Sofia

I walk into the kitchen to see if Muumu is here since we need to leave soon for the movie. She's sitting at the table, flipping through what looks like a photo album. She looks up and waves me over. Mina chirps her encouragement from her cage.

I sit next to Muumu. She points to a faded picture of a pretty girl my age wearing a light blue minidress. Her long blond hair hangs around her shoulders. "*Mä oon tossa.*" She points to herself then to a good-looking guy in tight red pants and a tight polyester shirt. "*Tos oon sun vaari.*" My grandfather.

After I get over how thankful I am no one dresses like that anymore, I study the photo. They're sitting on the grass by the lake, a tent to one side. His arm is around her and they're beaming at the camera.

In the next photo, they're sitting by a campfire with their friends. This time they aren't posing for the camera. It's a candid shot. Vaari still has his arm around her waist, but everyone is laughing and having a good time.

She flips the page. In this picture, they're walking along the pier where the Helsinki marketplace is located, holding hands. Their backs are to the camera but it's obviously them.

Muumu says something that is lost on me, but her dreamy tone gives away that she's remembering her early days with my grandfather, when they fell in love.

And they were still in love the day my grandfather died. That much I know from what Mom told me.

Muumu shows me more photos. A few are of places I've been to with Kyle. Some we haven't been to yet, and I mentally add them to the list of must-see locations. And with each picture we look at, she and my grandfather appear to be even more in love than in the photo before it. They're proof that happily-ever-after does exist.

Muumu glances at the clock and says something that I interpret to mean we need to go now if we're going to make the movie.

"*Kiitos*," I tell her, pointing to the album. I'm not sure what exactly I'm thanking her for. Showing me that love does exist. Showing me a glimpse of the fun-loving girl she was when she was my age. Showing me places Kyle and I need to explore. Or maybe a bit of everything.

The movie theater isn't busy when we arrive. We find empty seats near the middle and settle down for the show.

The movie is about a woman who has grown up with four brothers and is more comfortable tossing footballs as one of the guys than she is doing girlie things. But then her best friend convinces her to help with the friend's bridal consultation business. Great, if she looked the part. But she doesn't. So the hero, who is one of her brother's friends, takes it upon himself to help the heroine become more ladylike.

It's hilarious.

And it reminds me of Kyle.

The hero and the heroine spend a lot of time together, and learn more about each other and about themselves. Just like Kyle and me. Her makeover isn't lost on me either. In the end, she and I want the same thing—a fresh start to a bright new future. Except in her case, the funny sexy guy is an added bonus.

Muumu and I laugh at the banter between the couple. The woman then decides she's had enough of their innuendoes flinging back and forth. She kisses him—and he doesn't complain. Tensions between them become heated and the next thing I know, clothes are being flung across the room and they end up in bed together.

No, that's not awkward at all when you're sitting next to your grandmother. Nor is the part where my brain remembers some of my steamier kisses with Kyle, and my body is having its own little party at the memory.

I'll definitely need a cold shower if I plan to study tonight.

Once the movie is over, Muumu drives us home. My phone pings and I read the text from Kyle.

*You've had phone sex while watching* Star Wars. *True or false?*

I snort a laugh. *Isn't that like every guy's dream while watching Princess Leia in her bikini?*

*That was* Return of the Jedi.

*You're such a dork!*

*But a loveable dork, right?*

*Very.* Then I type, *Is this your way of saying you're watching* Star Wars?

*Is this your way of saying you want to have phone sex with me?*

My girlie parts between my legs perk up at the idea. I let out a slow breath and pray Muumu can't tell the affect Kyle's text is having on me. If I thought the semi-steamy scene in the movie was awkward, that's nothing compared to this.

*Goodnight, Kyle. :)*

Yep, my plans to study tonight are in serious trouble if my body has any say in it.

# Chapter Twenty-One

## Kyle

I'm doomed.

That's all I've thought about ever since I kissed Sofia last night.

Lucky for me the boys haven't noticed I'm distracted. Nor has Nik. "You all set for this weekend?" he asks, his sneaker-clad feet propped up on his desk.

"Yep. Thanks for inviting us. We're looking forward to it."

Nik smirks. "I bet you are." His phone rings. Dropping his feet from the desk, he answers the phone in Finnish, then leaves the office while still talking. Whoever he's talking to is pissing him off, judging from his tone.

I check my phone and mentally calculate the time back home. I still have twelve minutes before the boys' off-ice training session begins.

I call the Minnesota Bears head athletic trainer. "Brian Prescott," he answers.

"Hey, Brian, it's Kyle Bennett. Am I phoning at a bad time?"

He laughs. "There's never a good time to phone me, or so my wife tells me. What can I do for you?"

"A friend of mine is entering her final year in the athletic training program. Her practicum was canceled for the fall and now she has nothing to take its place. Is there any chance you can help her out with your connections?" I'm not sure what I'm asking for, but I hate to see Sofia miss out on a great experience because she got screwed.

"Let me call around and see what I can do. But I can't promise anything, Kyle."

"Thanks. I appreciate it."

"Is it true you're in Finland with Tikkanen?"

"Yes, but don't worry. I'm keeping up with my rehab here." Even though I know I'll never be fully recovered to play in the NHL again, part of me will never give up on that goal.

"I never doubted it for a moment. You're one of the most driven players I've worked with."

We talk for a few more minutes, then we both have to get back to work. The boys are waiting for me when I enter the gym. Like with all the strength and conditioning sessions, Nik's boys have joined mine.

"Five minutes of jogging to warm up," I direct them. "We're starting a new training program today." I send them off on their run.

"Do you wanna explain the drills to them?" I ask Nik.

"You're the one planning to be a coach. You can do it." His gaze drops to my injured leg. "I'll demonstrate."

I clench my teeth together. It's not Nik's fault he has to even suggest it. He's not the one I'm pissed at.

And since I don't want the boys to know I'm not thrilled with this arrangement, I release a long breath and will myself to get over it. Easier said than done.

After the boys finish their laps and we guide them through the stretches, I ask, "Who's heard the term plyometric training before?"

A few hands are raised.

"Hockey isn't just about being strong. It's about combining speed and strength to provide power behind your movements. Or in physics terms, the rate you can move an object with as much force as possible. With skating, that translates into how fast you can skate down the ice and therefore beat your opponent to the puck."

I explain what plyometrics are and why they're an important part their conditioning program. "We're only introducing you to them. Once you get higher up in your hockey career, they'll be a key part of your training."

After we guide them through the warm-up, Nik walks them through each exercise we want to teach them, starting with the standing long jump. I provide the necessary feedback. The workout is simple for now. The goal is to teach them proper technique.

I try to focus my attention on the boys, but memories of kissing Sofia sneak in. Memories of our texts before I showed up at the soccer practice also sneak in. Especially the text in which she jokingly asked if hers were turning me on.

I hadn't been turned on, but one question has bounced around in my head ever since: what is her stance on phone sex? This is usually followed with me wondering why I'm even thinking about it.

Following the afternoon session on the ice, I join the boys in the classroom to analyze the video of a NHL game from last season. Afterward, they're dismissed for the day, but one player remains. He shifts on his feet and looks everywhere but at me. Which is odd since Mikko is normally confident and tells it as it is.

"What can I help you with?" I ask.

"You understand physics, right?"

I nod. I've occasionally explained the physics behind a skill to show how the skill works. "Is there something you need help with?"

He hesitates for a moment and nods. "I'm taking the physics course this summer, but I'm not doing well in it. It makes more sense when you explain things to me."

One of the camp's features that makes it different from others like it—other than it's offered for eight weeks instead of for just one—is that the hockey aspect is combined with summer school. It enables the boys to reduce their course load for the school year so they can focus more on the sport during hockey season.

"If you want, I can try to help you Tuesdays and Thursdays after camp." The days when Sofia is too busy to hang out with me.

"That will be good. Thank you," he says. I walk him out of the classroom and meet up with the staff for our regular weekly meeting. By the time we're finished, Sofia's at the movie with her grandmother.

Nik has plans, so I head back to our apartment and read my

emails. My old agent sent me a message, checking up on me. He does that every so often. He hasn't fully accepted my career as a player is over. Before the accident, I was making two million dollars annual salary.

But this email is different from the previous ones.

*Hello Kyle,*

    *Hope things are going well with you. I wanted to let you know of two career opportunities I've heard about through the grapevine. Both would be perfect for you given your experience and background.*

He goes on to explain the positions. Both are with college hockey teams. One is for an assistant coaching position in Seattle. The other one is a scout in Texas. He tells me not to wait too long if I'm interested.

I email him back, thank him, and briefly fill him in on my stay here. Then I spend the next hour thinking about the two positions. Both are far from my family, not that Finland is a five-minute drive from their house. But Finland is temporary.

In the end, I update my resume, write cover letters for both positions, and email them to the contacts Ben sent me. At least if I land one, or something similar, I'll still be involved in hockey, even if it isn't as a player.

Sadness and pain grip my heart hard at the thought and I grab a beer from the fridge. Once it's finished, I drink a second one while watching mindless TV. It takes me a few minutes to realize the show's in Finnish.

*Get over it, Kyle. You need to move on. That's why you're here. Remember?*

Helsinki is a chance for a fresh start after my year of moping around, drinking, and screwing anyone willing to spread her legs. So far the only thing I've cut back on is the moping. I'm still drinking, just not as much as before. When it comes to screwing, other than the one time with Sofia, I haven't fucked another girl in a few weeks. Which is impressive when you think about it. I have a feeling it has more to do with Sofia than anything else. After tasting her, she's the one I crave.

Unable to stop thinking about her, I send her a text: *You've had phone sex while watching* Star Wars. *True or false?*

Sofia responds almost immediately. *Isn't that like every guy's fantasy while they're watching Princess Leia in her bikini?*

*That was* Return of the Jedi.

*You're such a dork!*

*But a loveable dork, right?* Oddly enough, her opinion matters.

*Very.* Then she replies, *Is this your way of saying you're watching* Star Wars?

*Is this your way of saying you want to have phone sex with me?* I can almost imagine her face turning that cute shade of pink it goes whenever she's embarrassed. It's sexy as hell.

*Goodnight, Kyle. :)*

Too bad we won't be the only ones at the cottage this weekend.

Or maybe it's just as well.

Sex between us will complicate everything. One-night stands are one thing. I'm used to those. Beyond that, Gabby was my first girlfriend and then my wife.

And the last thing I'm looking for right now is another relationship. Not when I need to focus on my future.

# Chapter Twenty-Two

## Sofia

The apartment door buzzes. "I'll get it," I call out, even though as far as Muumu's concerned, I could have said "there's a pink unicorn at the door."

Kyle's standing in the doorway, wearing jeans and a t-shirt, but the t-shirt hugs his body in a way that makes me want to rip it off him. Not because it says *Never trust an atom. They make up everything* and I want the t-shirt (which I do!). Not because I want to see his ripped muscles without the impediment, though I'm not complaining if this happens. It's because I want to be the one touching his body, his skin.

Although from the way his gaze roams *my* body, barely hidden under the white tank top and denim shorts, it's obvious he's thinking the same.

Yes, the lines of our friendship have definitely become fuzzy. Fuzzy in the least scary way.

"Hey." I pick up my duffel from the floor near the door. "*Hei, hei*, Muumu." Joni already explained to her that I'm spending the weekend with some friends. I didn't mention that it included Kyle—my supposed boyfriend—but I got the idea she figured it out on her own.

Muumu responds, either telling me to have a great time or telling me that Stockmann is having a special on kitchen knives.

Or since Mom decided to go along with my lie—after much

begging on my part—and Muumu still thinks Kyle is my boyfriend, she might've been warning Kyle to keep his man parts to himself.

Who knows?

Shutting the door, I step into the hallway. I barely have time to turn around before I find myself in Kyle's arms, his lips on mine. My bag slides to the floor and my arms, on their own accord, loop around his neck. The electrified buzz I felt the other day, when he touched my arm in the parking lot, hums through my body. Equally on its own accord, my body presses against his.

I open my mouth and welcome him inside. It's been four days since we last kissed, but it seems like forever. I breathe in his ocean scent and get lost in him and the feel of his tongue stroking mine. But just as things get heated between us, Kyle pulls back and pushes his hand through his hair as he looks away. The dark curls wrap around his fingers. His hand continues south and he rubs the back of his neck, deep in thought.

"We should get going," he says after several seconds. He picks up my bag and walks down the stairs. I hurry after him, confused at the sudden change in him.

"Is something wrong?" I say.

"No, why would you ask?"

"I don't know. It's just that we were kissing back there, and it was feeling good, very good"—I'm not sure why I'm saying any of this, other than lying isn't my forte, and the words are tumbling out—"and you suddenly stopped."

He pauses. "What? You wanna have sex in the hallway?"

I'm not sure if I should laugh or be concerned at how he didn't answer the question. But since I don't want to ruin the weekend by pushing him to talk about something he obviously doesn't want to talk about, I let it slide. "Good point."

I almost expect him to jump on how I responded to his question. I didn't say I *didn't* want to have sex with him. But if he caught that, he doesn't let on.

Heck, I don't even know if he wants to have sex with me. We've kissed a lot, he's gone down on me, but he's never indicated he wants to go further than that.

At his car, he loads my bag into the trunk before we climb into the vehicle. "True or false," I say as we drive along the road out of Vantaa. "You have a huge crush on Princess Leia, back when she was in the original *Star Wars* movies."

"What guy doesn't have a crush on her from back then?"

"True enough." And hence his text about phone sex while watching *Star Wars*.

"True or false." He taps his fingers against the rim of the steering wheel. "You crushed on your high school American History teacher."

I scrunch my face. "You've obviously never met Mr. Winters. He was alive during the American Revolution."

The corners of Kyle's mouth twitch up. "I take it he didn't preserve well."

Two hours later, as we get closer to our destination, Kyle becomes less talkative and we just listen to a classic rock station. An odd sort of tension grows and I squirm in my seat, thinking back to his reaction when we kissed at Muumu's.

"I'm sorry," Kyle says after our conversation has lagged for twenty minutes. I almost jump at the sound of his voice after not hearing it for so long. "I'm just worried about this weekend."

I turn down the volume on the radio. "Why?"

"'Cause I know how things are when it comes to Nik and his parties. He likes to drink. But off-season. While he's playing hockey, he knows to draw the line…" Kyle doesn't say anything else, but I manage to fill in the blanks. He doesn't know how to draw the line when it comes to alcohol.

"If you want, I can help you out. If you don't want to drink too much. I'm sure I can find a way to distract you."

Kyle laughs and my face heats up at how that must have sounded. "I bet you can." His smile fades and he steers the car into the marina parking lot.

"Nik's cottage is here?" I ask, looking around. Nothing in the area resembles anything close to what I would call a cottage—other than a small wooden building at the far end of the parking lot. The only other things around are the parked vehicles and boats. And when I say boats, I mean smaller boats, like rowboats, sail boats, motorboats.

"No. His cottage is on an island on the lake. We have to take a boat there."

"You mean a rowboat?" The voice coming from my mouth doesn't sound like mine. It squeaks.

"No, a motorboat." He climbs out of the car.

I scan the dock for Nik, but there's no sign of him yet. I open my door and join Kyle at the trunk. He grabs the bags from the back.

"What time is Nik meeting us here?" I ask.

"He and his friends are already there."

"B-but how are we getting there? Is someone dropping us off?"

"No, I rented a boat. Don't worry," he adds, taking in my panicked expression. "I know what I'm doing. Plus, Nik gave me a map and showed me how to get there." He studies me for a second. "Are you afraid of motorboats?"

"Nope, I'm good." But it tumbles out as a squeak again. At his raised eyebrow, I continue, "When I was eleven, I was in a motorboat with my uncle and cousins. He lost control of it and hit a tree that was in the water. I hit my head and nearly drowned." I wasn't wearing my life jacket.

"Was he going fast?"

I nod, again.

"Then I won't." He takes hold of my hand. "Will that make you feel better?"

I assume he means the speed and not the holding my hand part, although either way is good. I nod, and he leads me to a store near the dock. He tells the teen we're here for the boat, and fifteen minutes later we're ready to go.

"You'll want to keep off the water once the storm hits," the seventeen-year-old says in perfect English, reminding me once again that when they handed out language skills, I was taking a nap.

"Storm?" Kyle and I say in unison. I look at the clear sky and frown.

"Yes, there's a storm rolling in later this evening. You don't want to be on the water when that happens. The waves can become dangerous. People have died during storms."

Oh goodie. Just what I needed to know.

"Thanks for the warning." Kyle squeezes my hand to tell me I'll be okay. "We'll be off the water before the storm hits." While I know it's true, it doesn't keep my legs from going rubbery. And they'll stay that way until we're safely back on shore.

I secure my life jacket, not taking any chances. To my relief, Kyle does the same. We climb into the small boat. Kyle sits at the stern (or whatever you call the back of the boat), and I sit on the bench, facing him.

Flashing me a reassuring smile, he starts the engine and steers us away from the dock. As promised, he doesn't go fast, and the tension building in me drains to the point that I don't have to grip the side of the small boat so hard. Circulation returns to my fingers.

The warm wind blows gently through my hair, pushing loose strands of my ponytail into my face. That, along with the movement of the boat against the smooth waters, calms me to the point where I'm more relaxed than before I got in the boat. A memory of happier times on my uncle's boat bobs to the surface, and I allow myself to relax more. Kyle's reassuring smile has a lot to do with that, too.

"True or false," Kyle says. "You used to be a water-skiing stunt woman in movies."

I snort. "I think we've already established that I'm not good with boats."

"Water skiing and riding a boat aren't the same thing. Unless you're in a James Bond movie. Then I guess they both tend to fly through the air at top speed, pushing the laws of aerodynamics to their limits."

I laugh. "Yes, there's always that."

We arrive incident free at the part of the island where we're staying. I glance around as Kyle pulls up close to the beach, ignoring the dock a couple of yards away. We're the only boat in the area, other than the one further down the beach. But that one clearly belongs to the people staying in the other cottage, hidden slightly in the trees.

"If the only way here is by boat, where is everyone?" I ask.

"Good question." Even though he's wearing jeans, and not shorts like me, Kyle climbs out of the boat. The water laps his knees when he stands upright, turning the fabric dark blue. "Since it'll be stormy later, I'll leave the boat on the beach so it doesn't end up smashing against the dock."

I shift my body to the side, ready to climb out and help him. Seeing what I'm about to do, he holds onto the side of the boat and steadies it.

With my body weight low in the boat, I step over the side. Freezing water greets my leg. I gasp.

Kyle chuckles. "Guess I should've mentioned it's cold."

"It's not too bad." I've been in worse, although a warning might have been nice.

I climb out of the boat, the brisk water hitting me mid thigh, and help Kyle drag the boat ashore. My legs are a little rubbery from the ride, but it only takes a few seconds for them to switch back to their land-loving form.

Once the boat is far enough up the beach to be safe during the storm, we remove our bags and the supplies Kyle brought with us. We line them up on the sand, then I help him flip the boat over so the rain doesn't flood it.

He wraps his arms around my waist and plants a soft kiss on my lips. It's enough to banish any residual fear of traveling by boat. "I told you I'd get you here safely. You okay?"

I nod, not wanting the moment to end, even if a nagging voice in the back of my head warns me the happiness coursing through me can't last forever. I've learned that the hard way.

He lowers his mouth to mine and teases me with feathery kisses. The electric hum is back, traveling through every nerve in my body. I want him so badly. I want to touch him, to please him.

He gives my lip a gentle tug with his teeth, but before I can respond, he steps away and grabs our bags. I crouch and pick up a box with supplies.

"I can get that," he says.

"I know, but I'm capable of carrying it too." It's the other box I'm not so sure about. I peer into it. "Were you responsible for bringing everything?"

"It looks that way, doesn't it? Maybe that's why Nik invited me. I'm the pack mule."

The cottage is farther back in the trees and it looks exactly as I imagined it would. Small. As in, two rooms small, if that. Several yards away is an even smaller building that I know is the sauna. Every summer cottage in Finland has one. It's like a rule. Okay, maybe not a rule, but no self-respecting Finn would be without one, as Mom used to say.

"How many people are coming?" I ask, eyeing the building.

Kyle's eyebrows bunch together as he, too, takes in the place. "He said about five, including himself, plus us."

It will definitely be cozy for seven of us. This is further confirmed after Kyle unlocks the door and opens it. A small eating area and kitchen is located left of where you step in. At the back of the room is a single door. Other than the kitchen, dinner table for four people, a wood-burning stove, and the small couch, not much else fills the space. It's like it fell straight from a fairy tale. I wouldn't be surprised if three bears come through the door at any moment and wonder who ate their porridge.

I place the box on the table and open the other door. Inside the room is a queen-sized bed and that's it. "Are there any sleeping bags?" 'Cause we didn't bring any.

"Nik said we wouldn't need any. Why?" Kyle asks behind me.

I turn to him. "Because there's only one bed." Surely Nik doesn't expect us all to sleep in it. Or have an orgy.

"What the...?" Kyle pulls his phone from his back pocket. He waits for whoever he's calling to answer, then says, "Hey, Nik, where the hell are you?" Pause. "Yeah, we got in…And when were you planning on telling me this…? Yeah…yeah…okay." He hangs up.

"So where is everyone?"

"Not here. There is no get together planned. Nik set this up to make up for that asshole thing he did the other day with the dog tags. No one else is coming." He nods at the box on the table. "Which explains why I was supposed to bring everything."

"So we're it?"

He nods. "'Fraid so." He looks back at the bed, and an odd expression clouds his face. "If you want, we can go back…or—or you can take the bed and I'll take the couch."

I glance at the couch, which isn't long enough for either of us. I'm not sure if he's suggesting that because he's being gentlemanly, or because he really doesn't want to sleep with me.

"We can share the bed," I say. "I'm fine with that."

He rubs the back of his neck, but it doesn't seem to relieve how tied up in knots he is at the possibility of being in the same bed as me. He had a wife. It makes sense that he's not over her and isn't ready to go that far with me. But if that's true, why did he have the one-night stand with the woman from the club? Why has he been flirting with me? Why did he go down on me?

*Because he figures your ex-boyfriend must have cheated on you for a reason,* an annoying little voice points out.

I swallow down a bitter laugh at the irony. All this time I avoided being involved with anyone so I wouldn't be hurt again. Yet here I am. Different situation. Same rejection.

Needing to escape, I grab my camera bag and walk out the door.

# Chapter Twenty-Three

## Sofia

I stalk down the dirt path to the boat, but then change my mind. Kyle will be getting the other box and I need space to sort through my emotions. I turn, walk past the outhouse (oh, joy), and disappear into the wooded area that makes up the majority of the island.

It doesn't take me long to find the perfect location for photos. The clearing is small with the leaves redirecting the light and giving the place a mystical mood. I study the area, like I do whenever I get ready to shoot a scene, and figure out what I want my images to say. Right now dejected comes to mind, but I push it away. I close my eyes and remember the fairy tales Mom used to tell me. When I was a kid, I would imagine all kinds of magical creatures living in the woods near Muumu's. This place is no different.

I switch the lens on my camera to my favorite macro lens, and wander the area, searching for anything hinting mystical creatures are among us. I've been shooting a number of shots of a fallen tree trunk, while on my stomach, when a loud snap of a branch yanks me from my zone.

I gasp and scramble to my feet, almost expecting a troll to lumber out of the trees, hungry for a tall blond snack. All those childhood tales Mom used to read me aren't helping me here.

I creep backward away from the sound, my gaze locked in the direction it had come from. It could be a bear or something equally big and deadly. The back of my calves collide against a fallen branch and I lose my freakin' balance.

I land sprawled on the ground, the wind knocked out of me. It takes a moment to regain my senses before my gaze jerks up to meet Kyle's.

He crouches next me. "Sorry. Didn't mean to scare you. Are you hurt?"

My butt isn't exactly thrilled with what happened, but hell if I'm admitting that to him. "I'm fine. I didn't realize you were behind me."

Kyle, now wearing long khaki shorts, helps me to my feet. I run my hands over my sore butt and the backs of my legs, dislodging any forest floor debris that's made itself at home there.

Definitely not my finest moment.

"What are you doing out here?" I ask once I've removed the evidence of my clumsiness.

"I got worried when you didn't return. You've been gone for over an hour."

"I was taking photos." I hold up my camera, you know, in case he didn't believe me. At least only one us is dealing with a bruised ego and backside.

I walk to my camera bag and place my camera inside it. "So what now? You wanna explore or go swimming?"

"I started the sauna. It should be ready soon. Why don't we swim first?"

"You figured out how to start the sauna?" I guess it's not electric like the one in Muumu's apartment building. There is no electricity here. And that includes in the cottage.

"Nik told me how to do it." He shakes his head. "Because he knew he wouldn't be coming here with us." Wow, Nik really had everything planned out. The question is, did he know about the storm or was that an added bonus?

We return to the cottage and I change into my white lace bikini in the bedroom. I don't wait for Kyle while he changes into his swimming trunks. I'm already toeing my way into the water when he emerges from the building.

A brief glance at him is all I need to remind myself of the

power he has over my body. God, it's not fair. Just one look at him and my body aches for him to touch me again. I'm not talking about how toned his body is. I'm talking about how his gaze roams over my body in a way that makes me feel beautiful. If any other guy did that, I would have felt shy and self-conscious.

An army of emotions battles in me, with confusion in the top spot. One minute he's running cool and wants nothing to do with me, beyond being my friend. The next he's on fire and wants to devour me with his kisses. And let's not forget to throw in an extra order of how my body responds to his slightest touch. It's no wonder I'm lost as to what's going on between us.

And it looks like I'm not the only one struggling with this. The same battle of emotions warring in me is affecting him, too. He steps closer so our bodies almost touch. A mischievous look crosses his face. That's all the warning I get before he scoops me up in his arms and walks into the lake.

I squirm in his arms, which doesn't do much for the buzz zinging through me with his hard yet warm body pressed against mine. "Kyle, put me down." My arms go around his neck. "Please."

He tightens his hold on me and strides deeper into the water. I shriek as the cold lake laps my butt and my legs. He laughs and lets go of me.

I disappear under the water, the cold pressing in on me. My feet find the silty bottom and I push myself to stand. Kyle's chuckling when I emerge. I send a tidal wave of water at him. Laughing harder, he dodges it, then grabs hold of my waist and pulls me close so only a thin layer of water separates us. The water around us might be cold, but the water separating us is toasty warm. Kyle's toasty warm.

I take in his light blue eyes as they watch me from behind his glasses. My gaze drifts to the small scar under the outer corner of his left eye. As if drawn by it, my finger traces along the smooth surface. "How did you get that?" I whisper, too afraid to speak any louder and betray the longing flaring in me.

"It happened when I was nine. I was playing hockey and the

puck hit me in the face." His voice is low and deep, the sound of it velvet trailing across my skin.

The longing intensifies.

My fingers trace along the curve of his cheekbones down to the day-old stubble on his jaw. The magnetic drive between us strengthens and my lips crave to touch the same places my fingers explored. I press my mouth against his jaw and relish the roughness of his stubble against my skin. And then, as if my body is no longer interested in what my brain has to say, the tip of my tongue tastes his flesh and doesn't want to stop at just that. It keeps exploring him, along his jaw and his neck. And because that isn't enough, and my teeth want in on the action, I nibble his neck—something I never did with Ian.

A slight moan vibrates through Kyle's chest and makes me bolder. My mouth moves to his and I kiss him, deeply, taking everything he'll give me and so much more. Before I have a chance to register what's happening, Kyle's hands slide down the backs of my legs and in a smooth movement he lifts me. My legs go around his hips, grinding us together. Our kisses become more consuming, and any doubts I have that he wants me as much as I want him vanish.

At least it does until his mouth pulls away a minute later and he lets me slip back into the water. His expression is back to what it was earlier—the battlefield of emotions. "The sauna should be ready now," he says, voice strained. His gaze drops to my arms. "You're cold."

Disappointment and frustration course through me and I glance at my arms. Goose bumps cover my skin, but not for the reasons he thinks. Unable to look at him, I nod.

Without a word, I trudge through the water to the beach. He doesn't move for several seconds before splashing after me. The sound of him approaching kicks me into action and I run back to shore, pretending I'm just eager to get into the hot sauna after the cold lake. Okay, maybe not so much pretending.

A cool wind brushes against me, reminding me that the storm will hit us in a few hours. For a brief moment I contemplate telling

Kyle we should head back to the mainland, but then we're faced with another long drive home. It also means showing up a day earlier than planned, which will be hard to explain to Muumu. I have no one to translate for me, and this goes beyond what Joni has taught me so far.

Kyle doesn't say anything as we approach the sauna, but what is there to say? "Sorry, I'm just not that into you, even though I have no problems having sex with every other woman I meet." I yank open the door and a wave of heat hits me.

That annoying voice, the one that wants to be some twisted version of the voice of reason, reminds me that Joni is interested in me. Maybe I can hook up with him. I kick the voice in its backside. I don't feel for Joni what I feel for Kyle. Without that passion, that desire, things won't be any different than they were with Ian.

I sit on the top bench. Kyle sits next to me.

# Chapter Twenty-Four

## Kyle

Most teenage boys learn about the facts of life and dating from three sources: friends (not always the most reliable source at that age, in case you're wondering), sex education class, and parents (most notably the father). I was probably the only teen in existence who had The Talk with a plate of cookies and a glass of milk while sitting at the table with their grandmother.

I can't remember most of what she told me, mainly because I had been understandably mortified for the majority of it. But the one thing I remember is her advice to always treat a girl right. Good thing she isn't alive to see the kind of a man I've become in the past year.

I sit next to Sofia on the top bench.

What the hell am I going to do? All I want to do is kiss her senseless and burrow myself deep in her. Except she's my friend and I don't want to fuck that up. Not while I'm in Finland. Not while I'm having fun with her. Throw in the sex and this could all fall apart.

*Shit.*

I trace mindless circles on Sofia's thigh. Just touching her causes an electrical hum to vibrate along my nerves. Her gaze lowers to my left leg and the red scars forming a network across my thigh, the scars that I've managed to keep hidden until now, other than when I first met her in the sauna. But back then, she was so embarrassed that I was naked, she had avoided looking at my legs.

Some of the scars are thin, others thick. But one thing's for certain, they weren't from when I was a kid like I'd claimed. I can see it in her eyes; she realizes that, too. The accident I told her about, the one that causes my leg to stiffen when pushed too hard, it's all a lie.

"I was in a car accident," I tell her.

"And you prefer not talking about it," she says more to herself than to me.

I run my finger along the thickest line, the surgical scar. The others are from when the side window shattered and shards of glass dug into me. Sofia finds the one that is usually hidden under my t-shirt, the one on my shoulder. She leans over and kisses it as if that will wipe away the memory. I wish it would. I wish her kisses could erase everything about that night.

I cup my hands against her cheeks and lower my head to meet her soft lips. The heat squeezes in on us but that doesn't stop me from exploring her mouth, tasting the longing that fills me as much as it fills her. By the time we stop a few minutes later, we're panting from the dry heat as much as from the kiss.

She grins, but it isn't just a happy grin that tells you all is right with the world. It's a grin lightened by mischief. "Have you tried the birch branch experience yet?" she asks.

I frown. "The what experience?" Sounds kind of painful.

She grabs a small branch covered in leaves from next to her on the bench, and dips it into the bucket of water on the floor. She then slaps the branch and leaves against her skin. "It's supposed to bring the toxins to the surface, or something like that."

Okay. If she says so. Looks kinky more than anything.

Kinky or not, I take it from her and whack my body like she demonstrated. I can't say it does anything for me, but since it's supposed to be part of the sauna experience, and I'm all for new experiences with Sofia, I do it anyway.

We stay in here for a bit longer, until I'm squirming from the heat. "True or False," I say. "You would rather spend the next thirty minutes in here than jumping into the lake and cooling off."

She scrambles down from the bench. I join her, and we run the short distance to the dock. I beat her, place my glasses at the edge of the dock, and jump into the lake. The fucking. Freezing. Lake. It was cold before, but after the sauna, it's the equivalent of Antarctica.

I break the surface as Sofia leaps in. She reappears a moment later, shrieking, "Oh my God! It's cold!"

I swim over to her and wrap my arms around her. Shit, she's as sexy as hell with her wet hair pulled away from her face and her hard nipples pressing against the wet fabric of her bikini top. "I can warm you up."

She shivers. "Trust me. Nothing can warm me up. I'm ready to go back in the sauna." She squirms out of my arms and swims to the dock before hoisting herself up the slippery wooden steps. The weight of the water pulls down on her bikini bottom enough to fuel my fantasies for a month.

I follow her, grabbing my glasses from the dock on the way up, and we run back to the sauna. Fortunately compared to the water, the late afternoon air is a lot warmer. I have no idea how Finns manage this in the fall or winter. They must be crazy.

Sofia and I repeat the cycle of sitting in the sauna and jumping into the lake a few more times. We don't make out in the sauna again. It's too damn hot for that. But we do tell each other stories about when we were younger, while continuing our game, and share about things we have in common. Even after we're finished with the sauna, and we're sitting around the fire, cooking our dinner, we share about our life. Yet, I can't bring myself to talk about the accident and how I used to play for the NHL. I don't have any regrets about keeping the truth from her. It has nothing to do with Sofia, and I want to keep it that way, to keep our memories happy.

Sofia bites into her sausage. "Mmmm. I wish we could get these back home. I've been craving them since the last time I was here."

She's right. They are amazing. "When was the last time you were in Finland?"

"I was fifteen. It was just before my father cheated on my mom and the student went psycho bitch on him."

"Did your mom ever remarry?"

"No, but she recently started dating someone."

"Do you know him?"

She shakes her head. "She started dating him after I left to come here. She seems pretty happy but she didn't want to tell me much else, in case it doesn't work out…It just feels weird knowing she's ready to move on." A wistfulness sneaks into her tone.

Just like I need to move on after what happened to me. But like Sofia, I'm not sure I'm ready to yet.

I drink back some beer. At least with Sofia I don't have the burning urge to get lost in the buzz. She does that for me. She's like my guardian angel, sent to help give me a second chance at life. Too bad what we have between us is only for the summer.

Sofia glances at the beer and sadness washes over her face. "Are you okay?" She nods at the bottle in my hand.

"I'm fine." I stare at the fire crackling in the pit. Its flickering warmth mirrors the same warmth in my veins from sitting so close to her. Even with the smoke drifting in our direction, I smell the occasional whiff of her apple scent. "I have no reason to get wasted tonight." I press my lips against her temple, telling her she's enough for me. For now.

A small smile curves on her mouth then vanishes. "Someone I once cared about let alcohol destroy him." She places her cool hand against my face and strokes my cheek with her thumb. Her eyes lock with mine and I could get lost in her beautiful blue eyes. "I don't want the same to happen to you."

"It won't," I whisper.

The flicking light catches on her pendant. I reach out and finger the delicate silver swan.

"My parents gave it to me," she explains. "We were visiting Santa's Village in Lapland when we found it. Swans have always been my favorite bird. I used to want to be one."

"Santa has a village in Lapland? I thought he lived in the North Pole."

Sofia laughs. I fight a grin but lose out in the end and finish my sausage and beer. The wind picks up, sending the flames into a frenzied dance, and raindrops splash on our skin. We'd been so busy talking and eating, I hadn't noticed the storm clouds sneak in.

We jump up from the thick log we'd been sitting on. Sofia grabs our food and I douse the fire with the bucket of water. Then we hurry back to the cottage as the clouds release their load. The distance isn't far but that doesn't matter. We're soaked within seconds.

While Sofia changes in the bedroom, I search for something to keep us warm and for something to occupy us. By the time Sofia emerges from the bedroom, I've hunted down playing cards, a flashlight, plus oil and matches for the hurricane lamps.

"Your turn," she says, wearing a skimpy tank top and shorts with cartoon puppies on them. Her breasts press against the tight fabric and her legs are endless. My dick twitches against my zipper at the sight of her.

*Shit.* The beer and her outfit are making me want to rethink keeping our friendship simple.

She spreads a blanket on the couch. "I figured this would at least keep us warm."

Compared to the fire in my blood from thinking about all the things I want to do to her, the blanket has nothing on it. And I suspect being under it with Sofia will only lead to trouble for me.

"I found some cards. We can play poker." Except we don't have any chips, and strip poker isn't going to work. Not if we want to play for long. At most, she's wearing four pieces of clothing—five if we count the blanket—and unless she's a card shark in disguise, this game won't last long before I have her naked.

Not a good idea.

She nibbles her lips like she did earlier. "I don't know how to play."

Yep, definitely not a good idea.

"Can you play Go Fish?"

She nods.

Okay, Go Fish it is.

While I fill oil in two hurricane lanterns and light them, Sofia lays out our unfinished meal on the coffee table. She then snuggles under the blanket. I go to the bedroom and change into my shorts and t-shirt.

When I come out, Sofia's shuffling the cards. Her technique is a long way from Vegas ready. I sit next to her and shake my head at her offer to join her under the blanket.

Sofia deals the cards and we begin a heated game of Go Fish. The wind and rain battle against the windows and the roof. Thunder rumbles in the distance. Now we just have to hope the cottage stands up to whatever Mother Nature plans to hurl at us.

"Do you have eights," she asks, not the least bit nervous about the weather.

"Go Fish."

She makes an adorable face and pulls a card. We keep playing. Sofia wins the first five games. She might not be a card shark when it comes to poker, but damn the girl is good when it comes to Go Fish.

Growing tired of my losing streak, I remove the cards from her hands and place them on the table.

A sly smile breaks onto her face. "Does that mean I get my prize now?"

"What prize?"

"Well, I won five games. Five out of five. That means I'm the winner. So what's my prize?" She holds her hand out to me.

I kiss the palm of her hand. But I don't stop there. I keep moving up her arm, trailing kisses as I go.

She laughs. "Not quite what I had in mind, but it'll do."

It's not what I have in mind either. I'm aiming for a much bigger prize. Something that will ensure the largest of carnival prizes shrinks back in shame. Her laugh is cut off as my mouth finds hers.

I knot my fingers in her hair and deepen the kiss. She doesn't resist. She welcomes me in. Our tongues glide against each other and all I can think about is exploring her body even though that's the last thing I should be doing. My free hand pushes away the blanket from her shoulder and my fingers glance down the thin straps of her tank top. She shivers at my touch.

"Are you cold?" I ask against her lips.

"No, I'm perfect," she murmurs back.

Yes, she is.

I pull the straps of her tank top and bra down, my fingers brushing against her soft skin. I kiss her shoulder in the same spot she kissed me in the sauna, the location of my scar. I plant kisses along her shoulder, up her neck, and stop at her ear. My tongue travels along the outside of it before I nip the flesh between my teeth.

She moans and the heated sound of it is all the encouragement I need. I release her hair and skim my hand down her back. At the hem of her tank, I slide my fingers under the fabric and trace along the top of her shorts. Sofia's breaths come in rapid bursts, barely heard above the noise of rain pelting the roof. The sky fills with a bright flash of light followed by a loud crack of thunder.

Sofia leans back against the cushions. I readjust my body so I'm lying on top of her, my arms supporting my weight. Her leg skims mine and wraps around my hips, bringing me closer to the part of her that I long to touch, taste, tease. But instead, I rock against her, my entire body cheering me on. I want her so badly, I'm positive I'm going to explode.

I push her tank top above her belly button and swirl my tongue around it. A whimper falls from Sofia's lips and I smile inwardly at how she responds to the subtlest of moves. I continue pushing her tank top up and expose her bra. It's light pink and it suits her. While I can tell she's no virgin—she's not shy in the same way she would be if she were—I can also tell she hasn't had a lot of experience.

Sensing what I want, Sofia sits up and removes her tank top, drops it to the floor, then unhooks her bra. It quickly joins the tank top, as does my t-shirt.

# Chapter Twenty-Five

## Sofia

Kyle's t-shirt joins the party on the floor with my bra and tank top. But then he hesitates, as if deliberating what we're about to do. What the heck is there to deliberate? I want this, and judging from the bulge in his shorts, he wants this, too.

He pulls away and my body screams in frustration. I'm doing something wrong. That must be it.

I shift to sit and Kyle does the same. "What's wrong?" I ask him.

*Am I doing something wrong...or...are you feeling guilty because you're still love in your wife?*

He picks up the stack of cards forgotten on the table and shuffles them, not at all affected by the fact that I'm sitting next to him topless. Which I'll admit, if nothing else, is an arrow straight through my fragile ego.

"Nothing's wrong, Soph. It's just you're my friend." He continues shuffling the cards, his attention on them and not me and my breasts. "I don't want to fuck that up."

"Why do you think you'll fuck that up?"

"If we have sex, it will only complicate things."

I think on this for a moment, then remove the cards from his hands and straddle him. I place the cards next to us on the couch. "It doesn't need to complicate anything. We've got a month left together here. If we become..." Become what? Not boyfriend and girlfriend. Not with only a month left here. A fling? "...Friends with

146

benefits. It won't be complicated at all. This only has to last while we're in Finland."

There will be no strings attached, no hearts at risk of being broken. It will only be about having fun. And fun is exactly what the doctor prescribed for the new and improved me.

Something deep inside me cheers on this sudden burst of confidence. A month ago, I never would have considered doing something like this.

"You sure about this?" he asks, his gaze taking in everything about my face. My eyes. My lips. My desire.

"Positive." *Please say yes.*

He doesn't say anything, but there's no missing the want in his eyes. He needs this as much as I do.

Instead of saying it with words, he shows me. His hands cup my breasts, and his thumbs draw dizzying circles around the hard nipples. He lightly pinches one. The nerves between my legs go berserk with need. "Oh God," I groan.

Then his mouth crashes against mine. His kisses become frantic, filled with the same need coursing through my body. His hands—large, strong, warm—caress and explore my exposed skin. Every part of me he touches begs for more. I beg for more.

His thickness, straining in his shorts, presses against my super-charged center. I moan against his mouth, the sound barely heard over my pounding heart and the distant rumble of thunder.

He pulls away. "If you're sure about this…" he says, giving me one last chance to change my mind about what we'll be after this.

"I am. Do you have any condoms? I—I have some in my bag." Because that doesn't make it look like I was planning to have sex with him this weekend, even though we were staying here with five other people.

His lips curl into a sexy, one-sided smile. "Didn't think I could resist your magnetic attraction for long, huh?"

Heat rises in my cheeks. Not the look I was going for. He's used to confident, experienced women. I'm not exactly the poster girl for that.

"There's nothing about you, Sofia, I can resist. You had me the first day in the sauna, when you blasted me with the water." He threads his fingers through my hair and pulls me to him. His lips gently kiss me, setting free a crate of butterflies in my stomach. I want this moment to be perfect, but what is that exactly? Hot sex? Knowing all the positions and being adventurous? Or pouring everything you have inside you and hoping it's enough?

Even though I don't want to leave his embrace for even a second, the condoms are in the bedroom and I can't exactly levitate them over here. I scoot off his lap and offer him my hand. He takes it and I pull him off the couch, then lead him into the bedroom as I mentally go through the steps of how to put the condom on him.

I retrieve several foil packages from my bag and with shaky fingers, place the condoms on the night table. Kyle places the hurricane lamp next to them.

Okay, now what?

Kyle answers that for me. He comes up behind me and wraps his arm around my waist. His mouth blazes a trail of hot, wet kisses along my shoulder, and with his free hand, he nudges my hair back, exposing the skin on my neck.

The kisses continue along my neck to the shell of my ear and he nips it between his teeth. My panties grow damp.

As his tongue tastes and explores the outside of my ear and my jaw, his fingers do some walking…to the waistband of my sleep shorts. They slip beyond the elastic waistband and travel south, teasing my skin with their light touch.

They continue over my satin underwear, the ones Maija had recommended that I get, until Kyle reaches the throbbing part between my legs that has been cheering him on, remembering what happened last time he touched me here. Begging for an encore.

Kyle groans loud against my neck, sending an erotic hum through me. My body jerks back, pressing my butt against his hard length. Unable to help myself, I wiggle against him, tormenting him like he's tormenting me. His answering moan makes me grin.

He removes his hand from my shorts. The throb between my

legs pouts and cries no fair. But it changes its mind when Kyle shifts focus and slowly peels my shorts and panties down my legs. If he coaches half as well as he's seducing me, his players are bound to become great hockey players once day.

Once my shorts and panties are around my ankles, I kick them to the side and turn around. I'm naked. He's not. I plan to level the playing field. With clumsy fingers, I unfasten his shorts and slide them and his boxer briefs down his legs. There's nothing seductive in my movements. Kyle doesn't seem to care. He peers down at me, his eyes dark in the dim light of the hurricane lamp.

A sudden shyness overcomes me at seeing him naked, with his cock standing at attention. It's not like I've never seen a naked guy before, but right now it feels like my first time.

Before I can do anything else, Kyle's arms are around me again and he's kissing me. The shyness and nervousness melt away at the touch of his lips against mine.

He walks me backward to the bed and the next thing I know, I'm laying back on it with Kyle leaning over me. He traces his lips against my jaw, tasting me with his tongue. His thumb strokes my cheek then his hand drifts to my shoulder and slides to my chest. It stills over my rapidly beating heart. "You're so beautiful, Sofia. So, so beautiful." His voice is both husky and filled with warmth.

I spread my fingers over his heart, and relish its equally rapid beat against my hand. I'm affecting him the same way he's affecting me. That thought gives me a confidence I haven't felt since Ian's cruel words. Even before that. Kyle makes me feel like the woman I've wanted to be.

Kyle's fingers slide away from my heart and dip to an aching nipple that pleads for him to touch it again. Echoing what he did earlier, his thumb circles it, the circle growing smaller with each rotation. He pinches it again, and once more the nerves between my legs go berserk. I groan. Every cell in my body screams for more. My teeth gently sink into his shoulder, something I've never done before, but with Kyle it feels so right. So good.

"Fuck, babe," Kyle groans, and I'm more turned on than I ever thought I would be at his words. "That feels so fucking good." He kisses me once more. "I want to taste you again, Sofia. I've been wanting to taste you again since the first time."

I nod, unable to talk. I want that, too. I want everything.

Craving to touch every part of him, I wrap my fingers around his warm length. Kyle sucks in a sharp breath but doesn't say anything. He lets me continue to stroke his velvety hardness.

His fingers engulf my wrist, stilling my movements. "You need to stop now," he husks, "before I lose control. I'm not ready for that yet." I love that I have this effect on him.

He doesn't give me a chance to miss the contact. His hands brush against my inner thighs and spread them apart. He plants kisses along my skin until he gets to the throb between my legs. His tongue swirls around the swollen flesh and I gasp. Then he sucks on it and my gasp becomes a moan.

He slides a finger between my folds. "You're so fucking wet for me."

God, I never thought someone talking dirty to me could be such a turn on. I almost come right there.

His finger pushes inside and presses against me, setting off a new round of fireworks in my nerves. I grab hold of the sheet with both hands, afraid if I don't, I might explode.

Another finger joins the first and I'm beginning to think holding onto the sheet won't be enough.

"Babe, I want you to let go. I want you to come against my mouth."

I grip the sheet tighter. "No, I want you inside me."

He laughs against me and I swear I'm dying from the feel of it against the throbbing. "Don't worry. I'm not missing out on it this time. But I'm perfectly happy giving you multiple orgasms."

He sucks on the ache again and I can't hold back even if I wanted to. I scream, "Oh, God, Kyle," as I let myself go. Never. Ever. Did it feel this way with Ian.

The thought is barely out of my mind before Kyle kisses me, deeply. My tongue greets his and I explore his mouth as much as he explores mine. And my tongue isn't the only one doing its own exploration. My hand reunites with his hard length, and from the erotic sounds he makes when I touch him, it won't be much longer before he'll hopefully experience what I just did.

Still kissing him, I grope around the nightstand with one hand, blindly searching for the foil packages. Once I find one, I stop kissing him and I push myself up to sit. He lies back on the bed, watching me with hooded eyes.

I've never put on a condom before, but I've watched Ian do it. I rip open the package, careful not to damage the condom. Then with shaky hands, I slip the rubber onto his tip and begin unrolling it along his length. Sensing my nervousness, Kyle covers my hand with his and helps me guide it down.

And then I do something I've never done before...I lower myself onto him and let his width fill me. I rock back and forth, and Holy of everything hot does it ever feel good.

With his eyes open, watching me, Kyle grabs my hips and helps me find the rhythm that will push us both over the edge. It doesn't take long before I tighten around him and call out his name, the intensity of the climax as powerful as the last time.

Kyle comes seconds later.

I sag to the bed, boneless and drained, knowing I'll never been able to settle for less again.

# Chapter Twenty-Six

## Kyle

Sofia rests her head on my chest, our breaths still ragged. My hand draws lazy circles on her back. "You're amazing," I tell her. And I mean it. I hadn't pegged Sofia to be a fan of dirty talk. But she became more alive when I did that, like there was a neutron star buried deep, waiting to become a supernova.

"I am?" Her surprise fades to sadness. She glances toward the window, her mind anywhere but in this moment, her mind anywhere but with me.

I brush my fingers against her face. "What's wrong?"

Sofia looks back at me, the sadness still there. Instead of saying anything, she chews on her lip like she always does when she's uncertain. Gone is the girl who finds joy in even the smallest things.

"It's okay," I say. "You can tell me. Whatever it is we can deal with it together."

She nods and I snuggle her closer.

"I told you my boyfriend cheated on me." The sadness leaks into her voice and tears me apart. "He said he cheated on me because I was a lousy lay. He'd been bored of having sex with me, but didn't know how to breakup with me without hurting me, so he slept around on me instead."

"You're far from boring. Not even in the same galaxy as boring." I kiss her shoulder. "Can I ask you a question?"

She nods, not thoroughly convinced at my words. I'm not sure she'll be willing to answer my question, but I want what we have between us to be something more, something real. And for that to happen we need to be honest with each other.

"Did you ever climax with him?"

Blushing and without hesitation, she shakes her head.

"Did you just climax for me?"

She nods.

"In my apartment, did you climax then too?" I know she did, but I want her to see the difference between what we have and what she had with him. I want to make sure she doesn't have any doubts about how good we are together.

"Yes," she whispers and I brush my lips against hers.

"That proves he wasn't the right guy for you." I kiss her again, except now it's possessive, erasing all memory of the asshole and replacing each one with memories of how great we are together.

Our kisses become intense, and soon we're ready to fuck again. And this time, with Sofia knowing that everything she'd been told in the past was a lie, the sex is more mind-blowing than before.

• • •

I wake up to the sound of rain hammering against the roof and the windows. I don't open my eyes. I just lay listening to the noise, until I realize the rain isn't all I hear. Sofia's soft breaths cause an equally soft smile to sneak on my face.

I open my eyes to find Sofia watching me in the dim light. Although she's still covered with the bedding, she hasn't put her clothes on yet. Good, now I won't have to waste time removing them again.

"Mornin'," I say, voice low and husky with sleep.

She smiles back at me. The smile is shy, a little nervous, but I can't figure out what she has to be nervous about.

"Looks like we won't be going home yet." I nod toward the window behind her.

She laughs. "I guess you'll just have to teach me how to play poker."

I nibble on her ear. She moans which gets my dick excited at the prospect of what's coming next. "Only if I let you out of this bed. Maybe we can practice some more…" I don't finish the sentence with words. I finish it with my hand tracing along the silky skin from her hip to her waist.

Her eyes darken and she runs the tip of her tongue along her lip, her suggestion about playing poker long forgotten. "Practice is good. I could use lots of practice."

Before she had realized her ex-boyfriend had been way off base about how amazing she is in bed, she might've been serious when she said that. But this time, the unmistakable teasing to her tone makes me secretly hope it will storm for the rest of the week, just so that we're stuck on this island. If it weren't for my coaching job and her chance to work in the physical therapy clinic this week, I'd find an excuse for us to stay here.

Her hand shifts under the sheet and cups my ass, her thumb brushing against my skin. I moan into her mouth, then move away and explore her jaw with my lips and tongue. She tastes like heaven. Every part of her tastes like heaven. I keep traveling along her skin to her neck. She runs her fingernails lightly down my back and I hum in satisfaction against her. Forget a week. I wouldn't mind being stuck on this island for the rest of my stay in Finland.

I kiss my way to her perfect rose-colored nipple, hard and ready for me to savor. I tease it with my tongue, drawing tight circles around it. Then I close my lips around it and alternate between sucking and nipping it with my teeth. Sofia gasps. Her fingers trace the same circles in my hair that I drew with my tongue against her breast.

Needing to touch more of her, I let my hand wander over her body. She giggles and squirms as I hit her ticklish spots, and I mentally catalogue them for when I'm not about to make a claim on her. I switch to her other breast and tease it like I did the first. My fingers skim along her body, across her smooth stomach, and down to my favorite spot—between her legs. I slide my fingers between her folds, slick with need. "God, babe, you feel so good. So ready for me." I dip a finger in and press it against her heated lining, then pull it out and rub it against her clit. "Do you feel how wet you are, how ready you are for me?" I growl, returning to her mouth.

Sofia whimpers and I pinch her clit. Her whimper turns into an erotic moan against my lips that pushes me further to the edge and promises me a free fall to rival all others.

I've had sex with many girls. I'm not ashamed to admit it. But sex with all those one-night stands is nothing like sex with Sofia. Maybe there's something to be said about our relationship. It's not just about sex.

It's about friendship and trust.

And that makes a huge difference.

Sofia wraps her hand around my dick and squeezes lightly. I suck in a breath and will myself not to come in her hand like an inexperienced fifteen-year-old. Her grip slips up to the head and she runs her thumb around the tip, and all my plans for what I want to do her body check the wall. I pull away and spread her knees apart before shifting so I'm kneeling between them. With her eyes dark and hooded, her blond hair fanned around her head, she watches me, curious what I'm going to do next.

"God, you look so beautiful," I husk. "I want you to watch me. I want you to see how much you affect me." That should push aside any of her doubts about what she does to me.

She nods, her eyes darker pools than before, not at all embarrassed by my words. If anything, she's more turned on, and I didn't think it was possible. I slip on a condom from the night table and hoist her legs onto my shoulders. Her eyes widen.

I plunge deep into her and she moans that erotic sound of hers that has me almost coming. I still for a moment, doing my best not to close my eyes. I want to see her as much as I want her to see me.

I press my thumb against her clit. She bucks against me, letting out another sexy sound.

"Oh God, Kyle! I want you to…to fuck me…Now."

I pull out slightly and slam back into her. I swirl my thumb over the delicate tissue and slam back into her again. I continue the pattern until I'm certain we're both close to coming, then I pick up the pace until Sofia's softness grips tightly around me and she lets out a satisfied, "Oh, God, yes!" I wouldn't be surprised if the people in the next cottage heard her even over the storm.

That's the last thought I have before I come, and a guttural sound falls from my lips.

Once the intense tidal wave has crashed through me and some level of coherency returns, I remove her legs from my shoulders and lower them onto the bed, then remove the condom and collapse next to her. I pull her to me and whisper in her hair, "You're mine now and only mine." The words slip out so naturally even though they aren't technically true. Our friends-with-benefits arrangement doesn't make her mine.

Not even close.

"And you're mine," Sophia murmurs sleepily before drifting off to sleep.

I watch her, purposefully ignoring the slight thrill her words gave me.

# Chapter Twenty-Seven

## Kyle

Normally after I finish work on Mondays, I head to the sports center to work out, have a sauna, then spend time with Sofia. But because she's working in the physical therapy clinic this week, I won't get to spend time with her until the weekend.

I contemplate dropping into the clinic to check on her, but that's the last thing she needs. So, I spend longer in the sauna than I normally would and head back to the apartment.

"*Hei*," Nik says from the couch, a beer in his hand. The TV is on, with what looks like an American soap opera I've seen Mom watch from time to time. I've never seen Nik watch it before. "You want to go out tonight?" he asks. "I need a drink and some action."

"Sure," I say even though I shouldn't. I haven't been out since the first night I went down on Sofia. I've been too busy hanging out with her. But Nik really does look like he needs something. "You okay?"

"Nothing getting laid won't cure." He finishes his beer and gets up to leave.

We enter the sports bar and no sooner than we sit down, the waitress appears at our table. We order beers and she leaves, with Nik studying her ass as she walks away. I check out the menu. Nik does the same once the waitress is out of sight. A soccer match plays on the large screen TVs throughout the place. Unlike most of the patrons here, we don't bother watching it. It's just background noise for us.

The waitress returns a few minutes later with our drinks. As she places the beers on the table, she leans over, flashing her ample cleavage from above the low cut t-shirt. Nik practically drools on the table.

"Would you like anything else?" she asks, making eye contact with each of us in turn. We tell her our orders. I expect her to leave but she doesn't. "Where in America are you from?"

"Minneapolis," I say.

She nods. "You're Nikolas Tikkanen, aren't you?" she asks Nik.

"Depends if that's a good thing or not." But he says it in a tone suggesting 'your place or mine?'

She giggles. The sound is nothing like when Sofia laughs. It reminds me of a hyena. "It's a good thing." She looks me over. "You play for the Bears too, no?"

I open my mouth to answer but Nik beats me to it. "One of the best on the team."

I don't bother to correct him. There's no point.

She leaves to put in our order and I gulp back some beer. A few minutes later, it's no longer just Nik and I at the table. Two other girls join us. Like the waitress, they're pretty with large tits and tight, low-cut t-shirts. Typically, I don't care either way about breast size. Small, medium, large, they're all good. But for some reason my mind goes to Sofia and her perfect tits.

I chug back more beer as cheers break out throughout the bar.

"Are you in Helsinki for long?" Taala, the brunette, asks me. Laina is busy talking to Nik.

"Till the end of the month."

That makes Taala happy. She scoots closer to me and leans in as the waitress returns with the food. Before Taala can get close enough to touch me, the waitress's arm shoots between us and she lowers my plate onto the table. Her hip nudges Taala away from me in a move that's clearly intentional. I do my best not to laugh.

She places Nik's plate in front of him and asks if we need anything else. Nik and I order more beer. Taala's and Laina's glasses are still full. They excuse themselves for the bathroom.

I check the time on my phone. Sofia should be getting off her job anytime now. I text her: *How did your 1st day in clinic go?*

She responds a minute later. *Loved it! Much more fun than cleaning toilets.* I laugh. Just about anything is more fun than cleaning toilets.

I type: *You want to come over?*

*Have to pass. Need to go to bed.*

This doesn't surprise me. I dropped Sofia off at her grandmother's apartment around midnight last night, after we spent most of the day on the island. It wasn't until early evening that the lake calmed down enough for us to return to the mainland.

*Sweet dreams. Talk to you later.*

*Good night. :)*

I slip the phone back in my jean's pocket as Taala and Laina return. The bar is busier now even though it's Monday night. Busier and hotter.

Fortunately, the beer isn't hot. It's refreshing and cool. And before I realize it, Nik and I have had several more rounds. Taala talks but I can't hear her over the noise of cheering soccer fans.

She leans closer to me, but she doesn't repeat what she said. Her hand moves to my thigh. Nik and the blond have been making out for the past hour, and don't look like they plan to stop any time soon. His hand is on her tit and it doesn't take much imagination to know what will happen between them soon. The question is will it be her place or ours?

Taala's hand isn't content where it is, and she traces her fingers up my leg until her hand cups my package. Any other time this wouldn't be an issue, but now that Sofia and I have progressed to friends with benefits, I have no idea what the boundaries are. If she was my girlfriend, touching, kissing, sex would all be off limits. But what are the rules when it comes to friends with benefits?

The one thing I do know as Taala's tongue invades my mouth is her kisses do nothing for me. They're nothing like Sofia's kisses.

I pull away and remove her hand from my crotch. It doesn't matter what the rules are when it comes to friends with benefits and screwing other women, I'm not into Taala. I make a big deal about checking the time on my phone. "Looks like it's time for me to call it a night," I tell everyone at the table. From the way Nik and Laina are going at it, they either didn't hear me, or didn't care, or all of the above.

Taala pouts, which doesn't look half as adorable as when Sofia does it. "I can come with you if you want."

I fake a yawn. "Sorry, I have to get up early for work." Nik doesn't help my case since the women know we work together. I can see it in Taala's eyes as she looks over at him and her friend.

I indicate to the waitress that I want to settle my bill. She returns a few minutes later. I pay her and say goodbye to everyone at the table. Still in a lip lock with Laina, Nik waves. I push myself up from my chair. It's only then that I notice someone who looks like a blurry Joni. Shit, I'm more tired and drunk than I realized.

Except this blurry Joni is glaring at me in the same way I've caught the original doing.

Ignoring the warning bells in my head, I leave the bar and walk home.

# Chapter Twenty-Eight

## Kyle

I'm an idiot.

The pounding in my head fully agrees with that assessment. I should have known better when I went out with Nik last night. I thought I could handle it.

I was wrong.

But at least I've had more sleep than Nik, who looks like shit. Luckily he went to Laina's apartment last night instead of bringing her to our place.

"Okay, guys," I say to the boys after they've warmed up on the soccer field, "new coordination drill." I get everyone to partner off and grab a tennis ball. "Stand next to your partner, and toss the tennis ball back and forth between you."

They glance around, wondering if they're missing something. This drill is easy. I'm not known for easy drills. I let them practice for a few minutes. "All right. Now you'll do the same drill, but this time you'll run while tossing the ball back and forth to your partner."

The best part about being the coach is I don't have to demonstrate the skills. Especially ones like this. Which is a good thing given Nik's state. Okay, my pounding head wouldn't have appreciated it either, but I would've lived.

The boys get to work. I chuckle to myself at their missed attempts, but one of the best parts about the drill is that the boys have to learn to work together. It's not about screwing up the other person so you can win.

They continue the drill for a few more minutes. Once they're finished, Nik gets them to form two lines. I ask Kai to help me demonstrate the drill. I suspect my reaction time is currently a lot sharper than Nik's.

I have Kai hold the clear plastic ruler at the top. I place my hand so the ruler is between my thumb and index finger, but they're not touching it. "Drop it whenever you want and I'll catch it."

Kai does exactly that, and I quickly bring my finger and thumb together, effortlessly gripping the ruler. I calculate the distance between where my hand started and where I caught the ruler. I've done better, but it's been a while since I've performed the drill.

"During a game, you need to pay attention to so many different things. The puck. Your teammates. The opposition. The blue lines. The faster you can react to the appropriate stimuli, the better. We'll be working on that for the rest of the month. But first, Nik and I will measure your reaction times, so we have a before and after picture of your progress."

Nik translates for those who didn't quite get what I was explaining, then we proceed with the test. Afterward, I have the boys line up on the sideline and give them each a euro.

"Extend your arms with the coin clenched in your hand." I demonstrate and drop the coin. Then catch it. "The goal is to catch it before it hits the ground."

By the time the morning training session is over, I don't feel so drained and sluggish, and my brain is no longer pounding. Thank God for that.

The boys head to their summer school classes, and I finally have a chance to check my emails. First, I send Sofia a text.

*Thinking about you.*

Which is true. While the boys were busy with the drills this morning, I thought about her—and about how she feels with her legs wrapped around me.

Refocusing my thoughts, I read my family's emails. My original plan of coming to Finland for a break from their watchful eye hasn't worked nearly as well as I had hoped. Mom's email involves the usual mom questions. Am I getting enough sleep? Am I eating well? All the standard crap. I email her back and tell her the abbreviated PG version of what I've been up to. I haven't mentioned Sofia to her and I'm not about to start.

Next is my father. He's as subtle as a pissed off bull in a china shop. He tells me about a junior level marketing job I should apply for. "Great," I mutter, "if I'm interested in gardening supplies."

I avoid mentioning the two positions I did apply for. There's no point saying anything about them. I'm not the only qualified candidate, and I'm up against candidates who are more qualified than I am. Plus, I don't want to risk him saying anything to Mom and Cody.

Most of the remaining emails can be deleted unread. The one from Brian Prescott grabs my attention.

> *Kyle,*
>
> *If your friend is interested, and depending on her grades, the Bears organization would be willing to grant her a practicum for the fall as an athletic trainer. Just have her email me in the next day or two so we can move forward with this.*

When I had originally asked him for help, the last thing I expected was for the Bears to offer her a position. Sofia's going to be shitting herself when I tell her.

Even though my phone hasn't indicated an incoming text, I check to see if she has responded to my last one. Nothing. And there's nothing several hours later when Mikko shows up so I can tutor him in physics.

"What are you guys working on?" I ask him after we find an empty table in the corner of the local café, sodas in hand. The place is noisy, but not to the point where it's hard for him to hear me.

"Force."

We discuss force and work and how to calculate them. "Think of it this way," I say. "If you're playing a game of hockey and you're chasing the puck, but want to get to it before the opposition, what do you need to do?"

"Um, skate faster?" He shrugs.

"Exactly. The question comes down to how do you skate faster, and this is where we apply physics." I draw a dotted line with an arrow aiming to the top of the page. "This is the direction you want to travel." I draw two short lines at an angle to the arrow line. One is further ahead of the other. "These are the skates. The above one is the gliding skate, and the other one is the skate you're pushing off the ice with. As you move forward, the pattern is reversed. Does that make sense so far?"

Mikko nods. I go on to show him how to calculate the forward force depending on the angle of the pushing skate. His eyes light up as he gets it, and shit does that feel good.

He shows me his homework assignment.

"Can you translate it for me?" I ask. He does and we work through the equations. I don't give him the answers. I just help him get there.

By the time he's finished the assignment, we've worked for over an hour. And still no text from Sofia.

This doesn't surprise me. She has two more hours of work to go, and it's doubtful she'll text me before then.

I send her another text. *Have great news to tell you. Call me ASAP!*

# Chapter Twenty-Nine

## Sofia

With my least favorite chore for the day finished, I scurry from the men's room and collide into a wall of a person.

"*Anteeksi*," I say, taking a step back. Joni? "Hey, what are you doing here?" He's dressed in tanned pants and a buttoned-up dress shirt. Not the casual look I'm used to seeing him in.

"I need to talk to you, but it won't take long. Do you have a break soon?"

I shake my head. "I have lunch in thirty-five minutes. Can you wait that long?"

"No, but I should be back by then. I'm on a work errand."

"I'll meet you out front." Before I can ask him what it's about, he stalks off.

I continue my morning routine, puzzling the entire time what Joni could possibly need to talk to me about. I come up blank. Hopefully it's not about his soccer team.

I finish with the last of the women's bathrooms and head for the staff locker room.

I enter to find Maija at her locker, fiddling with her lock combo. She turns to me. "How was your morning?"

"Uneventful." I scrub my arms and hands in the sink. "I'm meeting someone for a few minutes, but I'll be back before the end of lunch."

"Would that someone be tall, dark, and wear glasses?" She wiggles her eyebrows. Ever since she figured out yesterday that I'd got laid on the weekend (translation: she guessed and my face heated up), she's been super excited for me. I haven't had the heart to tell her the truth about Kyle's and my relationship.

"No, it's not Kyle. It's Joni."

"That's too bad." From the way she says it, you'd think she's expecting Kyle to come over so he and I can have hot sex in the sauna (pun intended).

She does have a point though. It's only been two days since I last saw Kyle, but I already miss spending time with him.

I grab my lunch from my locker and walk to the main entrance. As I step out the door, Joni is striding along the pathway toward me. A thick blanket of gray cloud looms overhead, refusing to allow a single ray of light through. A few drops of water splash on my head and bare arms.

"*Hei*," he says. "Is there somewhere we can talk in private?"

Good question. "We can sit over there." I point to an empty bench overlooking the small garden and the half-full bike rack.

"So what's up?"

"Did something happen between you and Kyle this weekend?"

I squirm at the line of questioning. What Kyle and I did—and didn't do—isn't something I want to discuss with Joni. "Why are you asking?"

"Do you care about him?" He leans back against the bench, appraising me as if trying to read my mind.

"He's my friend," I say, "so, yeah, I do care about him."

"So that's all he is to you? A friend?"

I nod, confused where this is going.

Joni releases a heavy breath. "That's good." He taps the screen of his phone and hands it to me.

On the screen is a picture of Kyle kissing some blond who isn't me. It could be any of his one-night stands he hooked up with before he met me. *Except why would Joni have it?* "Where did you get this?"

"I went out with some guys from work last night. I saw Kyle all over the woman. But since he's not cheating on you..." He lets the end of the sentence hang.

Staring at the phone, I shake my head. "No, he's not cheating on me." So why are my eyes tearing up as if he were? We agreed to being friends with benefits. We didn't talk about being exclusive.

Kyle has every right to kiss anyone he wants, just like I do. But knowing that doesn't dull the pain clawing my heart. Stupid heart.

Blinking away the tears, I plaster a bright smile on my face and give Joni back his phone. The few rain drops from earlier are met by their buddies and it starts raining hard.

Joni curses under his breath in Finnish and glances at the sky. "I need to get back to work." He gives me a pity-filled smile. "Glad to see I was wrong about the situation between you two. I'd hate to see him hurt you."

"No, that's okay. You didn't know." I say goodbye to him, then race back to the main entrance. I'm a hot, wet mess by the time I enter the building.

I wipe my sneakers on the oversized mat, taking out my frustrations on it. I'm not even sure who I'm mad at: Kyle for making out with another girl after I told him I couldn't join him because I was going to bed—or maybe he was even making out with her before that. Joni for showing me the photo. Or myself for feeling this way when I have no right to.

As I make my way back to the staff room for a change of uniform, I check my phone. Kyle has sent me a text. *Thinking about you.* No doubt like he was thinking about me when he had his tongue stuck in that woman's mouth.

I ignore the text. Just like I ignore the one he sends hours later: *Have great news to tell you.*

I bet he does. He discovered the woman he was with last night is hot to do a threesome.

Awesome.

# Chapter Thirty

## Kyle

It's Wednesday afternoon and I still haven't heard from Sofia. Not even a simple text replying to the ones I sent her yesterday.

I phoned her last night and that went ignored, too.

Something's not right. Usually she responds quickly to my texts.

Not knowing if she's sick or injured, I drive to the sports center once I'm finished at the camp. I enter the physical therapy clinic and wait for the receptionist to finish with her call.

After what feels like several minutes, she hangs up the phone and rambles off a string of Finnish to me.

"*Hei*," I reply, "is Sofia Philips here today?"

Creases appear across her forehead. "Sofia Philips?" She checks her computer screen. "Is she a patient?"

"No. She's working with Rafu for the week. Blond. Pretty. A runner."

"Oh, Sofia. Yes, she's here today. She's busy, but I can tell her you are here. What is your name?"

I'm about to answer but change my mind. "That's okay. I'll come back at the end of her shift and talk to her then." For a second I consider asking her not to mention to Sofia that I was here, but that might not be a good idea. It might come off as creepy. Besides, there has to be a logical explanation why Sofia hasn't responded to my texts and call. Like she's busy and has a life outside of me.

It's not as if we have an exclusivity clause on our friendship. She could've been with Maija for all I know.

Since I have time, I head to the gym. My leg is tired and cranky, but that doesn't stop me from pushing it hard. Afterward, I spend time in the sauna, willing the minutes to move a little faster, but at the same time knowing that will never happen. But it also means they can't slow down, either. It just feels like they have.

Eventually my leg is no longer cranky, and I stumble from the sauna and head for the shower.

I'm almost there when a wave of dizziness hits. I place my hand against the tiled wall to steady myself.

# Chapter Thirty-One

## Sofia

I finish up with the last patient, a rugby player with a strained quadricep muscle. He climbs down from the table and I begin to tidy up the station as he walks away.

"Thank you, Sofia," Rafu says. "You're a great help."

"I'm enjoying it." It's nice to be doing something other than cleaning toilets while I'm in Finland. "I know I haven't been here long, but I was wondering if you could write me a letter of recommendation once the week is over."

"Absolutely. It's the least I can do."

"Thanks. I'll see you tomorrow."

He nods and picks up the patient file. "Can you give this to Kirsti on your way out? Thank you."

I take the file from him and head for the front desk. Kirsti's busy talking to the ruby player, so I place it on her desk. If I hurry, I can catch the next bus to Vantaa and squeeze in an hour of studying before exhaustion drags me down.

Those plans come to a crashing end when I walk out of the clinic. Kyle is standing near the door, but he's slightly pale and something looks off about him.

I nudge aside the hurt and rush to him. "Kyle, are you okay?"

He sways on his feet and I grab his arm to steady him. "It's nothing. I pushed myself a little too hard at the gym, and then spent too long in the sauna to make up for it. I just need to drink something and I'll be fine."

A bunch of questions leap to mind but they have to wait. "C'mon." With my hand on his arm, I lead him to the café in the sports center, and indicate for him to sit at the empty table in the corner. "I'll be right back."

I return a few minutes later with a sport drink and hand it to him. "Here you go."

Kyle opens the bottle. "Thanks." He gulps back at least half of it before making a face. "Christ, that's awful."

I shrug. "Sorry, I wasn't sure what was good. So why were you outside the clinic instead of here, rehydrating yourself?"

"Because I didn't want to risk missing you."

I frown. "You'd risk passing out for a booty call?" I didn't mean for the part about the booty call to come out. But now that it is hanging between us, time to deal with the truth of our relationship.

"Booty call? Why the hell would you think I was here for sex?"

"Then why are you here?"

The look he gives me is one you'd save for someone who is certifiable. "Because you never responded to my texts or voicemail message, and I wanted to make sure you were okay."

If a ladybug were to stand next to me, it would tower me based on how small I now feel. "I'm sorry. I didn't have time." That was almost the truth.

"I wanted to tell you about a practicum with the Bears as an athletic trainer for this fall, if you're interested."

My mouth flops open, positive I misheard him. "But how did you find out about it?" And how many others will also be scrambling for it once they hear about it?

"I called in a favor."

"A favor? Wait, are you telling me the position is for me?"

"That's exactly what I'm saying. I told the head trainer about your situation and he offered you the position. If you're interested and it depends on your grades."

Any other person would scream for joy at this opportunity. And under different circumstances, I would too. Working with a professional team like the Bears would be a tremendous boost for my career. Yes, I should be kissing Kyle and doing cartwheels, but... "Wait! I had sex with you then you get me a practicum with your former employer?" He could've slapped me and it would have hurt less. "Wow, I must be better than I realized."

The muscle in his jaw jerks hard. "It's nothing like that. I told him about you *before* last weekend. And I did it because you're a friend. And because I have that much confidence in you." He pushes himself out of his seat and storms off.

It takes a couple of seconds for what he said to sink in. "Kyle, wait." He stops and turns to face me, the space between his eyes pinched with lines. He's not the only one in the café to look my way.

Ignoring everyone else's curiosity, I rush to him. "I'm sorry. I shouldn't have reacted that way. Thank you so much. I can't even begin to tell you how much it means to me what you did for me."

His expression softens and his lips shift into my favorite one-sided sexy grin. "You could show me."

I stiffen. It's one thing to be his friend with added perks. It's another to become part of his harem.

"Is something wrong?" he asks.

"Why would you think something's wrong?" I glance around. No one's paying attention to us anymore.

"This weekend we were kissing and screwing, but now at even the slightest hint I want to do that again, you look ready to run."

He's right. I do want to run. Run and forget this arrangement between us.

"So what's going on?" he asks.

"When I agreed to our friends-with-benefits arrangement"—I lower my voice for the last four words, but it feels like I yelled them—"for some stupid reason I thought I'd be the only girl you're screwing around with. I didn't realize there'd be others."

Kyle's eyebrows draw together and I instantly wish I hadn't said anything to him about it. "What others?" he asks.

"Well, how about we start with the woman you were kissing Monday night, right after I told you I couldn't come over. Or maybe you were kissing her even before talking to me on the phone."

Kyle's eyes widened. "How did you know about that?"

At least he didn't try to deny it. Bonus points for him.

"I saw a picture of you two together, playing tonsil hockey."

He shakes his head. "It's not what it looked like."

"Yeah, I'm pretty sure it looked like you were kissing a girl. But don't worry about it. I understand. But you need to understand that's not me. I'm not comfortable being part of your entourage."

His eyebrows lift. "Are you finished?"

"Yep, that pretty much covers it."

"Like I said, what you saw wasn't what it looked like. She kissed me and I told her I wasn't interested." He steps closer. "And how could I be interested when all I could think about was you." His lips brush against mine. "How could I be interested when you're the only one I want to kiss." This time his lips don't just brush mine. They savor them. Our kiss deepens and I momentarily forget what we were talking about.

Then it hits me like an out-of-control train and I pull away, frowning. "So you weren't all over her?"

Kyle's expression mirrors my own, then it shifts as if he remembers something. He curses under his breath. "Where did you see the picture?"

"Joni showed it to me yesterday."

Kyle groans. "So the guy just happened to drop by and show you the photo?"

I nod, not getting where he's going with this. "He thought he was being my friend and protecting me. I guess he thought he was saving me from a broken heart."

"Right," Kyle says, except he doesn't sound too convinced. "Has it occurred to you he wants more from you than friendship?"

"Except he already knows I'm not interested. So you're wrong. He's just being a good friend."

Kyle tilts his head to the side. "Did you tell him we're involved?"

I laugh but it sounds a little off. "But we're not involved. We're just messing around. Having fun while we can." Moving on with our lives—even if they don't ultimately involve each other in the end.

"You know what I mean."

I roll my eyes. "You're reading way too much into what he did. Tell me, if places were reversed and you saw him kissing another girl, would you say nothing to me? Would you let him hurt me?"

Kyle's expression shifts, but I can't tell if he buys my argument. "No, I wouldn't do that."

Needing to redirect where this is headed, I say, "You never answered my previous question. So you weren't all over her?"

He shakes his head. "I promise you, other than when she kissed me and I told her I wasn't interested, nothing happened between us. She was only talking to me 'cause her friend and my roommate were going at it at the table."

I don't doubt for a second she wanted the same from Kyle, but I also believe he's telling me the truth. I see it in his eyes.

"C'mon," Kyle says. "I'll give you a ride home."

"You don't need to do that. It's still light out. I'll be fine."

"Well, I won't be. I've missed you, Sofia. So consider my giving you a ride home your way of saying thank you for the practicum."

I laugh. "Okay, if you put it that way." A warmth fills me that he hadn't wanted me to have sex with him to show my appreciation. I mean it's a given we'll have sex again, but it won't have anything to do with what he did for me when it comes to the Bears.

Kyle parks in front of Muumu's building. "I'll forward you the email about the position. Brian wants to get things rolling on this ASAP."

I kiss him. It's supposed to be a quick kiss to show my appreciation, but let's face it, it's easy to lose track of time while kissing Kyle. I'm breathless by the time we pull apart.

"You're still mine on Saturday, right?" His breath is heated against my lips.

"Yes," I whisper.

"Good, because I've got something planned."

"What?"

"It's a surprise." He winks.

# Chapter Thirty-Two

## Kyle

Sofia is already outside waiting for me when I pull up to her apartment building. She's wearing my favorite shorts—the ones that show off her long legs—and her light pink tank top.

She climbs into the car and places her backpack on the floor. Before I can say anything, she kisses me. It's a light kiss, but it's filled with promises of more heated ones to come.

"Toivo called to tell me he and Maija will meet us at the ferry," I say as I drive away from the building.

After deciding to take Sofia to Suomenlinna, an island known for it's old sea fortress, I mentioned it to Toivo and asked if he and Maija would like to join us. I guess I should have also mentioned to him the trip to the island was a surprise.

"Is Nik coming?" Sofia asks with a degree of trepidation.

"No, he's got plans." At her relieved breath, I say, "You know, he's not as bad as he seems. He's actually a good guy." Most of the time.

We drive to Helsinki, and I find a spot to park near the waterfront. Since the island has numerous locations where you can enjoy a picnic, we walk to the market to buy food first. It's Saturday, so the place is crazy with the crowds.

Sofia grabs my hand and pulls me through the bustle of people to the indoor market. Inside the building, we buy a loaf of bread, an assortment of cheese, reindeer meat, and sodas. Next, we wander around the different booths outside, and buy peaches, strawberries, and cloudberries to bring with us. The cloudberries are expensive but worth it.

Sofia's hand remains in mine the entire time. The reindeer meat, cloudberries, and marketplace aren't the only things I'll miss when I leave here. As it is, I missed her during the week, when I saw her Wednesday evening and that was it. We've texted back and forth a few times since then, but it's not the same as seeing her in person.

I check the time on my phone. "We should head over to the ferry now."

Toivo and Maija are waiting near the line to board the ferry when we arrive. Maija waves when she spots us, and she and Sofia hug.

Toivo laughs. "You saw each other yesterday. What will you do when Sofia goes back to Minnesota?"

Maija fake pouts. "Maybe she won't want to leave. I could introduce her to my cousin Haarti. It will be love at first sight."

Toivo bursts out laughing. "Your cousin looks like a troll. I don't think she'll want to stay in Finland for him."

Maija huffs, as if offended, then laughs. "I guess you're right."

After Sofia and I purchase our tickets from the machine, the four of us join the line to board the ferry and fall into an easy conversation while we wait.

Once onboard, we find empty seats outside on the top section. Sofia removes her camera from her backpack and starts shooting photos of the dock from the railing.

I join her and instinctively rest my hand on her lower back. It feels natural there. A warm, slight breeze brushes against her hair. Lucky wind.

"Someone's hungry," she says and points to a seagull flying overhead with a large piece of bread in its beak.

"Greedy more like it."

"I can take a photo of you two together, if you want," Maija says behind us.

We turn around and Sofia hands her camera to her friend. I pull Sofia against me, my arm around her waist. The breeze teases me with her apple scent.

Maija shoots several photos then hands the camera back to Sofia. Sofia checks them out as the ferry begins pulling away from the dock. In them, we look like a happy couple instead of two friends enjoying the added perks of our friendship. Not that we've had sex since last weekend.

But as much as I've missed it, I've missed Sofia that much more.

"Thanks," she tells Maija. "They look great."

As I turn back to look at the city, I spot Joni climbing the stairs to our level. What the fuck? "Why is Joni here?"

Sofia twists in the direction I'm looking. "He called last night and asked if I wanted to see a movie tonight. I explained I couldn't 'cause we were going to Suomenlinna today."

"So he decided to join us?" Again, what the fuck?

Joni surveys the area and his laser gaze lands on us. His jaw muscle briefly jerks before his expression adjusts into one that is thrilled to see me here with Sofia. He says something to the four people with him, and they walk over to us.

"*Hei*," he says to Sofia, pointedly ignoring me. "I didn't expect to actually bump into you on this trip. My friends are going to the island and asked if I wanted to join them."

If said friends weren't standing next to him, I would've questioned that, although it does seem to be too much of a coincidence for it to be true. But I'm hardly calling bullshit to his story.

Joni introduces us to his friends. From what I can tell, Erik and Hanna are a couple. He's on the skinny side with shaved short hair. She's curvy with chin-length red hair. The other two, Daniela and Lovisa, could be twins straight out of one of Nik's sexual fantasies. They're pretty, have long, straight blond hair, and are dressed like Sofia, in shorts and tank tops.

And they both have that look I'm familiar with. That look a puck bunny gets in her eyes when she goes after a hockey player.

Sofia introduces the group to Toivo and Maija, then Erik and Hanna excuse themselves to find seats inside. The other three stay with us.

One of the twins (Lovisa, maybe) stands next to Joni. The other one stands a little too close to me, and I get a weird feeling it's a test. I draw Sofia against my body.

Joni has already tried to screw things up between Sofia and me with the photo. Now he's trying to prove I'm the manwhore he's set me out to be.

The ferry trip to the island is quick. We disembark, but it soon becomes clear that Joni and his friends plan to crash our group. Sofia, Toivo, and Maija don't seem to have a problem with it, so I let it drop.

Toivo leads us to the oldest fortress first, created by the Swedes in 1748, when the country owned Finland. It's made of stones and mortar, with lots of above-ground tunnels, and reminds me of ancient castles. Parts of it are covered with grassy roofs.

We explore the tunnels, which are like stone passages with glassless windows to one side that allow light in. The group is just ahead of Sofia and me. No one is behind us.

Needing to taste her, I tug Sofia to the side, away from where everyone can see us, and pin her against the rough stone wall. My mouth finds hers and her gasp becomes a moan. Her tongue meets mine and her fingers pull through my hair.

At the sound of voices echoing in the tunnel, I reluctantly move away from her. "I guess we should catch up with them," I say, my voice holding a tell-tale huskiness.

I take her hand and lead her through the tunnel everyone else disappeared down. They're waiting for us when we get to the other end. Maija grins knowingly at seeing us; the twins and Joni don't. The rest are indifferent to our temporary disappearance.

After we explore the area some more, Toivo suggests we go to the beach. It's small and surrounded by a stonewall that separates the sand from the grassy area and trees behind it. A handful of individuals are lying on the sand. Half a dozen more are in the water.

We find an empty spot and lay out our towels. I park mine next to Sofia, but before Maija has a chance to put hers down on the other side, Joni's stakes claim to the spot. Lovisa straightens her towel next to mine. The girls strip to their bikinis, a point Joni doesn't fail to miss when it comes to Sofia. He doesn't leer at her, but he might as well have, given where I'm positive his thoughts now sit.

Sofia doesn't notice. She's too busy talking to Maija and Daniela. I remove my t-shirt and shorts and sit back down.

Big mistake. Lovisa leans toward me and says low enough so only I hear, "There's a great spot on the other side of the island I'd love to show you." She kisses my shoulder and flicks her tongue against the skin so there's no doubt what she's really hoping for.

I jerk away and scramble up from the towel. I catch the tail end of Joni's smirk. Asshole. Not wanting to give the twin another chance to try to test me, I join Sofia and envelop her in my arms. She's warm and soft against my chest. I could get used to this.

Now if only it were just the two of us. But we came with Toivo and Maija, and I have no desire to desert them because I want to get Sofia away from Joni. At least she's not interested in him, if that's what his game is all about.

"You want to swim?" Daniela asks us.

Before Maija can answer, Toivo sweeps her up in his arms and walks toward the water. His girlfriend giggles but doesn't try to escape.

"Don't even think about it, Kyle," Sofia says, laughing.

"What if I promise not to drop you this time?"

She studies me for a second, then her eyes give me the answer I'm waiting for. I scoop her up and carry her to the lake edge. I want to bring up my suspicions about Joni, but what will that prove? She'll just think I'm jealous.

In the end, I body check my suspicions aside. As long as I don't give him the opportunity to trip me up, he can't do anything to hurt me or Sofia.

Once I reach the water, Sofia asks me to put her down. Toivo is carrying a giggling Maija farther into the lake. The temptation to do the same to Sofia skirts around the edges, but I don't want to damage her trust in me. I lower her feet to the sand.

As soon as her feet touch the ground, she runs deeper into

the water, laughing. The chase is on. I run after her, the cold water splashing around us.

I can't run as fast as her, but her speed slows as she gets deeper and I easily catch up with her. We keep running until the water is waist high on her. I grab her around the waist and pull her to me.

Sofia tilts her head to the side. "I think Lovisa likes you." Her eyebrows scrunch into an adorable frown. "Or is that Daniela?"

I laugh. "I can't tell them apart, either. But you know I'm not interested in either of them, right?" Sofia and I might not be involved in a real relationship, but that doesn't mean I'll fool around with anyone else while I'm with her.

Her beautiful eyes become brighter. "Does that mean friends with benefits is an exclusive thing for you?"

I nod. "It does." I gently kiss her for a brief moment then rest my forehead against hers. "What about for you? Is it exclusive for you too?"

"It is," she whispers.

This time when I kiss her, it isn't so gentle. It's possessive. And I don't give a damn who sees me.

I'm so lost in the taste and feel of her, I'm oblivious to everything else. Which is why I don't register until it's too late what the girl's laughter from nearby means. A tidal wave of cold water splashes us, mostly hitting Sofia.

Shrieking, she jumps back, and because my arms are still wrapped around her, she almost pulls me into the water. Toivo and Maija burst out laughing...until we get revenge and douse them with water.

Maija shrieks something in Finnish that causes Toivo to laugh harder. "I'm done," she says and runs back to the beach. Sofia joins her, leaving me and Toivo behind.

"Are you and Sofia going to keep seeing each other when you return home?" he asks as we walk back to shore. Sofia and Maija are on the beach, rubbing themselves dry with their towels.

His comment surprises me. It's one I haven't thought about. "Are you asking or is Maija?"

"I'm sure Maija's wondering the same, but no, the question is mine." At my hesitation, he adds, "I understand if you don't want to tell me. Or if you don't want me to say anything to Maija."

"I really don't know what's gonna happen when I go home. I've applied for a few hockey-related jobs that are out of state." I had phone interviews this week for the coaching job in Seattle and the scouting position in Texas.

"But if you end up staying in Minneapolis...?"

If I were to stay in Minneapolis, I wouldn't want to keep up our friends-with-benefits arrangement. But I'm not sure what I want beyond that. I loved Gabby and lost her. Her loss just about did me in. Would I be willing to risk that again?

"I don't know," I say, more to myself than to him.

# Chapter Thirty-Three

## Sofia

After we spend time swimming and eating our picnic, we wander around the island, checking out the stores and the sights. We explore the Russian- and Swedish-designed buildings, the courtyard with the tomb of Augustin Ehrensvärd, King's Gate, the museum inside Vesikki Submarine, and the museum inside the old prison.

"Kyle," Toivo says, as we head for the café Joni recommended, "you should try the black-licorice ice cream."

I screw up my nose. Kyle laughs. "That bad, huh?"

"I've never been a fan of Finnish black licorice." Or any black licorice.

Of course Kyle, your typical athletic male, goes for the challenge. Once we're all outside with our cold treats, he holds the cone out for me to try.

"I'm good thanks." I lick my strawberry ice cream. "Yum."

"This isn't bad," he says.

I lick mine again, trailing my tongue slowly up the side of the sweet goodness. Kyle watches, and his Adam's apple jumps up then drops. "Still yummy," I say.

"I'll lick it, Kyle." Lovisa's gaze drops to his shorts and she takes a step closer to him.

Without warning, Kyle hooks his arm around my waist and yanks me in front of him. I stumble slightly at the quick move, but his arm keeps me from falling. Ignoring her, I turn to him, wrap my free hand around his neck, and kiss him. Our cold tongues slide against each other. This is as close to tasting the black licorice as I'm going to get. I still don't like it, but it tastes a little better when Kyle is involved.

His hand slips under the hem of my tank top and rests against my skin. I'd like to say the message is clear that he'd rather be with me, but he's been giving her not-so-subtle messages since it became obvious Lovisa wants him. She's either really dumb or really stubborn.

I pull away slightly and smirk at him. "My strawberry ice cream is still better."

"I might have to agree with you there."

I let him have a lick then kiss him again. It's not a long kiss, but it's enough to keep me satisfied until it's just the two of us.

We finish our ice creams and check out the art galleries and studios. It's late afternoon by the time we return to Helsinki.

"I can drive you home," Joni tells me as the ferry docks. The marketplace is packed up for the day, with a few workers still cleaning away the mess. Seagulls squawk and argue over forgotten scraps.

"That's okay," Kyle says, his hand resting on my hip. "I've got it."

Joni shrugs and leaves to join his friends.

"Did you want to go back to my place? Or do you want me to drive you straight home?"

I rest my hand on his arm, his biceps hard beneath my palm. "I'd love to go back to your apartment, but I need to study." I know if I go there, I'll have a hard time leaving and won't get any studying done tonight. "How about Monday?"

"How about tomorrow?"

"I'm spending the day with my grandmother, and I promised Joni I'd see a movie with him later on." A promise I made Joni two weeks ago when he started teaching me Finnish.

Kyle grunts. "You know he's trying to get into your pants, right?"

I feel my eyebrows jump up my forehead. "You mean like you?" The only difference is Kyle's been there. Joni hasn't and won't be.

"That's not how it is, Soph."

Close enough. "Hey, don't worry about it. It is what it is." Too bad a part of me wishes it isn't 'what it is.' Too bad what I'm beginning to feel for him has nothing to do with the benefits.

Once we're off the ferry, we say goodbye to everyone and head to Kyle's car. He drives me home but is quiet the entire way. It's a comfortable silence, so I don't make small talk or play our True or False game. He parks the car in the empty part of the parking lot, away from the main entrance.

My body instantly wishes I had gone back to his apartment for a while. It doesn't care about my certification exam. It only wants to feel Kyle's hands on it. It only wants to feel him in me.

Which is why I practically attack him when I kiss him goodbye. He returns my kisses with the same hunger burning in me. If the steering wheel wasn't in the way, I'd climb onto his lap and straddle him to get even closer.

I moan and my body begs me to take him right here. Only then does an irritating voice in the back of my head point out I need to stop kissing him before it's too late.

Reluctantly, I pull away. "I had fun today. Thanks." This time I give his cheek a light kiss. Before I can ravish him again, I escape the car and practically run to the building.

Muumu is watching TV when I enter the apartment. She asks me how my day was. She already knew where I spent it and who I spent it with. I don't mention Joni, but I don't need to. He's in some of the photos I took today.

She peers into the LCD viewfinder and sees him in the picture taken in front of a rusty old canon. He's not alone. He's with the twins. If Muumu recognizes the girls, she doesn't give any indication.

She does, though, smile at the pictures of me and Kyle that Maija took. "*Komea.*" Handsome.

I nod. "*Muy komea.*"

After I finish showing them to her, I grab my textbook and notes, and go onto the balcony. Shouts and laughter from the playground below greet me, but since I can't understand what the kids are saying, it all becomes white noise while I study.

By the time my brain decides it's had enough studying and calls a revolt, I've been working for four hours. It's still light out, but not enough to study by. Muumu has already gone to bed. I turn on the TV and flip through the channels until I find a show that looks interesting.

A few minutes later I realize it's not what I thought it was. It's soft porn. I've never watched porn of any sort before, but this one is mesmerizing. It wasn't created to get men off. It was written for females.

My phone pings and I read the text from Kyle. *What are you doing?*

My fingers hover over the keyboard as I contemplate what to tell him. *Watching soft porn.*

Seconds pass then my phone plays music. Kyle. Chuckling to myself, I answer it. What guy can resist porn, even if he isn't here to watch it?

"Was that autocorrect playing with my mind," he asks.

"Nope. I really am watching soft porn." The girl who is supposed to be a young fairy godmother moans in agreement as Prince Charming goes down on her. Not quite how I remember the fairy tale.

Her erotic sounds make the girlie part between my legs sit up and take notice. Instead of changing the channel, I say, "I wish I were with you." Except it comes out all breathy.

Several seconds tick by before Kyle says, "Me too."

More seconds and more moans from the fairy godmother. His previous jokes about having phone sex with me sneak into my memory.

"If…" My mouth suddenly feels dry and the word comes out as a croak. I swallow hard. This shouldn't be so tough. "If I were with you, where would you touch me?"

I can't believe I said that.

"Is this you saying you want to have phone sex with me, Sofia?" he asks, the level of huskiness in his voice making me weak all over.

"Yes," I squeak. Inwardly I groan. How am I going to do this if I can barely say a word?

I turn off the TV and move from the couch to the bed. With my lip trapped between my teeth, I close my eyes and imagine it's Kyle's fingers stroking the bare skin on my stomach.

"Are your clothes still on?" he asks.

"Yes."

"Remove your tank top and bra for me." His voice is low, preventing his roommate from overhearing him. At least I hope Nik can't hear him.

"Only if you remove your t-shirt." The squeak has changed into something sounding a little more seductive. I can do this…I think.

I place the phone on the bed and remove my top and bra. "Okay." Now what?

I pick up the phone and Kyle talks me through how he would touch me if we were together. I do the same to him as my fingertips lightly trace down my neck and my chest. They tease my breasts and my nipples. They continue south and explore every surface, every swell, every dip of my body. His deep voice guides me closer to the edge. It's his words and voice that do this to me.

"Oh, God, Kyle," I groan, straining to keep my voice down. From somewhere next to my hip, Kyle's cry of ecstasy meets my own.

Once the post-bliss aftershocks fade away, I lie still for a few moments, dazed and completely spent. It's not until Kyle says my name that I realize I dropped the phone at some point during my orgasm.

I scramble to pick it up. "Hello?"

"I thought I'd lost you for a second."

A languid smile stretches on my face. "No, I'm good…And thank you. I needed that." And not just for the orgasm, which was pretty damn good. Thanks to what we did, I can add another notch in the confidence belt.

"I can't wait to do that to you in person next time."

"Me neither. I'll see you Monday." My voice sounds drowsy and I fight to keep my eyes open.

"You know if you cancel on Joni, you can see me tomorrow."

I give up on the battle to keep my eyes open. "Goodnight, Kyle," I murmur and turn off the phone.

I'm tired, but not tired enough to miss the void in me at the absence of Kyle's arms holding me close as I fall asleep.

Nor am I too tired to notice the longing in me. The longing to find myself in his arms come morning.

# Chapter Thirty-Four

## Sofia

The following weekend, Kyle and I wait by his car for Muumu to join us. It's early Saturday morning and we have a four-hour drive to Joensuu, located east of the Russian border.

"Are you sure 'bout this?" he asks

"Positive," I say. "Joni told them you were coming and they're fine with it." Muumu and Joni's grandmother, Aino, decided it wouldn't hurt to have him come along. He would be a great addition to our mushroom picking expedition.

I wrap my arms around his waist. "Is your leg gonna be okay?" That's the only thing I'm worried about. We'll be doing a lot of crouching and standing. As it is, it will be tough for Muumu and Aino. That's part reason they agreed to have Kyle join us. They have no idea about his injury.

He kisses me briefly on the lips. "Don't worry. It'll be fine."

Muumu and Aino come down a few minutes later with Joni. He's carrying his grandmother's overnight bag. Mine and Muumu's are in the trunk of Kyle's car, along with the camping gear. Muumu and Aino are staying with Joni's great aunt. Joni, Kyle, and I are camping in the backyard.

Joni gives Kyle last minute directions, in case we get separated on the way. I catch Joni scowling at Kyle as my friend climbs into the driver seat of the rental vehicle. Muumu and Aino might be fine with the extra body to help out, but Joni clearly would've preferred if they had said no.

"True or false," I say as Kyle and I drive along the highway. "Your high school sweetheart was a fairy."

Kyle's mouth curls up to one side. We've long since tired of the boring first-date questions, and have progressed to the more bizarre ones. "I can't tell you. It's a secret."

"That means you have to take a dare."

"A dare it is then."

Except, what the hell do I dare him to do while he's driving that won't end in an accident? A shudder goes through me, and I steer my thoughts away from where they're headed. "I dare you to…I dare you to sing Twinkle Twinkle Little Star."

He throws me a that's-the-best-you-can-do? look. I shrug.

I've never heard him sing before, but the moment he sings the first few lines, my mouth flops open. His deep, rich voice sinks into every cell in my body, warming me like a fleece blanket on a chilling morning.

"I didn't know you could sing. Instead of the physics club, you should have been in the glee club."

Now it's his turn to shrug. "Singing never did anything for me. Not like learning how different hockey uniforms can affect your skating speed due their variation in aerodynamics. Or that skate blades are sharpened so only a small fraction of it touches the ice, which means less friction and faster skating speeds."

I pull my feet up on the seat. "I've mentioned how much your sexy physics talk turns me on, right?"

Kyle laughs. "But not my singing?"

"Oh, your singing definitely turned me on. But since we're spending the next forty-eight plus hours being on our best behavior"—and that includes at night, when Kyle and I will be sleeping in separate tents—"the last thing you should be doing is turning me on."

He chuckles. The sound of it warms me like his singing. "And maybe trying to turn you on, when we can't do anything, will make mushroom picking more interesting."

I pout. "Tease."

That only makes him laugh harder.

Four hours later, we arrive at our destination, a forested area near Joensuu. Kyle parks behind Joni on the side of the road, where a few other cars are parked, and we hike a short distance into the trees. Each of us carries a large basket. Muumu and Aino lead the way, trucking along with their wooden walking sticks. For once, they're uncharacteristically quiet, scanning the ground for their desired treasures.

A welcomed peace embraces us as we weave through the forest of birch and pine and along the worn dirt path. Leaves rustle in the warm breeze. Birds chat and sing their enticing song. I breathe in a lung-full of pine-scented air—and I feel like I'm home.

I glance over my shoulder to see how Kyle's doing. The narrow dirt path prevents us from walking together. Joni is in front of me, ever ready to assist his grandmother if she needs help.

We're not walking fast, but even at this speed Kyle is limping slightly. Not enough for the others to notice, but enough for me to know that his leg is bothering him.

I stop and turn around. "Are you okay? You're limping." I say it quietly so the others can't hear me.

"I'm a little stiff from the drive. It'll be okay once I've walked it out a bit." He indicates for me to keep walking, end of discussion.

We walk another fifteen or so minutes before Muumu calls out and points to the ground. Littering the area are mushrooms that look like yellow golfing tees but with slightly larger caps.

"Chanterelles," Joni explains.

Muumu hands me and Kyle each a paring knife, then she and Aino continue a few yards ahead of us. Joni finds his own patch of mushrooms to harvest not far from where Kyle and I are working.

"Only pick the chanterelles," Joni says, busying himself with the ones by his knees. "Finland has two thousand varieties of mushrooms. Many are poisonous. You wouldn't want to eat the wrong ones. You might end up with only a stomachache…or you might end up with something worse."

His glance flicks to Kyle and back to me.

"Why do I get the feeling he wouldn't mind if the latter happens to me?" Kyle mutters.

I let out a heavy sigh. "He just doesn't know you. It's not like you guys have tried to be friends."

"It's hard to want to be friends with someone who's interested in the same girl you are. We're dealing with a pretty strong conflict of interest here."

Kyle's words startle me. What kind of conflict of interest is his talking about when he and I are just friends with an added bonus? Not that Joni knows this. It didn't exactly come up when he and I went to see the movie earlier this week. If anything, he avoided the topic of Kyle.

"I don't think that's the issue. He thinks you and I are dating for real now."

Kyle snorts. "Trust me. It doesn't make a difference. If he likes you, he can't just turn off his feelings like that."

What Kyle doesn't say, but I can hear it in his voice, is that you can't just turn off your feelings for someone you love, even when she's gone. He might never be over his wife. He might never have room for me in his heart.

A dull ache fills my chest. I brush it away. What the heck am I thinking? This summer wasn't about finding love and a long-term boyfriend. It was about escaping the pain and betrayal back home. It was about becoming a new and improved me. It was about me having fun again, and that's what I'm having with Kyle. For now.

"So, Kyle," Joni says loud enough for us to hear, "Sofia said you're in Finland coaching hockey. What is it you do in Minneapolis?"

Kyle's knife slices through a mushroom. He places the chanterelle in his basket. "I'm currently looking for a job there. My old agent mentioned a few opportunities he'd heard about, and I've been looking into them." He avoids eye contact with me when he says it.

"Are they all in Minneapolis?" Joni glances at me for a second before returning to his task.

"No," Kyle says, "They're all out of state."

The ache in my chest becomes heavier, like a broken-down bus has parked inside the space.

I glance away, not wanting either guy to see the pain in my eyes. And that's when I realize the truth I've been ignoring for the past few weeks. What I feel for Kyle has nothing to do with our friends-with-benefits arrangement. Bit by bit, ever since the day at the amusement park, I've been falling for him. I've known from the beginning that what we have between us might not go beyond our time here. But hearing that Kyle might be leaving Minnesota only confirms it.

Blinking back the tears, I grab another mushroom. A sharp pain slices across my index finger. "Ouch!"

"Fuck!" Kyle says as blood appears along the thin wound and drips to the ground. "I'm sorry, Sofia. I didn't see your finger there."

"It's okay. I wasn't paying attention."

"Let me see it." Joni kneels next to me and removes his backpack. He drops it on the ground and examines my finger. "It doesn't look too bad." But despite that diagnosis, he glares briefly at Kyle, then rifles in his bag and pulls out a small first aid kit.

He opens it, then proceeds to clean the wound with an antiseptic pad, and covers the cut with a bandage.

A small laugh bubbles inside of me and bursts free. "I guess I'm not going to die after all."

"Hopefully there was nothing on the knife that could cause an infection." Joni checks the contents of Kyle's basket. "You only cut these mushrooms, right? You didn't cut anything else?"

Kyle nods. "Yeah, just these."

Joni visibly relaxes at Kyle's answer. "Just to be safe," he says to me, "you should work on those mushrooms over there with me." *So your boyfriend can't hurt you worse than he's already done.* He glares at Kyle one more time.

A shriek fills the air, startling us and a crow in a nearby tree. It takes flight, cawing. I don't see where it goes. All I see is Aino hunched over Muumu's body on the ground.

# Chapter Thirty-Five

## Kyle

At the sound of Aino shrieking, we all look over to see what happened. No one dares to move for the briefest of moments as we piece it all together. Sofia's grandmother is lying on the ground, clutching her chest.

Sofia is the first to come alive. She scrambles up and races to her grandmother's side. Joni and I are right behind her.

"What's wrong?" she asks, voice shaky.

Aino speaks. "She's having a heart attack," Joni translates.

A sob breaks free from Sofia. "We have to do something. Please, Joni, do something."

He crouches next to Tuuli and speaks to the woman in a soothing tone. I join Sofia on the ground. My leg isn't impressed with all this up and down stress placed on it. I push past the pain and rest my hand on Sofia's lower back, letting her know I'm here for her.

Joni pulls his phone out and inspects it. "*Vittu!*"

"What?" Sofia asks, voice splintering. "What's wrong?"

Joni rips his hand through his hair. "There's no reception here."

"*Mikä hätänä?*" Aino strokes the side of Tuuli's face, attempting to comfort her. Joni talks to her, and the tears she was holding back break free.

"We'll have to drive her to the hospital," I say. "Do you know where it is?" I ask him.

"No, but my grandmother does. She can direct me."

I shift closer to Tuuli and scoop her up in my arms. She

whimpers and a cold sweat covers my body. While Joni looks like he works out, I suspect I can bench press a lot more than him. And Sofia's grandmother isn't a frail old woman.

I stagger up, and pray with everything I have in me and more that my leg holds out at least long enough for me to get her into Joni's car.

Ignoring the sharp ache, I move as fast as I can along the trail. No one speaks, other than the occasional swear word from Joni ahead of me, as he keeps checking the cell phone reception, and the occasional word or two from the woman in my arms. I don't know what she's saying and I don't care. Just as long as she can still talk. Just as long as she's still conscious.

We arrive at the cars, my entire body shaking from the strain of carrying Sofia's grandmother and from the fear of being too late because I couldn't move fast enough. Sofia, looking pale and shaken, climbs into the backseat of Joni's vehicle, and Joni helps me transfer Tuuli into the back with her. Sofia's attention is fully on her grandmother, the woman's head on Sofia's lap.

I close the car door and turn to Joni. "I'll meet you at the hospital."

He nods and climbs into the driver's seat, and I watch them drive away. Once I can no longer see them, I drop to the grassy embankment, finally giving into the pain.

In the past, when I was in a lot of pain, I would self-medicate with booze. I haven't done that lately. I haven't needed to, until now.

I close my eyes and will the pain away. I have no idea how long I've been lying here—maybe a few minutes, maybe a lot longer—before I finally push myself up and limp to my car.

I drive to the hospital and park in the parking lot. Then stare at the building for five minutes. I should go in and be with Sofia. Be with her like Joni is. If something happened to her grandmother while I was dealing with my pain in the bar, I'd never be able to forgive myself. Sofia would never be able to forgive me.

Shaking away the thought that something bad has happened, I limp to a restaurant near the hospital. There, I call Sofia to tell her

I'm on my way but only get her voicemail. A couple of shots of something strong is all I need to take the edge off the pain.

"Hey, babe, I'm gonna be there soon. I had to stop off somewhere first." I end the call and enter the lounge, where I order four shots of whatever they have that is strong.

I shoot back the first glass. The dark liquid goes down smooth. I give it a few minutes before shooting back the contents of the next two glasses. My phone rings and I scramble to see who's calling. It's not Sofia. It's Cody. I place the phone on the table, unable to talk to him. Unwilling to hear the disappointment in his voice at what I'm doing. I shoot back the final drink and give it a few minutes for the buzz to numb the pain.

Once the pain is tolerable, I walk to the hospital and enter through the ER doors. I scan the waiting room and spot Joni and his grandmother sitting in the chairs against the far wall. Sofia isn't with them.

Joni stands as I approach, grooves stretching across his forehead. "Where the hell have you been?"

"How's she doing?"

The grooves deepen. "Have you been drinking?"

"None of your business."

Joni shoves my shoulder. "I'm making it my damn business. Sofia's grandmother had a heart attack, and you're getting drunk instead of being with your girlfriend." He spits the last word, the taste repugnant in his mouth.

"I'm not drunk."

He steps closer. I stand my ground. "I can smell the booze on you."

"That doesn't make me drunk," I bite back.

Aino stands and places her hand on her grandson's chest. Whatever she says to him is enough for him to take a step back.

I exhale slowly and look between them. "I want to see Sofia. Please."

Joni nods and indicates for me to follow him. He leads me to the front desk and speaks with the nurse on duty. She tells me in English where I need to go to find Sofia. Joni returns to his grandmother as I walk in the direction the nurse indicated. Hope pounds through me with each step that Sofia will forgive me for being late. Hope pounds through me that she doesn't notice I was drinking before coming here.

Sofia is standing next to her grandmother's bed, her face damp with tears. At the sight of her, something inside me fractures and threatens to destroy the last part of me that I've held onto for so long. The last part of me that had survived the accident and survived Gabby's death. I should have been here for Sofia no matter what, no matter how much pain I was in.

I wrap her in my arms and rest my cheek against the top of her head. She wraps her arms around my waist and holds on to me, tight.

Her grandmother's eyes are closed. I can't tell if she's asleep or unconscious. Behind her, a heart rate monitor beeps a steady beat. She's hooked up to an oxygen mask and IV, and I've never seen her look so frail.

"I'm sorry I'm late," I whisper. "How is she?"

"She's sleeping. The doctors said she was lucky. It wasn't a massive heart attack. They're waiting for an ICU bed to open up, then they'll move her there." She pulls away. "I need to call my mom."

"I can get Aino. She'll stay with your grandmother if you want."

"Thanks."

Sofia goes outside and I briefly talk to Joni before joining her. She's slipping her phone in her purse when I step out of the ER entrance.

"Did you get a hold of your mom?"

"Yes. She's making arrangements to fly out as soon as she can." Worrying her lip, Sofia glances at the sliding doors. "I'll probably be here a few days until she arrives. You can go with Joni to his great aunt's place for tonight, and head back to Helsinki tomorrow. I'll call you when I get back."

"I'm not leaving you." And especially not to go anywhere with

Joni. "I'll talk to Nik's uncle. I'm sure it will be okay if I stay with you a few days."

She averts her gaze and toes a crack in the sidewalk by her foot. "If I ask you a question, will you be honest with me?"

"Of course."

"Were you drinking before you came here? Is that why it took you so long?"

I ache at the sadness in her voice. All I can do is nod. My words, the ones she's waiting for, clog my throat with their dirty truth.

She looks back up at me, and the sadness in her eyes is almost my undoing.

"I'm so sorry, babe. My leg was hurting and drinking was the only way I could cope with the pain. I swear this is the only time I've done that since we've been together." The last time I drank too much—the night Joni took the photo of the girl kissing me—had nothing to do with my leg.

Her gaze searches my face, looking for the truth, separating it from the lies. "Did you drive here…were you…how did you get here after you'd been drinking?"

"I walked. The bar is across the street from the hospital. I would *never* ever drink and drive."

Her phone rings. She removes it from her purse and answers it. I'm about to leave when Sofia slips her fingers between mine. That's the only sign I need to know I'm forgiven for now, but if I screw up again, she'll walk away.

I don't want her to walk away.

She lets go of my hand and crouches while still talking to her mom. She digs around in her purse, removes a pen and crumpled receipt, then scribbles down her mom's flight information.

They talk for a few more minutes before she hangs up. "My mom's catching an early morning flight and will be here tomorrow night." She should feel at least a little bit relieved at the news, but it's like every problem in the world weighs her down, and she's about to collapse under the pressure. "I'm not sure what I'm going to do. My mom can't stay in Finland long, and someone needs to be here with my grandmother while she recovers."

And Sofia's the kind of person who would do that. She would throw away everything she's worked hard for to be there for the one person who loves her and who has never let her down.

I hold onto her, wishing I could hold onto her forever.

But wishes only exist in fairy tales.

# Chapter Thirty-Six

## Sofia

A week later in the staff locker room, I toss my dirty uniform into the laundry basket and swing my camera bag over my shoulder.

"How's your grandmother doing?" Maija asks.

"She's better. Thanks. She came back home yesterday." Mom's with her and is staying for the next few days to make arrangements for Muumu's care.

"That's great. Do you want to go shopping with me? To celebrate?"

"Sorry, I can't. I'm meeting up with Kyle." Well, more like surprising him. He's still working, but I'm hoping to get to watch him in action, which has to be a helluva lot more exciting than watching me at work.

She laughs shortly. "I think my boyfriend is in love with yours. All he can talk about is Kyle. He's a big fan of his."

"What's it with guys and hockey?" And why be a fan of Kyle just because he also loves it?

"I swear my dating life revolves around hockey games. If I didn't love Toivo so much, I'd be dating a guy who was into…um… lawn bowling."

"Lawn bowling?" I laugh. "Now there's a sport with lots of hot guy potential. If you're into eighty-year-olds."

Maija giggles. "Yeah, maybe dating a hockey fanatic is not so bad after all."

I lock my locker and, after saying bye to her, head to where Kyle works. The arena is cold inside and I instantly regret not bringing a hoodie. Seriously, what was I expecting? It's called *ice* hockey for a reason.

Rubbing my cold hands against my equally chilled arms, and cursing myself for wearing a tank top, I climb the empty bleachers to watch. My nipples prickle to stiff peaks, visible under my thin clothing and bra. *Brilliant going, Soph. That's now zero for two.*

Fortunately, everyone's too far away and too busy to notice my predicament. Trying to distract myself from the uncomfortable sensation, I remove my camera from my bag and switch lenses. I don't often use my telephoto lens since it's more suitable for distant shots. My father didn't know that when he bought it for me. It was a guilt present, another reason I don't use it much. But right now, it's the ideal lens for what I have planned.

Kyle is on the ice with a group of kids. They're all wearing their helmets and holding hockey sticks with the exception of Kyle. He has a whistle around his neck and a clipboard in his hand. It looks natural on him.

Two lines of pylons, evenly spaced apart on the ice, form a racecourse. Behind the goal line, the boys are divided into two groups. I watch as the first boy in each group races down the ice with their pucks, then skates around each pylon as if it's another player in the way. Once free of the pylons, they square up with the goal. The smaller boy is the first to take the shot. It easily flies into the hockey net despite the goalie's valiant attempt to block it. Boy #2 is a fraction of a second behind him. The goalie doesn't stand a chance against the rapid shooting, yet he somehow manages to knock the puck away.

I adjust the aperture and shutter speed for the optimal shot, and wait for the next two boys to race. I zoom in closer so I can capture their individual facial expressions as they speed around the pylons. I shoot several dozen more photos.

At the sound of loud cheering, I have an idea. I keep my lens on the teammates at the other end while the next boys skate down the ice. I shoot several photos of them cheering their teammates on.

The best ones are when the pucks go into the net or when the goalie manages to catch it. I laugh at their pained expressions of defeat.

For my final round of pictures, I focus on the one person I've tried not to look at too much. Kyle. My heart is ready to strap on skates and race around the rink at the sight of him. Even if it would probably slip and land hard on its left ventricle if it tried.

I'm not sure if he's seen me yet; his attention is on the boys navigating through the pylons at top speeds, somehow managing not to lose control and careen across the ice on their butts. He's grinning like I've never seen him smile before, pride clear on his face. And it's not just for these two boys. I watch him for the next two and the two after that. He cheers them on loudly. Nik does too, but the enthusiasm isn't as great as it is with Kyle. With Nik, I get the impression this is only a job for him, like cleaning the bathrooms at the sports center is for me. It doesn't mean the same as it does for Kyle.

My cell phone rings in my pocket. Thinking it's Joni, I answer without checking. "Hello?"

"I can't believe I actually got a hold of you," Claire says. "How's your grandmother doing?"

"She's fine." I update her on Muumu's condition and that my mom will be returning to Minneapolis in two days.

"But...?" she says after I finish, knowing me too well.

"But I'm not sure my grandmother should be left alone." I swallow back the ache and wish for the billionth time that my best friend could be here with me. I miss her so much. "I'm thinking of staying here. At least for the next year or so."

"But what about college? What about Kyle?"

"I've talked to the university. They can grant me a leave of absence for the year." But it means turning down the practicum with the Bears, and if I do that, I might never have a chance at it again. "As for Kyle..." The ache in my chest tightens. "He might not be returning to Minneapolis. He's got some job leads out of state." We haven't talked about it since Joni brought it up, but I can't expect him to throw away a chance at the career he wants just to be with me. It's not like we've discussed where things are going between us once we leave Finland. And now that he might end up out of state, there's no point having that discussion.

The boys finish racing and Nik calls them over. They take their positions on either the ice or the bench.

"Enough about me," I say. "Don't you have anything exciting to tell me?" Something to distract me from my own problems.

She hesitates, then tells me about her crazy weekend and her equally crazy date. Kyle picks that moment to look in my direction. His eyes are enough to cause every female's heart in a twenty-mile radius to stop beating.

Claire has to go, so we end the call, and I return to what I came to do. Even though I don't have many frames left on my digital card, I continue taking photos. The game lasts fifteen minutes, much to the boys' disappointment. The coaches have them cool down and stretch, then send them to the locker room. Nik skates off but Kyle doesn't join him. He calls out a name and a boy who's been struggling to keep up with everyone turns around.

Kyle gestures for him to return to the bench. The boy does, but like in the race and the game, his heart is not into it. Even I can skate faster than him, and that's not saying much. It doesn't make sense. Kyle told me these are some of the best players for the age group in Helsinki. The way that boy played, you'd think the opposite.

While Kyle talks to the boy, who must speak enough English to understand him, my phone rings again. This time it really is Joni.

"Hi," I say after answering.

"I hope I'm not interrupting anything," Joni says.

"No, you're good."

"Remember that wedding I told you about?"

"Yes, your cousin's wedding." He told me about it when we saw the movie. It's near Jyväskylä, a place I've always wanted to visit.

"Lovisa was supposed to go with me but she can't make it. Would you be interested in going with me?"

"I'd love to, but I can't be gone that long. I need to look after Muumu."

"It was her idea that I take you. Actually, she insisted I take you. She said you're driving her nuts and she needs a break from you." He chuckles. "I just think it's her way of making sure you have a good time, Sofia, and that you get to see more of Finland while you're here. And you wouldn't want to disappoint her, right?"

I guess this doesn't surprise me. She also knows I wanted to check out Jyväskylä. They have an amazing sports research center at the university. I might have mentioned it a few times to her.

The boy Kyle was talking to skates off to the locker room. Kyle skates toward me. If I go to Jyväskylä, it means less time with him before the summer is over. Given the situation surrounding our relationship, it shouldn't matter—but tell that to my heart.

# Chapter Thirty-Seven

## Kyle

The sound of skate blades scraping against the ice fills me with the usual thrill as I cheer the two boys racing down the ice. The usual thrill combined with an overwhelming sadness that this is no longer part of my life. I don't mean as a coach. I mean as a player. It's the same feeling I get every time I set foot on the ice with the boys. Eventually that feeling will go away. I just wish that day would hurry up.

A weird sensation that someone is watching us pokes at me, and I look up to find Sofia sitting on a bench on the other side of the rink. She watches the boys for a minute then lifts her camera. I tear my attention from her and go back to coaching my group. Pride charges through me at how hard they're working.

The pride shifts to concern as I watch Kai go through the drill, but unlike with the other boys, his heart isn't in it. The opposite to when he first began the camp. He was the most driven player back then.

After the last player has gone through the drill, Nik and I organize them into a quick game. I do my best not to look at Sofia even though seeing her makes me feel lighter. Lighter than I've felt in a while. When we were stranded at the cottage three weeks ago, it was as if the anger I struggle with over what happened last year had temporarily burned away. And it wasn't due to the marathon sex session that came from not having much else to do. It came from the hours of talking to Sofia, playing our True and False game, sharing abstract physics facts that popped into my head. It came from the hours of laughing with Sofia. It came from holding her. She's a small burst of sunlight between thick gray clouds.

Nik's yelling snaps me back to the game in time to witness my team score. Ignoring the growing ache in my leg, I jump up and down, cheering the guys on the ice and high-fiving the ones on the bench.

The game ends and Sofia is still sitting on the other side of the rink, watching us intently. I want to join her but can't yet. There's something important I have to deal with first.

Nik dismisses his boys. They whoop and holler and skate toward the change room. I call mine over.

I high-five them as they approach the bench. "Great game guys. Your slap shots are really coming along. Remember to transfer your weight from your back leg to your front leg, and then to your stick as you hit the ice. Does anyone know why you want to hit the ice and not the puck?"

They exchange curious glances, waiting to see if anyone else knows the answer, already knowing that they're about to get another physics lesson.

"By hitting the ice, you bend the stick like a bow. This stores up extra energy. When the stick snaps off the ice, there is a transfer of stored up energy from the ice to the puck. This causes the puck to shoot forward. The more stored energy, the greater the momentum of the puck."

"Why can't you be my physics teacher?" Mikko says. "You at least make physics interesting."

I smile at the unexpected compliment. "Physics is interesting when you're able to apply it to real life examples that mean something to you." I dismiss them, and with excited chatter, they skate to the other side of the rink.

Kai follows them, not interacting with anyone like he did the first few weeks of camp. He's shutting down. I recognize the feeling.

Before he disappears into the locker room, I call his name. He looks back and I gesture for him to join me.

He glances at the last of the boys as they step off the ice, then skates over, avoiding the ruts in the surface. "You want to talk to me?"

I indicate for him to sit on the bench and I sit next to him. "You wanna tell me what happened out there?" I keep my tone casual, nonjudgmental.

He doesn't look at me or say anything. He just fiddles with his stick.

"You know, talking about it might help." When he still doesn't say anything, I go for a different approach. "It's obvious something's bothering you and it's not healthy to keep it bottled up. You need to tell someone you can trust." And if it isn't me, then hopefully he has someone else he can turn to.

He continues fiddling with his stick. I don't say or do anything. I wait for him to decide what he wants to do next.

He eventually stands but continues to avoid eye contact. "I have to go." He steps onto the ice and skates toward the locker room. I don't join him. I leave Nik to deal with the guys and slowly skate across the ice to Sofia. She's staring at her phone, contemplating something.

"Hey, you okay?" I ask.

She slips her phone into the front pocket of her backpack. "Sorry, I didn't see you there," she says, avoiding my question.

"Is something wrong?" I nod at her bag.

She bites her lip and I can tell she's deliberating how much to tell me. She glances at her bag. "Joni asked me to go with him to his cousin's wedding. Lovisa was supposed to be his date but she can't go now."

"And you don't want to go?" It could be worse.

"It's near Jyväskylä. I have to spend the weekend there."

Several emotions flare in me. I was right. It could be worse. What Joni has planned *is* worse. He knows she's battling with the decision of whether she should go back to Minneapolis at the end of summer or stay with her grandmother. We haven't talked about it since she brought it up at the hospital, but I know she's thinking about it.

"Why would you agree to that?" I snap.

She gapes at me for several seconds. "Because he's my friend. And because the University of Jyväskylä has a world-renowned athletic research center. I mean, it's not like I'll get to do anything there, but it's still cool to check out the place." And no doubt Joni knew all of this before he asked her.

She looks at her watch and scrambles up. "I need to go. I'll talk to you later." She doesn't look at me as she gathers her stuff and I don't try convincing her to stay a little longer.

I just watch her walk away, taking a piece of my heart with her.

A piece of my heart I've unknowingly, bit by bit, been giving her.

# Chapter Thirty-Eight

## Sofia

The next day, I step out of the sports center, practically bouncing off the walls after a meeting with Rafu this morning. Kyle is waiting near the road, watching cars drive past.

"Hi?" I say, unsure where we stand after yesterday.

He reaches for me and pulls me close, then murmurs in my ear, "I'm sorry for being such an asshole yesterday."

I wrap my arms around his neck, our bodies pressed together. "Apology accepted. This time." Even though I say the last two words with a teasing smile, there's no missing what I'm really saying—as long as he doesn't think he has the right to tell me who I can hang out with.

He kisses my neck, and the familiar electrifying warmth spreads through me.

"God, I've missed you." His mouth finds mine before I can reply.

The kisses start out gentle, small tastes of what the other person has to offer. But the sweet samples aren't enough, and the kisses become heated, to the point where I'm surprised we haven't evaporated on the sidewalk. Who knew friends-with-benefits kisses could be so hot?

We wander along a side street, checking out the small stores on the lower level of the historic low-rise buildings. These aren't the stores that draw tourists, who prefer sticking to the city's core. But they still showcase designs unique to Finland—jewelry, dishware, glass vases and bowls—with their simple lines and geometric shapes. Kyle's oddly quiet. He doesn't even mention anything to do with physics.

"Rafu tracked me down this morning," I say, the excitement from our conversation still bubbling inside me. "He did his Masters in Sports and Exercise Medicine at the University of Jyväskylä, and has arranged for someone to introduce me around. And I'll get to talk to some people there about their current research." The news comes out so fast, I'd be surprised if Kyle understands half of what I said.

"Hey, that's great."

"Work is giving me two days off so I can do this." I was going to catch a train back to Helsinki, but Joni said he's fine staying a few extra days to visit family.

For some reason, this part of my news isn't met with the same response as when I told Kyle about what Rafu said. He points to a store with handcrafted glassware in the window. "Let's check in here. I want to get my mom a present."

We end up at a display of glass birds in an array of shapes and sizes. I stroke the head of a swan, its neck long and graceful. Next to it are the cutest little birds. They're similar to the swans, only a lot fatter and neck-less. And unlike the swans, they come in a rainbow of colors.

"How about this one?" I point to a royal blue bird the size of a large apple. Its head is clear colorless glass.

Kyle picks it up and pays for it. Despite finding the perfect gift for his mom, his mood hasn't changed much. Unable to hold back any longer, I finally ask him what's wrong as we continue exploring the area.

"It's nothing."

I stop and shake my head. "My last relationship was nothing but lies. I don't need you lying to me too." Because if that's what it's going to be about, then I'll walk away, permanently.

"Don't worry, it's nothing." He looks toward a small park across the street, where several teenage boys are playing street hockey on the concrete surface. He grabs my hand and leads me over there.

On the other side of where the teens are playing, Maija is sitting on the bench with a girl who looks to be six or seven years old. She waves at us and we join them.

Kyle glances at the teens, a look of longing on his face. It's the same look he wore the other day when I watched him coach.

Maija talks in Finnish to the girl before she says to us, "This is my niece, Emilia. My nephew is playing hockey with his friends." She nods at the teens as a tall, gangly fourteen-year-old heads our way. His eyes widen and he speaks rapid Finnish to Kyle.

Before Kyle can respond, Maija replies to whatever the boy just said. He nods and says to Kyle in halted English, "Would you like... like to play with us?"

The life that jumps back into Kyle's eyes is breathtaking. "I'd love to."

While he plays street hockey with the boys, I take out my camera and shoot dozens of pictures. The joy on his face warms me more than the warmest day ever could. The game pauses a few times while he gives them pointers. The boys eagerly ask questions and one of the older ones appears to translate. Otherwise, Kyle mimes what is lost in translation.

As I take pictures, Maija and I talk about our job and the funnier things that have happened. Like Maija "accidentally" spilling dirty water on the shoes of the jerks who had been harassing me. Fortunately, they haven't bothered me again since the day Kyle confronted them. Emilia watches my camera with great interest, and I show her how to use it. She shoots a picture of her brother that's pretty good, even if she did tilt the camera so it looks like he's falling over. It adds to the artistry.

Kyle saunters up to us and holds out his hand to me. "Your turn. I'm gonna show you the finer points of street hockey."

"I don't think that's a good idea. I'm not very good at it."

He lifts an eyebrow. "Have you tried it before?"

"Um, well, no."

"Then you can't know if you're not good at it."

I snort. "Trust me, I know. I suck at all team sports. I'm better at sports like running and Nordic skiing."

He beckons me forward with his finger. With a resigned sigh, I hand my camera to Maija and walk with him to join the boys. One of them hands me a hockey stick and Kyle points to where he wants me to stand. I've seen enough ice hockey games with Claire in high school to know how to play. Kind of. At least I don't have to worry about slipping on the ice and landing on my butt. Running around is much more my style, and I can concentrate on stealing the ball away from the opposite team. I succeed a few times, but end up passing the ball to my teammates. The other team knows I'm beyond the weakest link. They don't even have to try very hard to steal the ball from me. It goes to them by its own free will.

I do, though, manage to get it in front of the net at one point and shoot the ball, without really aiming it at anything. I was just attempting to keep the ball away from the teen who was determined to steal it from me. I don't know if his goalie felt sorry for me or had been overly confident the ball wouldn't go anywhere near the net. All I know is the ball somehow finds its way in and I score.

Shock at what happened rams into me and I stand there, gawking at the net and the ball. It's not until Kyle sweeps me up in his arms and swings me around that I snap out of it.

"Did you see that?" I say. "I scored!"

He laughs. "You did. You're a natural." He's kidding but I don't care. I. Got. A. Freakin'. Goal.

I fling my arms around his neck and kiss him hard. He lifts me and my legs hitch around his waist. The adrenalin flowing through me turns me into a mess. The way our bodies touch isn't helping any either. Maybe it's the exhilaration of the moment, but I'm incredibly turned on.

I pull away slightly. "Are hockey players usually this horny after they score?"

He grins, barely suppressing a laugh, and I suddenly realize what I said. I giggle, my unexpected success making me giddy.

At the mocking groans from the teens, Kyle releases me. He doesn't let go of me right away. We just stand here for a minute or two, absorbing each other with our gaze, my arms still around his neck.

Giving up on us, the boys resume their game and play around us. Kyle threads his fingers with mine and we return to Maija. She hands me my camera and after we say our goodbyes to her and her niece, we head to Kyle's building.

"I need to take a shower," he says after we step into the quiet apartment. He flashes me one of his trademarked sexy smiles. "You wanna join me?"

I'm about to say no, but a voice whispers in my head, *Think of it as part of the 'new you' experience.*

And shower it is.

Kyle grabs a change of clothes and condoms from his bedroom and leads me into the bathroom. He turns on the shower while I stand next to the door, uncertain what to do. He straightens and steps closer to me before whipping his t-shirt off over his head. It lands on the floor. I don't have a chance to add my clothes to the pile. Kyle slowly bunches the hem of my t-shirt up my stomach, his fingers brushing against my skin. My supersensitive skin that craves his touch.

My t-shirt joins his soon after. It's barely settled on the ground before Kyle unfastens my bra in the front and slips his hands between the soft cotton and my skin. He lightly squeezes my breasts, then his thumbs scrape against my nipples.

I whimper, unable to hold back the sound even if I wanted to. Just the thought of him claiming me in the shower is enough to push me to the ledge—and we aren't even in the shower yet.

He must have sensed it because my bra is quickly removed and before I know it, he has peeled my shorts and panties off. I step out of them and kick them to the side. He kneels and kisses the skin next to my belly button, then nips it between his teeth. I suck in a sharp breath, barely heard over the water hammering against the bathtub.

He stands and his gaze worships me in a way no guy has before. I'm not sure what it means, given our arrangement. All I know is that I don't want it to end.

Unlike Kyle, who's still wearing his jeans, the only thing I have on is my swan pendant. He fingers it for a moment, studying it even though he's never seen the charm before, but at the same time recognition and wonder fill his eyes.

And then he's kissing me again, but this time the kisses feel different. Vulnerable. Tender. Sweet.

They continue until I'm left feeling breathless and boneless. I'm floating. I'm free. I've never felt better.

Kyle slides his jeans and boxer briefs down his muscled legs and removes his glasses. His length springs free, erect and ready. He takes my hand and leads me into the bathtub. We stand under the warm water as it rains on us, Kyle's body shielding the water from my face. I rest my hands against his chest and stroke my thumbs against his nipples. He groans, the sound making me feel more desirable, more powerful than I've ever felt before.

Needing to show him what he's done for me, I wrap my hand around his hard length. I smile against his lips at his moaned reaction. Without giving it a second thought, I go down so that I'm kneeling in front of him and look up at his beautiful blue eyes that are dark with surprise and longing. His fingers thread through my wet hair.

"I've never done this before," I say with a confidence I didn't have a month ago. Not before my first time with Kyle. "You have to tell me what to do."

I slide my lips over his tip, taking in as much as I dare. My other hand gently grabs his balls and I carefully squeeze them. Kyle tightens his grip on my hair as a sound that's part loud groan and part "Sofia" powers from his mouth.

And the Pulitzer goes to *Ten Ways to Please a Man*, which I read in a fashion magazine two months ago.

Not sure what else to do, I flick my tongue just below the tip, tasting his subtle saltiness. That, too, gets a positive reaction out of him. As does moving my mouth and the hand around him simultaneously. I alternate between flicking my tongue, and sliding my mouth and hand back and forth along his length.

Just when I think he's going to come soon, he pulls away,

removing himself from my mouth. "I want to come deep inside you," he says, his voice thick with need and desire.

I stand, my breath and heart rate racing each other. He rolls on the condom, runs his hands down the backs of my thighs, and lifts me. I wrap my legs around him; my arms go around his neck. He adjusts us so my back is pressed against the far wall, his tip rubbing against my entrance. He then thrusts deep inside me, pushing me closer to the moment we're rapidly approaching.

My head falls back against the tiles, leaving my neck exposed. His mouth is on me in a flash, his body perfectly still. He nibbles and flicks the tip of his tongue against my skin, tormenting me further. I attempt rocking against him, telling him what I want, what I need.

"Sofia," he growls. "I'm not going to last much longer if you keep doing that."

"Good. Because I want you now." My voice is low and filled with longing.

Kyle pulls back then burrows himself deep in me again. He only has to repeat this several more times before the softest part of my body clenches around him and a tidal wave of euphoria sweeps through me. I scream Kyle's name, which is amplified by the bathroom's acoustics. Before the euphoria has a chance to fade away, Kyle joins me on the wave with an erotic, guttural grunt.

It takes us a minute before the world, or rather the shower, comes back into focus. Even longer before our breathing returns to somewhere close to normal. And once it slows enough, our lips meet, again, but this time with soft, intimate kisses.

"You're incredible," Kyle murmurs, but the way he says it, he's referring to more than just the sex we experienced.

I lightly pressed my mouth against his for a heartbeat. "You are too."

We kiss for another minute or two before I slide off him, and move to stand under the water while he disposes of the condom. He joins me soon after and we spend the next five minutes soaping each other to up to the point we're ready to have sex again.

Kyle had grabbed one of his t-shirts for me when he was in

his room. Once I'm dry, I slip it over my bra and shorts. The soft royal blue fabric, with the emblem for the Minnesota Bears on it, brushes the tops of my thighs and reminds me of him with his familiar scent. I'm tempted to sniff it, because I love his scent, but that would probably look a little crazy.

"It looks better on you than it does on me," he murmurs in my ear. Between that and the way his hands are skimming my body, relearning all my curves, the familiar electrical hum spreads through me again.

Kyle opens the door and I follow him to the living room where we had planned to watch a movie. Nik isn't due home until later. But when we enter the room, it becomes obvious pretty quickly that not only did he change his plans, he heard us having a less-than-innocent shower.

"Dude, that was hotter than porn. Both times. Just wish I had beer for the second period."

Kyle picks up the nearby cushion from the couch and hurls it at Nik.

Nik catches it with one hand and chuckles. "Do you need me to leave so you can go at it on the couch?"

A volcano couldn't get any hotter than my face right now.

"We're going to watch a movie." At Nik's crass grin, Kyle adds, "A regular movie, not porn. So you're more than welcome to leave if you want." I can't tell if he means it or not, or said it to further amuse his friend. If it's option B, then I'd say Kyle has succeeded.

Kyle indicates for Nik to move over and sits. He pulls me down so I'm snuggled against him. I have no idea if snuggling is normally part of the friends-with-benefits experience. It really should be. Since I don't want it to stop, I avoid asking Kyle. Instead, I allow myself to pretend Kyle is my boyfriend. As long as I remember where things really stand between us, everything should be okay.

I'll be okay.

I hope.

• • •

Back at Muumu's apartment, I walk into the kitchen to check on her. She's sitting at the kitchen table, studying her old photo album again. The album she showed me with pictures of her and my grandfather, back when she was my age. I kiss the top of her head and check if she needs anything. Then I return to my room, turn on my laptop, and download the pictures from this afternoon's photo shoot. I flip through the images, marking down my favorites. It's not until I'm almost finished going through them that I discover Maija was busy while I was playing hockey. Like when we were on Suomenlinna, she shot a bunch of pictures of me and Kyle together. Some of them are funny with me attempting to play the game. Others are of the intimate moments between us after I scored the goal. The pictures leave me breathless and give me an idea.

I grab my phone and dial Joni's number.

"*Hei*," I say after he answers. "Where can I get photos developed in Vantaa?"

# Chapter Thirty-Nine

## Kyle

Fully clothed, I pull open the door to the men's sauna and the dry heat blasts against my body. Sofia is bent over, her sexy ass in the air, as she scrubs the top bench. Who knew an ugly brown uniform and rubber boots could look so hot?

She hums a familiar song that's a little off tune. It's another of those things I love about her. She doesn't care that the song isn't quite right, as long as she's entertained while doing her job.

I step behind her. "Christ, you're hot," I say, placing my hand on her hip, the heel of it touching her ass.

She shrieks, and in one swift move, spins around and sprays me with the hose. Cold water hits my face with its stinging touch, and drenches my t-shirt and shorts.

I remove my glasses and attempt to find a dry piece of t-shirt to dry them with.

"Oh, God," she says and aims the hose in the opposite direction. "I'm so sorry." Her gaze sweeps over me and her teeth press into her lower lip. But she's not doing it because she's uncertain. She's trying not to laugh.

"You know, you have a really bad habit of doing that."

The corners of her mouth twitch up and the battle to keep a straight face is lost. She turns off the water and drops the hose onto the lower bench. Once she's no longer armed and dangerous, I pull her against my wet body, and my hand skims down her back and cups her ass. The tip of her tongue runs along her lower lip.

"If this weren't such a public place," I say, voice low so no one walking pass can hear me, "I'd bend you over that bench and see if we can go for an electric potential to rival that of a lightning storm."

She laughs, the sweet sound doing all kinds of crazy things to me. "Oooh, I love it when you talk all sexy like that."

"And I love talking sexy to you." At the sound of my husky tone, Sofia's eyes darken. Any other girl would have given me that standard God-you're-such-a-nerd look. Not Sofia. She has a way of making me feel like none of that matters.

I kiss her. "I'll meet you outside."

"But you're all wet."

"So I've noticed. Don't worry, I'll figure something out." It's not like she's much better, thanks to my wet clothes pressed against hers.

When I meet up with her again, I'm wearing the dry t-shirt and basketball shorts I bought at the front desk. Since she's leaving tomorrow to attend the wedding with Joni, I've planned a quiet evening, just the two of us. Nik has other plans for tonight, which fortunately don't involve the apartment.

After we wander around the Helsinki marketplace, to pick up groceries for dinner, we make our way back to my place. Once there, Sofia peels and slices the carrots while I sauté the thinly cut chicken strips. She tells me about her day and I tell her about mine. Even though this is the first time we've cooked together, not counting at the cottage when we grilled sausages over the fire pit, we work together perfectly side by side.

I pour her a glass of white wine.

"I've got something for you." She leaves the kitchen and returns with a small book, which she hands to me. "I made this for you."

"For me? Why?"

"Open it." She worries her lip, her gaze on the book in my hand.

I flip the cover open. It's a photo album. The first picture is of me at the arena. The boys are standing around me, listening to me explain the physics behind hitting the puck into the net. I turn the pages. More photos of me coaching.

Sofia points to one picture. "This is one of the things I love about you. You're great with these boys. Even though they don't always understand you, they worship everything you say. And I can tell you care as much about them as they do about you."

I don't say anything, the words immobilized at the back of my throat. *This is one of the things I love about you.* She said it so casually, as if she didn't realize what she had said. Does she love me, like I'm starting to fall for her? Or did I misunderstand what she said?

Afraid of discovering the truth and finding out it's not what I'd hoped, I turn the page. The next couple of pages are covered with pictures of me and of us when we were at the cottage and when we were on Suomenlinna. We look happy. We look like a couple.

I flip the page to find another picture of her in my arms. We're looking at each other like nothing else exists. Which is exactly how I'd felt at that moment.

"I love it," I whisper. And I do. No one has ever given me a gift like this before.

I turn to the next page. Again, it's of me and Sofia playing street hockey. We're messing around and laughing. Sofia doesn't know me as a NHL player or an ex-NHL player or a has-been. She only cares about the side of me that's been missing since even before the accident. I was so driven to live up to everyone's expectations, including my own, I'd forgotten the meaning of having a good time. After the accident, I thought I was having a great time, drinking and having sex with all those girls. But I wasn't. That's Nik's idea of a great time. It isn't mine.

"I really do love it," I whisper. My mouth finds Sofia's, and everything in this world feels right again, at least for now. At least until I have to tell her my news about the coaching job I was offered. Starting in two weeks. In Seattle. I don't want to give Joni a chance to use that against me, to use it to convince her to stay in Finland longer.

I place the book on the counter, my lips still attached to hers and turn off the stove. My palms slide down her hips to the backs of her thighs, and in an easy move I hoist her up. Her legs hook around me, and I carry her into the bedroom and to the bed. Sofia releases her legs and places her feet on the floor.

"What you said earlier…in the sauna," she says. "Do you…do you wanna try it that way?"

I rapidly sort through my memory of what I had said. "I don't care how we do it, as long as it's you I'm with." I stroke my thumb against her lip, eager to suck it between mine. "Do you want to try it that way?"

She nods, the movement small, her gaze focused on my mouth. "Yes," she whispers. Her voice isn't filled with uncertainty or nervousness. It's laced with curiosity, desire, inner strength.

This time I suck her lip between mine as my fingers find their way under her t-shirt and slide up her flat stomach. She squirms, my fingertips brushing against her ticklish zones. If I could do this every day for the next two weeks, I'd be a happy man.

Sofia lifts her arms and I pull the t-shirt off her. I toss it to the floor and my t-shirt joins it soon after. I pull her to me, our skin barely touching, yet it's enough to send every nerve in my body tingling. And judging from her reaction, she's no more immune to this than I am.

I tease her nipples with my fingers, drawing circles around them until they become stiff peaks. My mouth remains against hers, tasting her and enjoying the moans and whimpers escaping her lips and vibrating against mine. I squeeze her nipple between my fingers and I swear her legs almost buckle under her as she lets out a sound so erotic, so hot, I come close to pushing up her skirt and taking her now.

I undo the snap of her denim skirt then unzip it. I slide my hands to her hips and turn Sofia around. I pull her toward me, her back against my chest, and nip her shoulder with enough pressure to cause her to buck into me and whimper again. Fueled by her sound and by the feel of her, I cup her breasts in my hands and swirl the tip of my tongue against the faint bite mark. Her head falls back onto my shoulder and she moans.

Never in a hundred years will I ever get enough of hearing that sound.

Once I've finished entertaining myself with how her nipples

respond to my touch, I trace my hands across her stomach to her hips. My fingers hook the waistband of her skirt and I pull the clothing down her legs, exposing her pale pink cotton underwear that matches her bra. While I'll be the first to agree satin underwear is hot, the same can be said about what Sofia's wearing. She might come off as innocent, but what's beneath her skin is screaming to be anything but that.

I slowly stand again, trailing my hands up the outside of her legs. My fingers slip under the edge of her panties, then between her legs and her slick folds. "Christ, Sofia," I moan in her ear, "you're so ready for me. So ready for me to fuck you." My fingers against her clit mirror what the one on her breast is doing. It doesn't take long before she's panting with need.

Not to be outdone by me, her hand slips between us and she settles it against my dick. The warmth of her hand soaks through the fabric of my shorts and boxers, and she squeezes. The throbbing intensifies. "Shit," I groan.

My fingers move to the waistband of her panties and I pull them down. Once they're around her ankles, she steps out of them and kicks them to the side while I yank my shorts and boxers off. My dick springs free, ready to join Sofia's warmth. I toss my clothes halfway across the room.

"Bend over," I breathe in her ear, "and put your hands on the bed." She does and my fingers return to her clit from behind. "You look so hot from where I'm standing." I grin at her light moan. She's getting more turned on than I ever thought she would when I first met her. And just knowing that is having the same effect on me. It's as if being with Sofia has given me a new level of awareness that had escaped me for so long. A new level of awareness that makes me feel stronger than I've been in a while.

I slip a finger inside of her. She's so wet, so responsive. I add another finger and press them against her. Her breath draws in quickly. It won't take much more for her, for me, for us to get there.

I remove my fingers and position my tip against her entrance. I push it in just enough to torment her, to excite the nerves there. My fingers find her clit again, circle it and pinch it.

"Oh God, Kyle," she groans. "I want you to fuck me."

The grin on my face doesn't resemble the one from earlier. That was the sun peeking from behind a cloud. This one is a full on beam. She sounds even more innocent, more desirable when she says it. I open a condom and roll it on, then thrust into her and groan my satisfaction as her body welcomes me.

With my fingers still tormenting her clit, I slam into her again and again and again. It takes every ounce of control not to come before she does. Luckily I don't have to wait long. Her body clenches tightly around my dick as she screams out my name. I come soon after, drowning in her—but drowning in a good way.

Once I return back to earth, I fold myself over Sofia's back and rain it with soft kisses, giving her something to remember while she's with Joni this weekend.

I rein in the anger threatening to storm its way in. There's nothing to fear. She's mine. Joni doesn't have a claim on her. Sofia's been hurt by a cheating boyfriend. She would never turn around and do that to someone else.

It's Joni I'm more worried about. He's taking advantage of the situation before she's made her decision about whether or not she'll stay in Finland. I wouldn't be surprised if he spends the next four days trying to convince her that staying here would be the best for everyone concerned, including me.

I nip on her ear. "That was incredible." Her panting is her only reply.

I kiss her neck and pull out of her. She watches me through hooded eyes as I dispose of the condom. The bedroom door clicks open behind me. Sofia shrieks and scrambles under the sheet, her gaze ever watchful on the door. I whip around. Nik leers at her from the doorway, ignoring me.

"What the hell are you doing?" I stalk over to him and shove his arm. That's enough to pull his attention from Sofia.

"Sorry to interrupt," he says without a hint of remorse. "Just wanted to let you know about the change of plans."

"What change of plans?" I ask as a brunette Sofia's age appears next to him. Her gaze wanders down my body, reminding me that I'm naked, then it darts to where Sofia is sitting. The girl licks her lower lip, her attention still on Sofia, and talks to Nik in Finnish.

Nik laughs. "My friend wants to know if you're interested in a foursome."

I don't even have to look to know Sofia's blushing. She might be learning to be adventurous, but even she has limits, and a foursome is definitely beyond both of our limits.

"We'll pass. And FYI, dumbass, that's my food in the kitchen. We're about to make dinner."

Still chuckling, Nik raises his hands. "Got it. We're going to be busy anyway. She brought her camcorder with her." Great, we'll get to listen to them make porn.

Nik turns to leave and I begin to close the door. His friend waves bye to Sofia as I shut it.

"Is it just me or was she totally checking me out?" Sofia asks, eyes wide.

I join her on the bed and crawl under the covers with her. "What she was hoping for would've proven to be interesting. No way would anything have happened between me and Nik, and with the way she was eating you with her eyes, I have a feeling it would've been three-on-one action if we had agreed to it." And hell if that would have happened. Joni is enough competition for me.

"I-is that what you want to do?" If I thought her eyes were wide before, that's nothing compared to now. And her face is several shades lighter.

"No. God no! That's definitely not my kind of thing."

She lets out a long slow breath, blowing out the tension like it's a candle flame.

The question is, what are we going to do now? Listening to Nik and the girl go at it for the benefit of her camera doesn't make it to my list of fun-filled activities.

"Do you want to go out for pizza?" I ask.

Sofia looks at the door and nods. "Can we shower first?"

By shower, I'm guessing she doesn't mean a repeat of the one we had last week, where the sex was hotter than the water. At least with the water running, we can't hear the other two in Nik's bedroom.

Silently cursing him for changing his plans and screwing up mine, I climb out of bed and grab my favorite physics t-shirt for her to wear to the bathroom. And yes, the sight of her in it, and the sight of her only in the t-shirt, will fuel my sexual fantasies for while she's away.

After a quick shower, we escape the apartment, but not before we hear the girl scream out in ecstasy as I shut the door.

• • •

*"I'm thinking of applying to the speech pathology graduate program for next fall," Gabby says.*

*I take my eyes off the road and look at her for a brief second. "Are you sure?"*

*"This is the perfect time to do it. You're away a lot for games. If I'm studying all the time, I won't have time to miss you so much."*

*We've had this discussion before. It was because of my traveling schedule that she hadn't been excited to apply just yet.*

*The traffic light is green and I continue through the intersection. Gabby screams and before I can react, an SUV plows into her side of the car. We're sent flying sideways, flying, flying, flying, until we smash into a lamppost. Glass showers my body and metal tears into my left leg.*

*And I momentarily black out.*

*When I regain consciousness, every part of me is screaming in pain. I hear yells from what sounds like miles away but can't understand what they're saying. My eyelids have been turned to lead, but somehow I manage to open my eyes a crack.*

*It takes me a few seconds to piece everything together. The darkness. The glow from streetlights. The caved in driver's door. The people running toward the car. The sirens in the distance.*

*Gabby. I turn my head to see if she's okay. But it's not Gabby. It's Sofia. Fear floods my body. God, no! Please not Sofia. I reach out to her. She's white in the pale light and covered in blood.*

*"Sofia. It's going to okay. Hold on for me, babe. Can you do that for me? I love you and you're going to be okay. I promise." But even as I say the words I know it's not true. The part about loving her is. I've been falling in love with her from the first day we met; I just didn't realize it until now. That part is true. The part about everything will be all right is a lie.*

"Kyle, you're having a nightmare," Sofia says from the distance.

She strokes my cheek and the awareness of what happened creeps in. I slowly open my eyes, almost afraid to in case she's another dream and I'm too late.

My eyes adjust to the dim light of the moon. Sofia's leaning over me, her eyes bright with concern. Needing to prove to myself that she's real, I thread my fingers through her hair and guide her mouth to mine.

I just want to hold and kiss her. I never want to let her go again. Except I don't know how to do that. I don't know how to keep her and how to have the new future I've been working hard for. I don't know how to have them both.

I don't say any of this to her. Instead, I relish the feel and taste of her mouth, of her skin. I relish each of her moans as my hands explore her body and her sounds as she comes.

I relish making love to her while I still can.

Sofia falls asleep in my arms soon after. I watch her sleep for a few minutes as the sky clears, and the moonlight pours into the room and glows around her. She's an angel. An angel who has buried her way into my heart. But is it enough? She's more than enough for me.

But am I enough for her?

# Chapter Forty

## Sofia

My steamy dream starring Kyle fades and I open my eyes. It takes a few seconds to understand why I was dreaming about him, the arm around my waist and his chest against my back being my first hints.

We did go out for pizza, but returned to his apartment to find Nik and his female friend had left. Not wanting to go back to Muumu's so soon, I'd stayed to watch a movie. The next thing we knew, it was too late to drive home.

I blink the sleep from my eyes and check the alarm clock. Then shoot upright, the sheet tumbling down and pooling around my waist. Crap. It's already 9:07 a.m.

"Hey," Kyle murmurs, and I'm not sure if he's complaining about me moving or if he's saying 'hi' in Finnish.

"I've gotta get going," I tell him, the words rushing out in one long word. "Joni's meeting me at my grandmother's place, and I still have to shower and pack."

"Or you can stay in bed with me and forget about the wedding."

I can't tell if he's serious or kidding, although the temptation is there to do as he suggests.

I kiss Kyle's shoulder. "As tempting as that sounds, I do need to go." I grab my clothes and head for the bathroom to have a quick shower before Kyle decides to join me.

Which is exactly what he does, but this time he's on his best behavior and doesn't do anything other than gives me a quick kiss.

I leave him in the bathroom where he's toweling off and return to his room. I straighten his bedding, and notice an envelope from the athletic department at a university in Seattle.

"You almost ready to go?" Kyle asks behind me.

I whip around, still holding his pillow in my hand. He looks from the pillow to the envelope on the table. There's no missing that I've seen it.

"I've been offered a job there. An assistant coaching position."

Everything inside of me crumbles, but I manage to pull off a grin. "Oh, wow, that's awesome, Kyle. You're perfect for the job." I wrap my arms around his neck, give him a quick kiss, and rest my head on his shoulder so he can't see the tears in my eyes. "I'm so proud of you. You deserve it."

I don't even know why I'm reacting this way. It's not like we've made plans to be together after the summer is over.

He holds me close, and I can only hope he doesn't notice I'm shaking "When do you start?"

"They want me there in two weeks."

"That's good. You'll be finished with your coaching job here by then." I pull away. "We should go now."

An odd tension lies heavy in the air as Kyle drives me home, neither of us saying anything. I try asking him a True or False question, but he doesn't answer. The rest of the trip is spent in silence, other than the radio.

Joni is walking to the entrance of Muumu's building when we pull up. Kyle honks his horn and pulls into a spot, then walks with me to where Joni is waiting.

"I just have to pack," I say. Both guys follow me into the building and walk behind me on the stairs. I can feel them glare at each other as we climb the steps.

I unlock the apartment door and open it. Muumu is standing in the hallway and I hug her, needing her more than ever to keep me together. Even though she has no idea what's wrong, she squeezes me tight.

I leave everyone in the hallway and begin packing my bag. The front door buzzer intrudes on my thoughts, which is followed by the familiar voice of Joni's grandmother. I rejoin them, and both guys move to grab the bag from my hands. Kyle is standing next to me so he wins this round of Testosterone Wars. I roll my eyes at the smirk he levels in Joni's direction. Kyle follows us downstairs to Joni's car. Before I can offer to sit in the back, Aino dives into the backseat, forcing me to sit up front with Joni. Kyle loads my bag into the trunk and walks me to the passenger side.

I kiss him, the moment too brief. "See you Tuesday."

Kyle knots his fingers in my hair, keeping me close, and his tongue darts along my lips. Without meaning to, I open my mouth and let him in. My arms wrap around his neck and I get lost in the kiss. Time loses all meaning. Everything I'm supposed to be doing is no longer important. All I can think about is the taste of him, the warmth of his soft lips against mine, and the strength of his arms around me.

It's not until someone politely coughs that I snap back to the moment and remember we're standing next to Joni's car, with everyone watching us. Kyle's wearing a smug look aimed at Joni. This time when I kiss him, it's a quick peck on his cheek. I wave goodbye to Muumu and climb in.

The journey isn't too bad. Aino talks the entire trip, and Joni is forced to translate, but she's funny and has lots to say. I spend a lot of the journey laughing, despite the battle of emotions inside me. The last thing I want is to ruin the trip for everyone. I push past my pain, remembering the reason why I'm going to Jyväskylä with Joni.

Joni and I don't have a chance to say much to each other. A few times I get the feeling he wishes he could zip his grandmother's mouth shut since she loves sharing embarrassing tales about his childhood, which he translates even though it's obvious he would prefer changing topics.

After we drop her off at a family member's house, and tell her we'll see her in two hours, we drive to the hotel where Muumu, instead of Joni, booked our reservations. Or rather, the small inn where she booked our reservations. It's quaint, with flower boxes bursting with bright blossoms under all the windows. It's the kind of place you would bring your loved one for a romantic hideaway. I mute the alarm in my head. Just because it looks like that kind of place doesn't mean Joni expects this to be a romantic weekend between the two of us. As weekends go, this will be the opposite to when Kyle and I were stranded on the island during the storm.

Joni opens the trunk and I grab my backpack before he has a chance. He removes his bag and follows me into the building. The only person in the lobby is the girl behind the desk, tapping keys on her computer. We walk over to her.

"*Hei*, we have two rooms booked," I tell her, temporarily forgetting Joni could have told her this in her native language. "One for Sofia Philips and the other for Joni Kurri."

She punches on a few keys, frowns, and taps on a few more. "We only have a reservation for a Mr. Joni Kurri and guest. With a king-sized bed."

"There must be some kind of mistake. My grandmother booked us two rooms not one." At least I'm pretty sure she would have booked two.

The girl shakes her head. "Sorry. This is all I have booked under those names."

I give her Muumu's name, but the result is the same. She either booked the one room or they made a mistake with the reservation. "Can I book a room then?"

She shakes her head, again. "We're all booked up. You could try elsewhere but there's a convention in town. Everywhere has been booked for months. You were lucky to get this room." Which explains why Muumu ended up booking only the one room. She trusts Joni isn't going to try anything or hurt me—otherwise she never would've let me go with him.

"Okay, we'll take the room," I say.

Once we're checked in, we climb the stairs to the first floor. It doesn't take long to track down the room, and I stand by my original belief. This room is a perfect getaway, with the fireplace, two armchairs in front of it, and the roomy bed.

"I can sleep on the floor," Joni says, frowning and looking around the room.

"Don't worry about it. There's plenty of room on the bed." And plenty of pillows to build a barricade between us, in case he forgets it's me in the bed and tries to cuddle—like Kyle has a habit of doing. "I'm going to have a shower."

I have a quick shower and re-apply my makeup. As I step out of the bathroom, I catch Joni sneaking glances at me in my pale yellow sundress while he pretends to read a brochure. My face heats and I rush over to my bag to find my sandals.

While Joni gets ready, I call Kyle. Because we're being honest with each other, I tell him about the mistake with the room. The last thing I need is for him to accidentally find out from someone else, mostly notably Joni. Then he'll never trust me, even if it really doesn't matter in the end. He's leaving Minneapolis and I'm probably staying in Finland.

"I trust you," Kyle says after I tell him nothing will happen. "It's him I'm not too sure about."

"He's not going to try anything. I'm sure he'd prefer his own room than share one with me."

Kyle mutters something that sounds like, "That's what you think."

"Everything's gonna be fine, I promise."

"Just be careful. And kick his ass, hard, if he tries anything, okay?"

I laugh, and any previous trace of nervousness about how Kyle will respond to the news slips away.

We talk until Joni is ready to leave. I almost tell Kyle that I love him, but catch myself at the last second. I can't do that. He's leaving soon and this summer will amount to nothing more than a summer fling.

The evening with Joni's relatives is entertaining, the view of the lake breathtaking, with the forest of pine and birch skirting the water and providing privacy from the neighboring houses. His aunt set up a long table containing various foods and drinks, and as the evening wears on, the laughter grows louder, as does the music and singing. The gathering consists of at least twenty people. The older adults chat around the fire not far from the water's edge. The aroma of grilled Finnish sausage links fills the air.

Joni and I hang out near the red barn-style house, with a few of his relatives who are close to our age. All speak various levels of English and are happy to practice it…and teach me inappropriate words in Finnish. Luckily for me, Joni warned me that's what they were doing. It would've been a little embarrassing if I had said the words to Muumu. Oh, who am I kidding? Saying "pussy" to her would be mortifying.

I glare at the male cousin who can't stop laughing after I said the word perfectly, thinking he told me something else. Joni slings his arm over my shoulder and tells his cousin off. Or at least I think that's what he's saying. He says it in Finnish while frowning, and his other cousins burst out laughing.

I sip the fruity punch Joni fetched for me while I was increasing my list of vocabulary words. Whatever alcohol is in it gives it a nice little kick. I take another sip. Correction. It gives it a nice big kick.

One girl, who's about seventeen years old, smiles shyly at me before speaking to Joni. She's the opposite to the rest of them. She's quiet and doesn't speak English. She nods at me. He shakes his head but she doesn't see it.

"What did she say?" I ask.

"It wasn't important. Let's dance." Without giving me a chance to respond, he grabs my hand and pulls me to the makeshift dance floor between several small trees that look like Tinkerbell sneezed pixie dust on them. The miniature lights twinkle in the dimming sunlight.

The fast-paced song ends as we reach the small space, and a slower song takes its place. His grandmother is practically glowing. If Muumu was into texting, I wouldn't be surprised if she and Aino would be gossiping to each other about this. I silently groan.

Joni puts his arms around my waist and mine automatically go around his neck. I sway in his arms, my gaze focused on the lake.

"It's pretty here," I say, needing a distraction.

"Yes, it is," Joni says. But he's not looking where I'm looking. Even in my tipsy state, I feel his gaze burning into me.

I continue to watch the lake, you know, in case a mythological beast crawls out of it. Which might not be a bad thing. It would give everyone something else to talk about, other than talking about me and Joni.

The song ends. "How about we go for a walk?" he says. "I could use a break from everyone."

"What are they talking about?"

"My ex-girlfriend. They like you better. Let's just say they're not much different to my grandmother. They think it's time I settle down."

"They know I'm seeing someone, right?"

"I did mention it a few times."

I glance over his shoulder. Everyone's still watching us.

We walk along a narrow path skirting the lake, until we can no longer see anyone. The laughter and music fades into the background, accompanied by the chirping of frogs. With the sun low in the sky and shimmering off the water, this is easily one of the most romantic locations around.

Joni clears his throat.

I turn to him and his lips are suddenly on mine.

# Chapter Forty-One

## Sofia

Joni's lips are only on mine for a second, but the moment they pull away, I turn and run. Deep down a voice tells me I'm overreacting. I ignore it.

I need to run. It's the only way I know how to deal with the battle of emotions over Kyle's news, Joni's kiss, my need to make a decision whether I'm staying in Finland or not, and my fear of trusting a guy only to be hurt again. Joni calls out my name but doesn't come after me.

Running in sandals...never a good idea. I stop long enough at the fork in the trail to slip them off while deciding which way to go, then I bolt along the sandy path parallel to the lake. I keep going, no doubt trespassing on private property belonging to the neighbors, but that doesn't stop me.

No, what stops me is a sharp pain slicing into the bottom of my foot. An equally pained cry stumbles from my lips. Crap. I lift my foot. Blood drips onto the sand and the evil chunk of broken glass sticking up.

I half walk, half tip-toe a few feet and drop onto a large flat rock half in the water. I lower my injured foot into the lake, and wash off the blood and sand while inwardly cursing myself for being such an idiot. The cold temperature bites into my skin and soothes the stinging.

Once I'm satisfied it's numb enough, I lift my foot out of the water and rest my ankle on my knee. The cut is deep, but I can't tell if I need stitches, or if it just looks worse than it is. Blood oozes from the wound and mixes with the water. The way my luck is going, I wouldn't be surprised if a blood-loving, mystical creature jumps from the water and latches onto my foot. It's been that kind of day.

"Sofia!" Joni calls from farther up the path.

"Watch out for the glass!" A warm breeze ruffles strands of hair into my face and mouth. I push it behind my ear and consider my options.

Joni says a word that I've long since guessed to be a swear word. I glance over my shoulder to find him staring at my bleeding foot. He bends to inspect it then unbuttons his shirt.

And now it's my turn to stare. At his body. I knew he was in good shape, but I never realized he's in this good of shape. Not that this changes anything between us.

I look at my foot, again, worried he'll get the wrong idea if I check out his body for too long. Behind me the ripping of fabric tears through the air. Before I have a chance to see what's going on, Joni kneels and starts wrapping the fabric around my foot.

"You need stitches," he says, his attention focused on what he's doing. He ties the ends so the knot is on top of my foot. "The hospital isn't far from here."

"But you've got your family thingy going on. You can't leave." And honestly? I've had enough of hospitals to last me a while.

His lips attempt a smile but only sadness reaches his eyes. "Considering it's my fault you ran and cut your foot..." His smile fades. "I'm really sorry. I mean, I'm not sorry for kissing you. I'm sorry for upsetting you."

Now it's my turn to look away. "I shouldn't have reacted that way."

He chuckles. "So you're saying slapping me would have been a better option?"

I look back at him. "I'm just confused about everything and you kissing me didn't help."

His mouth slides up to one side. Amusement gleams in his

warm brown eyes. "Does that mean you like me more than you're letting on?"

My gaze drops to my bandaged foot and the blood beginning to seep through the white fabric. "It means I'm falling in love with Kyle but it doesn't matter."

"Why?"

"Why doesn't it matter or why am I falling in love with Kyle?"

Joni laughs shortly. "Maybe a little of both, although I'd prefer you skip the part about falling in love. Especially since he's all wrong for you."

I decide to ignore the last part. I'll never convince Joni otherwise. "Kyle was offered a job, but it means he has to move away to another state. And I've got to think about Muumu. She needs me." Joni knows I've been thinking of staying here for the year to help out. He doesn't know about the experience with the Bears that I'll lose out on. "So like I said, it doesn't matter that I'm falling in love with him. It will never work out."

He's silent for a moment then asks, "If you stay here once the summer is over, will you be allowed to still work at the sports center?"

I shrug. "I have no idea. I have a feeling I won't be. It was only a temporary position." And my work visa will no longer be good if I lose that job. Which means I'll need to find a new job and apply for a new visa. Neither will be easy to do.

"You know if you need help, just let me know and I can see what I can do." He brushes a strand of hair behind my ear, his fingers lingering on my skin.

"Thanks." I stand, not wanting to talk about this anymore, not wanting to think about what he's really offering. "My foot should be fine now."

Joni gently grabs hold of my arm. "I'm driving you to the hospital and they can decide if your foot is fine or not. And whether you want to hear my opinion or not, you don't have a choice. He's wrong for you. You're a sweet and amazing woman, Sofia. Kyle's the kind of guy who could end up bulldozing over you, especially if he starts drinking again."

The sad thing is I know he's right about the last part. But Kyle deserves a chance to prove himself. I'm just not sure if I should give it to him—or if doing so will only lead to more heartache.

# Chapter Forty-Two

## Sofia

I wake up to find Kyle's arms wrapped securely around me. I blink my eyes clear and take in the bedroom bathed in the early morning sunlight. The bedroom that doesn't belong to Kyle. The bedroom that doesn't belong to me. The bedroom that looks familiar but I can't figure out why.

And then everything about last night comes back to me. The kiss. The broken glass. The several hours spent in the ER. The stitches in my foot.

I groan and don't bother to turn around. Even without looking, I know it's Joni's arm pinning me from behind. I glance down and exhale a relieved breath at the sight of my sleep shorts and t-shirt, which I now remember changing into once we returned from the hospital.

Wiggling myself free, I slide off the bed. Joni doesn't stir. It's still early in Finland, but it's the perfect time to phone home. I grab the crutches, which I'm supposed to use until my foot is healed, and collect my phone from my purse. Then I quietly leave the room, shutting the door behind me, and crutch my way down the hallway and the stairs.

Outside, I sit on a bench overlooking a small pond shaped like a wonky heart. Several orange fish dart around the lily pads. On the other side, a statue of a young girl pours water in the pond from a jug. At least she doesn't have men problems. The worst she has to worry about is birds pooping on her head. Lucky girl.

I call mom first and go straight to voicemail. I end the call without bothering to leave a message. Next, I call Claire since it's too early to call Kyle. Besides, it's my best friend I need to talk to more than anyone. She'll know what to do about Kyle, about Joni, about Muumu.

"Hey you," she says after the second ring. "Aren't you at the wedding?"

"No, it's not for a few more hours."

"So? How's it going?"

"It's going great." I toss the words at her with a side order of sarcasm. "Joni kissed me last night and I ran off and cut my foot. So we then spent several hours in the ER while I waited to get stitches."

"You ran off? A hot guy kisses you and you ran off?" She's not sure if she should laugh at a predicament that only I could get into, or be worried for me. The laugh wins. "I'm sorry," she says through her giggles. "I'm having the most boring summer of my life with you gone, and you've got some sort of lopsided love triangle going on and I'm not there to witness it. So is it official yet? Are you and Kyle dating when you return here?"

I let out a long breath. It does nothing to extinguish the emotions battling inside me. "I haven't decided if I'm returning yet."

"But what about Kyle?"

"He accepted a great coaching job in Seattle. So there is no more Kyle and me. Not after the end of the summer." We were nothing more than a summer fling in the end.

And even if he wasn't moving away and we were willing to make our relationship work, I need to know Kyle won't slip back to being the guy he was before he came here. I need him to be more honest. I have a feeling he's holding something back from me. Until his walls are completely down, our relationship will never last.

"Have you not heard of long-distance relationships?" Claire asks. "I mean, we're not talking about you having a long-distance relationship with Joni. A long-distance relationship with Kyle is still doable."

"I guess you're right."

"Of course I'm right." Her words are barely heard over the loud chopping that just started. I glance around. A man is standing in a wide-legged stance at the end of the garden, next to a pile of firewood. He lifts the ax above his head and whacks the log with such force, I jump at the thunderous crack of splitting wood.

Unable to talk to Claire any longer because of the noise, we end the call, with her telling me she can't wait to hear about the next exciting episode of my love life.

Joni is already awake, freshly showered, his hair damp, when I return to the room. I don't mention how he was spooned up next to me this morning, and he avoids the topic, too. Or maybe it was just an innocent action and he didn't know he had done that.

We arrive at the pavilion by the lake where the wedding is taking place and sit in the back row. Joni's grandmother is ahead of us, but she turns around and waves. I wave back. The wedding ceremony takes place without any problems. Or I assume it does. Since I don't understand a single word spoken, I spend the entire time trying to look thrilled for the bride and groom instead of bored. The end can't come soon enough for me, and when it does my smile is genuine, even if the reasons for it aren't what everyone thinks.

The wedding party leaves for photos. All of Joni's relatives from last night keep coming over to me and asking about my foot. It's not until forty minutes later that I can finally slip away to call Mom again.

"Aren't you at the wedding?" she asks. A man speaks in the background and I cringe. Mom's on a date? God, did I interrupt them making out? Ewwww.

"Who's there?" I blurt even though I don't really want to hear the answer. I should be happy for her, but this is my mom we're talking about. I can't picture her with another man who isn't my dad. I know they're never getting back together but still.

"It's your father."

Huh? I couldn't have been more surprised if she had said in a breathy, Darth-Vader voice: *It is your father, Sofia.* "Why is Dad there?"

"We talked and realized we still care a lot for each other. So we went out on a date. And one thing led to another. We've been seeing a marriage counselor for the past month." And that's why he'd phoned to see how Muumu was doing after the heart attack. It was also because he wanted to talk to Mom.

I'm too stunned to speak. After everything she went through, the shame and humiliation, she's willing to forgive him. Maybe even fully trust him again, one day. She's willing to leave the past in the past. Maybe I should do the same. Maybe I can take the risk that things will work out for me and Kyle, and that he'll never hurt me like Ian did.

Even if we aren't living in the same state.

But this is all assuming he still wants to see me once he moves to Seattle. I guess it's time we have that conversation. Right after I decide if I'm staying in Finland or not.

But first, before I can do that, I need to survive this wedding.

Aino gestures at me. "Come. Come."

# Chapter Forty-Three

## Kyle

Kai stick-handles the puck to an open spot and takes a shot. When I first started working with the boys, it would've been an easy shot for him. He has the talent to go far in the game, but he's lost the heart for it and it's showing no signs of returning.

The puck flies past the open crease, straight to the skates of a player from the other team. I glance at my watch and blow my whistle. The shrill sound grabs their attention and they groan.

"Sorry, guys. That's all we have time for. I'll see you tomorrow." As they skate toward the locker room, I call out, "Kai, can I talk to you for a second?" I haven't pulled him aside since the last time I talked to him a few weeks ago.

He stops in front of me but doesn't say anything. Eyes averted, he chips away at the cracked ice with the side of his blade. I indicate for him to follow me, and we enter the box and sit on the bench. Kai removes his helmet and since he can't pretend to study the ice anymore, he studies his helmet instead.

"Kai, you're a very talented player. I saw that when we first started camp. But something's obviously bothering you, and I can't help you if you won't let me."

He remains silent and I add, "I want to help you. I know what it's like to feel as if the world is against you, and it's easier shutting down than dealing with it."

He eyes me for a moment, the need burning in his gaze to tell someone what's going on, mixed with confusion as to whether or not to deny it. He eventually nods. "It's my dad. My mom recently died. She had cancer. And he's changed."

"In what way?"

"He does not talk to me now. He lost his job…He does not eat much…And every time he looks at me, he hates me and wishes I were dead and not her."

My stomach turns to lead and struggles against the force of gravity. "I'm sure he doesn't feel that way. Grief can change us. It can make us lose perspective and it can consume us." But even as I say it, I wonder how anyone can make their own child feel that way, even if they are so overwhelmed with grief. "But if you show him you're there for him, and let him know you need him as much as he needs you, it'll be the first step in helping him. In helping both of you."

My words come from the heart. My family did this for me when I first struggled to cope with Gabby's death and with the loss of my dreams. If they hadn't shown me they were there for me, would I have gotten over my grief? My family saved me.

"I don't know…" Kai says. His shoulders are hunched, carrying the weight of several large planets. No kid should ever feel that way.

I proceed to tell him the abbreviated version of what happened to me and how my parents helped me. I skip the parts about the sex and how I was still drinking more than I should until recently.

Once I'm finished, Kai smiles. The movement is small, not noticeable by most. It's more about hope than happiness. And for the first time in a while, hope stirs deep in me, as if woken from a long hibernation. Hope about my ability to be strong despite everything I've lost.

Hope about my future.

Hope about Sofia.

Kai skates back to the locker room. I don't feel like heading there yet. Nik can keep the boys out of trouble while they get ready to go home.

Other than me, the rink is empty. And just like I used to do when I was trying to figure things out, I start skating laps around the ice. My leg aches, but I don't care. I just keep going, shifting back and forth between skating forward and backward.

Eventually I stop, the fatigue in my leg burning too much. I skate off the ice and enter the empty locker room. I remove my skates and strip off my sweaty athletic clothing, then grab my towel and head for the showers.

Closing my eyes, I duck my head under the stream of water and rinse the sweat from my hair. Once I'm finished, I shut the water off and turn around.

At the sight of the last person I expect to see in the men's locker room, I startle. "What are you doing here?" I ask Lovisa—or Daniela. I still can't tell the twins apart.

But it doesn't matter if it's Lovisa or Daniela, I'm naked...and so is she. *Fuck.*

I snatch my towel off the hook. What the hell am I supposed to do? Cover myself up or throw her the towel so she can cover *herself* up?

I toss her the towel. She catches it but isn't in a rush to cover herself. I attempt to block her view of my package with my hand.

"I wanted to say hi, Kyle."

"Great, you've said hi. Now put on your clothes and go."

Pouting, she wraps the towel around her chest and takes a step toward me. I step back, maintaining the distance between us. "What part of 'now go' are you having trouble with?" I ask.

"You don't have to be shy with me."

"I'm not being shy. This is the men's locker room."

Her gaze drops to my hand covering my package. "So I've noticed."

"And you can't be in here."

She takes another step forward, cornering me. "Sure I can. Ever had shower sex? I thought we could try it out. Together."

"I have a girlfriend." I don't know if it's true or not, but this isn't the time to get into those semantics. And as far as Lovisa knows, I'm dating Sofia. Which means why in hell is she in here? "Weren't you supposed to be in Jyväskylä with Joni?"

"Plans changed."

So, she's definitely Lovisa.

The sound of the locker-room door opening mocks me. Shit. The good news, if you can call it that, is she's still wearing the towel.

"You and I will be hot together," she whispers. Damn shower acoustics. Even though she whispered it, her words are heard by the occupants in the other room.

Nik and his uncle enter the shower area. Nik's face holds an edge of amusement. His uncle is less than impressed.

"What's going on here?" Alvar Tikkanen says.

Before either of us can respond, he tells Lovisa, "I don't care who you are, get out of here or else I will have you charged for trespassing."

Lovisa doesn't stick around to find out if he's bluffing. I release a relieved breath. Hopefully that's the last I'll see of her. One thing I'm certain about is that not only does Joni knows about this, but he'll make sure Sofia knows, too.

"What the hell were you thinking?" Alvar says, his face red, nostrils flaring.

I open my mouth to tell him it's not what he thinks, but he doesn't give me a chance to defend myself.

"You're lucky we walked in when we did, and not when you and the girl were having sex. And you were lucky it was us who walked in on you and not one of the boys from the camp. Do you realize what your careless indiscretions could have done to the reputation of the camp? If I had known you would do something stupid like this, I never would have given you those recommendations."

He pauses his rant long enough for me to get a word in. "I didn't invite her in here. Nor did I plan to have sex with her. I didn't even know she was in here until it was too late."

Alvar digests this. His stance is still stiff, but I can tell he believes me. "Do you know her?"

I nod. "Not very well. I just met her once, and I have no idea how she knew where to find me." Although I do have a strong suspicion how she knew enough to track me down.

244

"Do you think she'll be a problem again?"

I have no idea. Who knows what else Joni has planned. "Hopefully not."

"Well, for you own safety and for the safety of the program, you're to ensure you're never alone in here." He looks at his nephew. "If he's in here, then you're in here."

"Yes, sir," Nik says, his face a mask of seriousness. Deep down he's laughing that he now gets to babysit me.

Alvar leaves and I change into my regular clothes. Joni and Sofia should be leaving soon to drive back to Vantaa. I send her a text. There's no easy way to put it so I simply type: *Hope you had a great trip. Just want you to know that Lovisa came into the men's locker room at the arena while I was showering. Nik and his uncle saved me from her. Miss you.*

As I'm gathering up my stuff, Sofia replies.

*Glad you're okay. Miss you too. Talk to you soon. :)*

Nik slaps me on the back. "Okay, loverboy. Let's get out of here before anymore of your fangirls show up, naked." Although from the way he says it, he wouldn't be opposed to it.

# Chapter Forty-Four

## Sofia

The arena door opens and a group of boys exit. I recognize them from when I watched Kyle work the day I took photos for the photo album. The boy Kyle was talking to that day, after practice, leaves with two other boys. All three of them are laughing. I almost don't recognize him. The last time I saw him, it looked like someone had died.

They walk past, talking in rapid Finnish. Eventually Kyle and Nik exit the building. It takes everything in my power not to run to Kyle and jump into his arms. Everything in my power, along with a pair of crutches.

The crutches I never told Kyle about.

His eyebrows draw together in a dark line. "What the hell happened to you?" He doesn't have to say it; I can see it in his eyes. He thinks what happened is Joni's fault, and in a small way it was. Except I have no intention of telling Kyle that. Yes, I want us to be honest with each other, but telling him that Joni kissed me is like wrestling with a hungry bear. Not the brightest of ideas.

"I didn't see some broken glass in the sand and stepped on it. It's really nothing. I just needed a few stitches." Well, more like six.

Kyle takes a crutch and hands it to Nik. He wraps his arm around my waist and hands Nik the other crutch. Then his lips are on mine just like I'd fantasized all weekend, and everything else is quickly forgotten.

Who knows how long we've been kissing when Nik says, "Dude, I do have someplace to go."

At first I can't figure out what he's talking about. Why does he have to wait for us to finish kissing, which if I had my way would be never? Then I remember why: he's still holding my crutches.

Thinking that Kyle's going to let go of me so I can take the crutches from Nik, I attempt to pull away. Kyle's arms remain locked around me. Before I can say anything, he scoops me up and walks toward the parking lot. His clean ocean scent, which I've missed more than I thought would be possible, welcomes me. I bury my face into his shoulder and breathe him in.

Nik doesn't have any other choice but to follow. He smirks at me like he knows exactly what's going to happen soon enough. He's right. I plan to make love to Kyle and make up for being away from him for so long, even if it could be one of the last times I might be making love to him.

A crushing pressure in my heart warns me that saying goodbye to him in the end will be the most painful thing I've ever done. I've never been good with goodbyes, and this one will be so much worse.

I push the fear aside and dwell on this moment, on this man.

Kyle carries me to the arena parking lot and lowers me next to the passenger side of his small rental car. He takes the crutches from Nik and places them in the backseat, then opens the passenger door for me. I climb in.

If it weren't for my foot, we could have walked along the sea front by the marketplace. I can still do that with my crutches, but clearly Kyle has other plans in mind. He drives me back to his apartment as he asks questions about the trip and about my visit to the university. He seems as excited about my time at the university as I was about being there.

Normally we take the stairs to his floor, but given my situation, we're forced to ride the elevator. The incredibly slow elevator. Or at least it's slow until we're inside it, kissing. Just as our kisses turn full-out hot, the damn elevator door pings open.

In his apartment, we can barely keep our hands off each other.

A trail of clothes extends from the front door to his room, leaving us in only our underwear. And even that doesn't last on us for long.

Kyle scoops me up again and I let my crutches fall to the floor. He lowers me onto the bed and joins me a heartbeat later as his lips find mine once more.

"God, I've missed you," he murmurs against them.

I kiss him back. "Good. I've missed you too."

"I've thought about nothing since you left other than tasting you." His tongue traces its way along my jaw and down my neck. Jolts of electricity fan out from each point of contact. I moan and my fingers draw a line down his back, relishing the strength of each muscle. I flash back to my first year anatomy class. If only that class had been this much fun, this exciting. If it had been, I might've gotten an A.

While my fingers explore his back, his explore another part of me. The mere touch of his fingers against the aching throb is enough to set off a small round of fireworks. It's as if my body has been in a half-aroused state all weekend and his touch, his taste, his scent are all that was needed for me to ignite.

There's something I want to try, but I'm not sure how to bring it up. Kyle knew what I wanted to do last time without me having to say it, but this time I won't get so lucky. I open my mouth to speak, but the words are stilled on my tongue as he pushes my legs apart and his tongue sets off another round of fireworks.

"Christ, you're so goddamn hot." His equally hot breath blows against the aching throb as a finger slips inside me. It presses against me and another finger joins it.

His fingers don't move, other than to apply pressure while his tongue continues its sweet torment. Once he's close to bringing me to the brink of the abyss, he pulls away and kisses his way up my stomach.

Inch by slow inch, he makes me feel so desirable, I swear I'm about to explode from the intensity of it. But it also gives me the strength to be in charge for once, to let him know what I want.

I push myself up, forcing Kyle to sit, confusion on his face. He thinks I've changed my mind and I don't want to have sex after all. I swirl my thumb against his tip, my eyes locked on his. Then I run my hand down his length and give it a light squeeze. The combination of lust, pride, need in his eyes sends a power-filled shudder through me. If there's ever been a moment when I've felt incredibly sensual, this is it.

Kyle doesn't move, as if sensing I want to take the lead on this. His half smile radiates pride at the person I've become in the last two months. I open his night-table drawer, and remove a foil package. Carefully, I rip it open, confidence bubbling inside me. No matter what I do, Kyle isn't judging me. He's encouraging me with each sound he makes, with each look of utter joy.

I roll the condom onto him, straddle his hips, and lower myself so his tip presses against my entrance. Then I slowly slide my body down the length of him, taking him deep.

Kyle releases a sound that is part groan, part my name. We keep our gazes focused on each other, nothing else in the world existing, and I move along him. He grabs hold of my hips and helps set the pace. I want to kiss him but I don't want to tear my gaze from his. The fire in his eyes is pushing me closer to the edge and I don't want to risk stumbling back and lose this incredible feeling. I'm so close, but I do hold back, not wanting to go over before Kyle is ready.

"Let go, Sofia," he breathes. "Don't hold back for me."

Just hearing him say those words proves to be too much and I clench around him, screaming out. For a brief moment, I stop moving as I regain my senses. But then I remember I'm not on this journey alone and move against him again. Every nerve fiber in my body is on heightened alert. It doesn't take long before the fire consumes me once more, only this time Kyle joins me.

He squeezes his eyes shut and I watch as a mix of pain and bliss washes over his expression. "Oh, God, Sofia." The sound is guttural, erotic. I can't help myself. I kiss him, long and hard, even though he probably wants nothing more than to collapse on the bed.

His hands travel up my back. One hand holds me tight against him, the other tangles in my hair. We kiss for a good minute or so before we drop to the bed, with Kyle still in me.

"I don't want to move," he murmurs in my ear. "I want to stay like this forever."

"Sounds good to me," I murmur back, one leg wrapped around his hip. But we can't stay this way forever, as nice as it might sound.

Kyle rolls off me and disposes of the condom before joining me back in bed. We cuddle close, Kyle on his back, me half slung across him. His heat and delicious scent blankets me. Leaves me drowsy. The caressing circles his fingers draw on my back don't help either.

I inhale a long slow breath. Maybe this isn't the best time for what I have planned, but after what happened between us—the connection. The honesty. The trust—it's time we talk.

"Can I ask you a question?"

"Anything." His voice is as drowsy as I feel.

"What's gonna happen to us once the summer's over?" I brace for any sign that what we have will end once we leave.

It doesn't happen. He tightens his hold on me. "I was hoping you'll be my girlfriend. For real—even if it's long distance for a while."

"But you're struggling with so much, and until you trust me with what you're going through, there'll always be a wall between us. And it won't go away if you're living in Seattle and I'm living in Minneapolis." Or Finland for the year.

His hold on me loosens and his runs his hand over his face. I've lost him. I pushed too hard and instead of him being ready to let me in and help him, he's pushing me away. Part of me screams out to beg him to ignore what I said. That I'm willing to accept whatever he can give me, even if it ends once he leaves Helsinki. But the rest of me warns not to be an idiot. Ian's and my relationship was a mess because he wasn't honest with me. I need Kyle to be honest with me.

"I told you I was in an accident last year."

I nod even though he can't see me. Turning to my side, I take in his pained expression.

"My wife and I were driving home from a party and a fucking drunk driver didn't stop at the red light. He hit my car and killed Gabby." His tone is a wreckage of anger. My insides tighten at his words as a memory leaks to the surface.

"When was this?" I whisper.

"A year ago last May," he says, and my insides tighten so much, I can barely breathe. "The asshole and his girlfriend also died in the accident."

Tears cloud my vision but Kyle is too busy glaring at the ceiling to notice.

"I used to play hockey with the Minnesota Bears. I had a promising future until the fucking asshole took it away from me."

*"Sofia," Mom had said through my bedroom door the morning after the party. She'd been in bed when I finally came home after crying for hours in a playground not far from our house. "I need to talk to you."*

*I wiped my chooks dry and sat up. Whenever she told me, "I need to talk to you," it was never good news. "Okay."*

*She opened the door and hesitantly stepped in. Her gaze settled on the corkboard that was once filled with photos of me and Ian, as well as photos of my family and friends. Yesterday morning you would have been hard pressed to find patches of cork peeking between the photos. Now half the board was empty, Ian's pictures crowding the trashcan.*

*She sat next to me on the bed. "Ian's mom just called."*

Great, Ian's mom knows what happened and phoned to say she was sorry. *The image of Ian's tongue down the blonde's throat crashed into my head, and I almost doubled over in pain. "Ian was in a car accident last night." She kissed my forehead. "I'm sorry, Sofia. He didn't make it."*

Kyle is so lost in thought about the accident, he doesn't notice I'm dying inside. In the end, it doesn't matter if he's moving away or if I stay in Finland for the year, that's not what will destroy what we shared between us.

I choke back the sob building in me. I should leave. I should find some excuse and go back to Muumu's apartment and try to forget the last year ever happened, try to forget this summer happened. But I can't.

So I stay and watch a movie with him. Stay and pretend everything is all right. And when I can no longer keep pretending, I peel my body away from his. "I should go back home and make sure Muumu is okay."

Kyle nods and pushes himself off the couch. "I'll drive you."

I give him a quick kiss. "You can just drop me off at the bus station." I need to talk to Claire, and I'd rather not do that at home.

I give him the best smile I can muster, which must have been convincing enough because he smiles back. The sight of it breaks my heart and I can barely hold back a sob.

# Chapter Forty-Five

## Sofia

In Norse Mythology, there are female beings known as the Norns. Like with the Fates of Greek Mythology, they determine the future. It's also believed in Norse Mythology that along with the three main Norns, there are many lesser known ones. Some cause all the tragedies in the world, some protect us.

But in my case, they're sitting somewhere having a good laugh at my expense.

"You sure you don't want me to drive you home?" Kyle says as he pulls up to the central bus station in Helsinki.

"No, this is good."

He parks the car in front of the terminal, in the passenger unloading zone, and leans in to kiss me.

I pour every emotion storming inside me into the kiss, wishing it's enough to take away all the pain Ian caused Kyle. Wishing it's enough to turn back time so that somehow I can change the past, even if it means I never would have met him. Even if it means Gabby would be the one making love to him instead of me.

But no amount of kissing or wishing will make it come true.

Breathless, I pull away. "I'll talk to you later." I scramble out of the car before he can say anything, and crutch my way to my bus stop.

My bus isn't here yet. I sit down on a bench and call Claire as Kyle's car pulls away.

"Hey, what's up?" she asks.

An elderly woman walks up to my bench and I move my crutches so she can sit next to me. The benches on either side are occupied with teens talking and texting. "I need you to look up something for me."

"Sure what?"

"The victims of Ian's accident. Did the media release their names?"

"I think so. Give me a second and I'll tell you."

It takes more than a few seconds. While I wait, I listen to the muffled sounds of whatever dance song is playing in the background.

"Here it is. They did release the names."

"What were they?"

"Ian, of course. The two other dead victims were Samantha Green and Gabriella Bennett." A chill creeps through me at the second name.

"What about the survivor? What was his name?"

Silence hangs over me for what feels like an hour before she whispers, "Oh my God."

"What?" I ask even though I know what she's going to say.

"Morris Handover, general manager of the Minnesota Bears, has confirmed that right wing Kyle Bennett is listed in serious condition."

I close my eyes, and what's left of my world that hasn't already crashed in on me does so now. Kyle lost everything because of Ian. His wife. His beloved hockey. His life, so to speak. Everything.

I sniff, and work hard to keep the sob hovering near the surface from breaking loose. I want to say something, anything, but the words are unable to form. I can only stare at the dried piece of gum on the ground a few feet ahead of me.

"Kyle Bennett," Claire says. "That's your Kyle, isn't it?"

I nod even though she can't see me.

"Sofia?"

"Yes, that's him." My voice comes out as a cracked whisper.

"Does he know Ian was your ex-boyfriend?"

I let my head drop forward, the weight of the truth too heavy

254

for it. "He knows my ex cheated on me, but I never told him anything more than that."

"Are you going to tell him?" she asks, the sound of her voice a warm hug from a million miles away.

"I can't," I choke back. "He'll hate me."

"Why? It was Ian who hit him. You weren't even in the vehicle."

My ribcage feels like it's trapped in a vice, and someone is slowly tightening it, preventing air from entering my lungs. Crushing my heart in the process.

My bus pulls up to the stop. "I have to go. My bus is here." I hang up before she can say anything else, and I wipe away the tears, grateful that the elderly woman next to me probably didn't understand a word I said to Claire.

But I don't get on the bus.

I phone Maija and ten minutes later she pulls up in front of the bus stop. I never told her what was wrong. She'd heard it in my voice that I'm an emotional train wreck.

I climb into her car. "*Hei.*"

"No one is at my place. Why don't we go there, eat lots of ice cream, and you can tell me what happened?"

All I have the energy to do is nod.

At her parent's apartment, we flop down on the couch, each with a bowl of strawberry ice cream and cloudberry sauce. We don't talk about what's upsetting me at first. But eventually, after the last of the ice cream and sauce has been licked clean, I open up and tell her everything.

Until now, I've been doing a good job keeping the crying to just a stray tear or two. But the memories of Kyle's scars, of all the times the pain in his leg became too much and he was reduced to limping, of his struggle with drinking, of the dog tag from his wife overwhelm me, and the sob I've been holding back bursts free. I cover my face with my hand and don't bother to try stopping it. Maija hugs me.

I cry for a good five minutes…or maybe even longer. Maija

strokes my hair as she tells me it will be okay. Everything will be all right.

"I'm sorry," I finally say, scrubbing my fingers under my eyes to remove any traces of makeup that transferred there during my sob fest. God, I must resemble a natural disaster times two.

"You love him, don't you?" She doesn't sound too surprised.

"I need to go," I murmur, more to myself than to Maija. She's right. I do love Kyle, which is why this is so hard.

Maija puts her hand on my arm. "You don't need to go yet. Stay. Just a little longer."

"No, I need to go."

She hugs me again. "Okay, I'll drive you."

I shake my head. "No, I mean I need to go somewhere that isn't here. I need to figure out what I should do. I have to figure out if I should stay in Vantaa"—And be haunted by the memories of Kyle and what could have been—"or return home."

And be haunted by the same and so much more.

# Chapter Forty-Six

## Kyle

It's been forty-three hours and still no word from Sofia. She never called me after I dropped her off at the bus station the other night. I've sent her several texts and voice messages. Those all went unanswered. What the hell's going on? Shit, if something's happened to her or her grandmother, I doubt Joni would bother to track me down and tell me.

I need to know the truth. I need to know what I did to upset her. I've been through our last conversation so many times and still come up blank. All I can think of is that she was upset I never told her that I used to play for the Bears. She already knew about the accident and that Gabby was dead. But it doesn't make sense that she would be upset over my history with the team.

It has to be something else. *Like she's already written me off because of the job offer in Seattle.*

There's only one other person who would know what's going on.

I call Toivo. After he talks to someone who I guess to be Maija, he tells me to meet them in the pub I've been to one other time with them and Sofia.

"Is Sofia okay?" I ask. "Is she hurt?"

"I don't know all the details. Maija will fill you in when you get here."

Toivo and Maija are sitting at a small table in the corner of the patio when I arrive. I take the empty seat. "So what's going on? Where's Sofia?"

"She went to Rovaniemi," Maija says. "She needed time to figure stuff out and couldn't do that here."

"Rovaniemi? Where the hell is that?"

"Lapland. In northern Finland. It's a city on the Arctic Circle."

I remember Sofia and I talked about Lapland at one point. Her parents took her there as a kid. It's where she got the swan pendant she loves so much. "What stuff did she need to figure out? Is this about her trying to decide if she should stay here another year?"

"You really don't know, do you?" she asks.

"Know what?"

She glances at Toivo, who nods at her and says, "He deserves to know the truth."

Every cell in my body turns to ice, making it hard to breathe or think. What the hell's going on? "Is Sofia okay?"

Maija nods toward the waitress walking toward us. "You will need something strong once you find out the truth," she says.

The waitress shows up and growing more nervous by the second about what Maija has to tell me, I order a beer.

After the waitress returns with it, Maija says, "What do you know about Sofia's ex-boyfriend?"

I shrug. What the hell's this got to do with anything? "Not much. He was an asshole who cheated on her. But I'm not him. I would never hurt her." Then the words I've longed to tell Sofia for the past few days tumble out free and unabashed. "I love her."

Maija smiles, but it's not the happy smile I would expect after I've declared I'm in love her friend. It's a smile filled with pain. "Do you know what happened to him?"

"No, she never told me. Why?"

"So she never told you his name?"

What is this? Twenty Questions? "No, she never told me his name. What the hell does it have to do with anything?"

"His name was Ian Fischer. Does that ring a bell?"

A bitter chill spreads through me, rapidly numbing my body. *Shit.* "He was the drunk who killed my wife."

I wait for her to go on, but she doesn't. She drinks her beverage, waiting for me to solve the puzzle as to why Sofia refuses to talk to me. "So he's her ex-boyfriend. What does that have to do with her ignoring my calls and texts? And what does it have to do with her going to Rovaniemi?"

"The night her ex hit your car was the night Sofia found out he was cheating on her. She was afraid you wouldn't be able to look at her again the same way after you found out the truth. She was afraid she would always be a painful reminder of the life stolen from you. Of the wife stolen from you."

Double shit. How could she even think that? "But why go to Rovaniemi?"

She glances at Toivo again and he takes her hand. "Do you know what Sofia does best?"

I have a few thoughts but they don't explain why she went to Rovaniemi. I shake my head.

"When things are too much for her," she explains, "Sofia runs. She came to Finland because she was escaping her memories of the accident, and now she's running again." She takes a slip of her drink, giving me time to allow this all to soak in. "Now you know the truth. The question is, what are you going to do about it?"

What *am* I going to do?

Another voice reminds me how similar Sofia and I are. I didn't come here just to coach those boys and gain experience toward a new career. I was trying to escape my memories and demons back home, like she's been doing. Shit. If I hadn't been so messed up. If I hadn't held onto my hatred for what the asshole drunk driver did to me and Gabby and our families. If I hadn't told her about the accident, I wouldn't be losing the one person who can help me move on. The one person who made me want to move on.

And what was the point of staying angry this past year? Did it bring back the dead? Did it mean I could play for the NHL again?

There's only one thing I can do. "I'm going to Rovaniemi to see if I can find her. I need to talk to her and figure out how to keep her in my life."

Maija narrows her eyes at me. "Even though you're moving to Seattle? Even though she might stay here for a while?"

"I'm not going to Seattle. I turned down the job. And if our relationship must be long distance until she goes back to the States, then we'll make it work."

• • •

Early the next morning, with my backpack stuffed with clothes to last me two days, and no idea where to look once I get to Rovaniemi, I drive to the airport. Fortunately, Rovaniemi isn't Minneapolis, with hundreds of hotels. But what difference will it make? It's doubtful they will tell me if she's staying there. All I can do is leave a note at each one and hope wherever she's staying will pass it on to her.

In the boarding area, I pace back and forth, waiting to get on the plane. The overhead speaker crackles and an announcement is made in Finnish. Judging from everyone's expression, it's not good news. People gather their belongings and walk to the counter.

"Ladies and gentlemen. Due to mechanical issues with our plane, we will be canceling flight Air Finland 245 to Rovaniemi. If you approach the check-in counter, we'll do our best to reschedule you for a later flight today."

Shit. The line's already long. No way will I be on the next flight. Knowing I don't have much choice, I join the end of the line. It takes a while before it's my turn. Most of the passengers before me don't look too happy as they leave the counter.

"The next available flight we can get you on is this afternoon at three o'clock," the woman at the counter says after checking the computer. "Do you want it?" A sinking feeling consumes me. That's not for another seven hours. But since it's over twelve hours via train, I don't have a choice. "Yes."

# Chapter Forty-Seven

## Sofia

I sit next to an elderly woman on the wooden bench and wait for the bus. A cool morning wind brushes past, making me glad I'm wearing my jeans and hoodie. The oversized mosquitoes buzzing around my head also make me glad I'm dressed like this. If I hadn't left my crutches in the youth hostel, I could have swung at the mosquitoes and hit a home run. They're that big.

Trying to ignore the irritating buzz near my ear, I check my phone. Maija sent me a text to ensure I'm okay.

*Sitting at bus stop to see Santa's Village,* I text back.

*Make sure you remind him that I've been good this year.*

I laugh and the woman, who could be in her late sixties, smiles at me in that way where you know she has no idea what I'm saying if I were to talk to her.

*Or maybe it's Toivo I should be reminding that you've been good. :)*

*You have a good point!*

The phone rings and I answer it. "Hey mom. Is everything all right?" She knows I'm in Rovaniemi, she just doesn't know why. I haven't told her yet that I'm considering staying in Finland. I have two days to decide before my return ticket to Minneapolis expires. Two days to decide what's the right thing to do. Two days before I'll have to tell the Bears that I won't be able to do the practicum. The practicum that Kyle helped me get. Not because he used to work in their marketing department—but because he used to be one of their players.

I thought being in Rovaniemi would help me figure things out. But it hasn't.

"What's this about you staying in Finland once the summer is over?" she asks.

"Where did you hear that?" I haven't mentioned it to Muumu. Despite Joni helping me learn the language, that discussion is well beyond my abilities.

"My mother. And she had to find it out from Joni." An odd strain marks her voice. She's not happy I'm considering this option.

"Muumu needs me. She needs someone who can help her while she recovers."

"Sofia, you don't have to worry about that. Your father and I made arrangements so that she would be taken care of. It's up to you, but I don't want you to feel obligated that you have to stay there."

Hearing this is like a weight I didn't realize existed on my shoulders is suddenly knocked off. Now I really do have a choice. "Thanks, Mom. I'll let you know tomorrow what my decision is. Okay?"

"All right. But if my vote counts for anything, I miss you and I want you to come home."

I laugh. "Okay, I'll take that under advisement." I end the call and stare at my phone. I've read and listened several times to the texts and voice messages Kyle left me since I last saw him. And I still don't know what to do. I love him and everything about him. I love his random physics facts and how he gets excited when I tell him he's sexy whenever he talks about them. I love how he makes me feel, whether he's kissing me or touching me. I love how he makes me laugh and how my confidence has grown from being with him.

And I miss him more than I thought possible.

"What would you do?" I ask the woman after pouring my heart out, knowing she doesn't understand anything I'm saying. The entire time I was talking she nodded, pretending to be enthralled with everything I said.

"I think you already have the answer," she replies and I shriek as if a dead body just spoke to me.

"Y-you understood everything I said?" I ask, eyes wide.

"What? You didn't think I spoke English?"

My face heats a thousand degrees. "Well, yeah, no, I didn't. My grandmother doesn't speak English so I assumed you didn't either."

She pats my hand. "You're changing the subject. We were discussing your boyfriend problems. Have you tried calling him?"

I shake my head. I've thought about it a million times, but I chicken out each time my finger hovers over the keypad. "What I have to tell him isn't something that can be explained over the phone. It's complex."

"There's nothing complex about love." I open my mouth to argue the part about me being in love but she stops me short. "It's on your face. That's how I know. Have you even told him how you feel?"

I shake my head, clearly unable to say anything intelligent. Heck, clearly unable to say anything, period.

"Maybe it's time you do."

I snort. "You want me to tell him on the phone that I love him? Isn't that kind of impersonal?"

"Maybe so, but something tells me that pouring your heart out will do you and him some good. And from what you've told me, you've got nothing to lose. You don't have to tell him everything now, but you do need to eventually be honest with him."

The bus that drives past Santa's Village pulls up to the curb and the woman stands. She climbs on and I follow. The bus is crowded so even though I wouldn't mind getting more advice on my love life, I can't. A man stands up, allowing the woman to take his seat. I continue to the back of the bus.

I find the only other empty spot available and sit next to a guy with a pierced lip and a sleeve of tattoos. The last person on the bus I expect to be a love expert, although I could be wrong.

I remove my phone from my backpack and study it for several minutes, as if the answer to what I should do will flash on the screen. Or Kyle will sense that I want to talk to him and phone me this very second. Or this second.

Or this one.

When that doesn't happen, I scroll through the texts Kyle has sent me since the day I ran. He hasn't texted me in the past twenty-four hours. And why should he? It's my turn to reach out, not his.

Not wanting to pour my heart out to Kyle while on the bus with Tattoo Guy sitting next to me, whether he understands English or not, I return the phone to my purse. I spend the rest of the trip watching the houses become fewer and fewer, to be replaced by pine trees as we drive along the highway.

Santa's Village comes into view. The squat wooden buildings, joined in a line, with their arched windows, haven't changed since the last time I was here with my parents, when I was a kid. Nor has my belief changed that the pointed roof on the taller building, which makes up the main entrance, reminds me of an angular wizard hat with Santa's picture on it.

The bus comes to a stop and a swarm of tourists climb into the aisle and exit. A few people, including Tattoo Guy and the elderly woman remain behind.

"Don't forget to call him before it's too late," she says as I walk past. I promise her I will and join the rest of the tourists milling around the front entrance. While everyone goes inside, I remove my phone from my purse. Before I can change my mind, I find Kyle's number and call him. *Answer. Please answer.*

I get his voicemail.

"Hi. It's me. Sofia. I just want to say that I'm sorry for not calling you back sooner." I stumble over the words, not too sure what to say. "Something happened. Well, more like I found out something that has to do with you and me. And I got scared that you would hate me after you discovered the truth. So I left. And I'm in Rovaniemi and I'm not sure if I'll see you again, because after this I'm going back home. But—but I wanted to tell you that I love you. And I'm sorry about everything. I really am." The words come out so fast I barely realize what I'm saying. He won't understand what I'm talking about, but it'll have to be enough.

I hang up and enter the building somewhat lighter. I can't keep running. No matter what happens or doesn't happen between me and Kyle, I'll have to face the truth and deal with it.

With no real destination in mind, other than to explore the entire village, I wander through the stores. I'm not searching for anything specific, other than maybe a few gifts for my parents and friends.

It's not until I'm looking through the various gifts made out of reindeer antlers that I find the perfect gift for Kyle, if he ever forgives me for not facing up to the truth and telling him who I am.

I pick up the small knife and slip it from the leather case made out of reindeer skin. The handle is made from reindeer antler. The knife is a symbol of how much I trust him, with my heart and with my body. I take it to the cashier and she asks if I want them to engrave anything on the blade.

"To Kyle, love Sofia." The words come so easily, like they've been waiting patiently for me to say them. I've spent the past several years exploring the world through my camera lens. Looking for the world no one else sees because they are too busy looking at the wrong things. When it came to me and Kyle, and the truth about the night of the accident, I was no different to everyone else. I ignored what was in front of me. I ignored the other truths.

After I write down the message I want engraved on the knife, I pass time waiting for it by studying the various glass birds on display. The birds, including the swans, are the same as the ones I saw with Kyle a few weeks ago. They even have the fat little bird he bought for his mom.

It doesn't take long before the knife is ready, and I walk to the next store. My phone buzzes, and my heart rate accelerates, clearly thinking that maybe it's Kyle texting me. But it's Maija.

I read her text. *Are you still at Santa's Village?* Then reply, *Yes. But I haven't told Santa yet what I want for Christmas. Or that you've been good.*

I pick up a hand carved reindeer made from wood. I'm definitely aiming for a reindeer theme here.

My phone buzzes again.

*Turn around.*

# Chapter Forty-Eight

## Kyle

Sofia turns around and her expression transforms through a range of emotions. It settles on her staring at me, her mouth open, eyes wide. She doesn't move and she doesn't speak. She's been turned into a gold statue.

I walk up to her, mouth dry, mind racing. In hockey, before I hit the ice for a game, I could focus on what I needed to do. Win. But winning a hockey game, even if it is during the Stanley Cup playoffs, is nothing like winning the love of the girl who means everything to you.

"Hi," I say.

Her mouth closes and she blinks. "You're not really here." Her voice is soft, as if she's afraid I'm a figment of her imagination, and people will think she's crazy for talking to the empty air in front of her.

I chuckle. "No, you're not imagining me." I cup her cheek in my hand and run my thumb along her lips. The lips I've fantasized about kissing during the seven hours I was stuck in the Helsinki Airport and during the flight here. And then the hours I had to wait until today, this morning, while Maija located her for me. The image of my lips against hers was the only thing that got me through the ridiculously long wait.

"But how?" she whispers. "How did you know where to find me?"

"Maija. She told me everything. Including who your ex-boyfriend was."

She nods slowly, bit by bit processing what I've told her.

"I wish you had told me when you first realized the truth," I say.

"I wasn't positive until I talked to my best friend back home." Her eyes gloss up and she sniffs. "When you mentioned the car accident, I never realized it was the one Ian caused. I never realized he was the one who had caused you so much pain and suffering."

A tear breaks free. I catch it with my thumb and wipe it away. "The only one who caused me so much pain and suffering was me. I let my anger over what happened consume me. It was my hatred toward him that made me screw up again and again and again. He didn't make me drink and he didn't make me use sex as a distraction. That was all me."

My thumb wipes away another tear. "But it was you, Sofia, who helped me find the strength to get past it. Since coming to Finland and spending time with you, I've become the guy I used to be." A lopsided smile slips onto my lips. "And I don't know about you, but I think I'm kind of adorable this way."

She laughs. The sound of it warms me up for the first time since she left Nik's apartment. "Yes, you're definitely adorable this way." She cocks her to the side. "So you were the one texting me, not Maija?"

I chuckle. "No, that was her."

My mouth lowers to hers and I brush a feather-light kiss against it. "I love you too. And I'm willing to wait for you if you decide to stay in Finland for a while. You're worth the wait."

While I might've been going for a feather-light kiss, Sofia has other plans. Her mouth crashes into mine. I'd be a damn idiot not to kiss back with everything I have inside of me and so much more.

When we finally pull apart, we're both breathless. I'm vaguely aware of tourists sneaking glances at us, but I don't care. All I care about is one thing right now, and she's standing in front of me.

"I love you," she says, and a warm glow fills my heart at her words, adding to what was there from when she said 'I love you' on voicemail. "But I'm not staying here. I've decided to return home. My parents have made arrangements so that my grandmother will have someone to help her. I want to go back to my life in Minneapolis and start moving past what happened. To create new memories. To rebuild my life."

I might've been fine with a long-distance relationship if she had stayed in Finland, but I'm more than thrilled that we don't have to deal with that after all. Now I'll be able to hold her, kiss her, be part of her life every day, if she'll let me.

"And at least Seattle isn't as far away from Minnesota as Finland," Sofia says. "I'll be able to see you more often."

"I'm not moving to Seattle. I turned down the job." I thread my fingers with hers.

"But why? I thought you were excited about it."

I shake my head. "I thought I would be, but I realized coaching isn't what I want to do with my life."

"But you're so good at it. I saw how those boys responded when you were coaching them. You were great with them."

"I know, but it killed me that I wasn't the one doing the drills or playing hockey competitively. I want to be a physics teacher. I loved coaching them, but I loved teaching them about the physics behind hockey even more. I loved seeing their faces when something I said made sense because I explained it in a way that interested them. I wouldn't get that coaching at the collegiate level."

She grins, her beautiful light-blue eyes sparkling. "You'll be a great teacher. You are a great teacher." She pulls her hand away from mine and fishes around in the plastic bag in her other hand. "I had no idea if I would ever see you again, or if you would even want to talk to me after I called you and left the message—but I got you this."

She hands me a long package wrapped in paper. I open it. Inside is a knife, its handle made of reindeer antler; the blade is encased in a leather case with the picture of a reindeer on one side.

"The blade's engraved," she says.

I pull the knife out and grin at the words, and what the knife means, especially after I almost sliced her finger off while we were mushroom picking. She trusts me. She loves me and she trusts me not to hurt her, both emotionally and physically.

My lips find hers to show just how much I love the gift and the meaning behind it. I pull away after a heartbeat. "It's only fitting I give something to you, since this is Santa's Village."

She opens her mouth to protest. I place my finger against her lips. "Uh, uh. No talking. And close your eyes."

Once her eyes are closed, I remove the gift from my backpack. "Hold out your hands."

She does it without hesitation. I smile at the simple gesture of how much she trusts me, and place the package in her hands. "Okay, you can open your eyes."

Sofia looks at the gift, confusion and wonder in her eyes. Then like a little girl on Christmas morning, she unwraps it and reveals the swan from the store where I bought my mom the glass bird. The smile on Sofia's lips makes me love her even more.

The swan represents everything about us. Her beauty and grace, both inside and out. And my transformation from ugly duckling to something much much better.

"I'll going back to college to get my teaching degree." I've talked to the university about the courses I need, and registered for them in the upcoming school year. Which means I'll be going to school with Sofia. "So, it looks like we'll see a lot more of each other this year. Can you handle that?"

Sofia wraps her arms around my neck, the swan still in her hand. "Let me think about it." She presses her lips against mine for a heartbeat, then winks at me. "Yes, I definitely think I can handle it. As long as you continue all that sexy physics talk."

Before I can tell her, "Damn straight I will," her lips are on mine again.

For news on Stina's upcoming releases and to read two exclusive bonus chapters from *Heat It Up*, sign up for Stina's newsletter: **wp.me/P3RjVE-7g**

Find Stina online at:

stinalindenblattauthor.com

Facebook.com/StinaLindenblattAuthor

Facebook reader group:
on.fb.me/1N4m1FT

Twitter.com/StinaLL

Instagram.com/stinalindenblatt

Pinterest.com/stinall

# Acknowledgments

Authors come up with ideas for their books from the least expected sources. Sometimes it's inspired by a real-life event that happened to them. Who would have thought that my work-exchange experience cleaning toilets in a recreation center in Helsinki, when I was twenty-one years old, would one day result in this book? And because of this, I want to thank my (now deceased) grandparents for putting up with me, especially since my Finnish sucked and the only English they knew was "very good."

Before I thank everyone involved in bringing *Heat It Up* to life, I want to express my undying gratitude to the readers and bloggers who have fallen in love with my characters along the way. I love every tweet, email, and Facebook message that you send me, sharing your experiences and your love for my books. And if it weren't for my publicist, Nina Bocci, none of that would be possible. She's the one who helps keep me sane in this crazy world of publishing.

Thanks go out to my agent, Marisa Corvisiero, for believing in *Heat It Up* and for her enthusiasm over it. And to my editor, Randall Klein, for helping me make the book much stronger. He challenged me and I enjoyed every moment of it. And then there's the cover. *Heat It Up* wouldn't be the same without the great cover designed by The Killion Group. From what I've been told, the model has a very sexy Russian accent. I also want to thank everyone else with Diversion Books who worked hard to get the book out there.

Before a book ends up in an agent or editor's inbox, numerous other individuals have contributed their time, their suggestions, and their encouragement to help make the book better. They are the cheerleaders that a writer can't survive without. Christina Lee has been by my side for more years that I can remember. I'm thrilled to have her as my critique partner, best friend, and general partner in crime. The other wonderful individuals who provided feedback on the book and who have been with me on every step of this journey include: Tracy Buscemi, Jayden Abello, and Laura Pauling. Thanks also go out to Lia Riley for her feedback on the earlier version of *Heat It Up*, for talking me off the ledge when I got stuck, and for brainstorming potential plot solutions with me.

There are also two other writers I need to thank. Cherylanne Corneille is my ice hockey guru and has a strong appreciation for Finland...especially the fine hockey players the country produces. She's the one I can always turn to with my hockey questions. Suzanne van Rooyen is my guru for all things related to Finland and the Finnish language. Suzanne helped ensure that I got the Finnish phrases I used in the book correct. Yes, Google Translate is not always your friend.

And finally...to Ralph, Anton, Stefan, and Anja. I know being married to an author and having an author as a mother isn't always easy. Your love and support always makes my day that much brighter. Thank you!

Printed in the USA
CPSIA information can be obtained
at www.ICGtesting.com
JSHW031709140824
68134JS00038B/3611